The Faber Book of Modern Fairy Tales

THE FABER BOOK OF
Modern Fairy Tales

edited by

SARA AND STEPHEN CORRIN

illustrated by Ann Strugnell

FABER AND FABER
London and Boston

First published in 1981
by Faber and Faber Limited
3 Queen Square London WC1N 3AU
Printed in Great Britain by
Fakenham Press Limited
Fakenham, Norfolk

British Library Cataloguing in Publication Data

The Faber book of modern fairy tales.
1. Children's stories, English
I. Corrin, Sara   II. Corrin, Stephen
823'.01' 089282 [J]   PZ5
ISBN 0–571–11768–6

Contents

Acknowledgements

We are grateful to the undermentioned authors and publishers for permission to reprint the following stories:

"The Iron Man" reprinted by permission of Faber and Faber Ltd. from *The Iron Man* by Ted Hughes

The Squirrel Wife by Philippa Pearce, published by Kestrel Books

"The Clumber Pup" from *The Little Bookroom* by Eleanor Farjeon, published by the Oxford University Press

"The Young Man with Music in his Fingers" by Diana Ross

Where the Wind Blows by Helen Cresswell, published by Faber and Faber Ltd.

"Prince Rabbit" by A. A. Milne, reprinted by permission of C. R. Milne and The Canadian Publishers McClelland and Stewart Ltd. Toronto

"A Harp of Fishbones" by Joan Aiken, published by Jonathan Cape Ltd.; copyright © 1974 by Joan Aiken

"A Wind from Nowhere" reprinted by permission of Faber and Faber Ltd. from *A Wind from Nowhere* by Nicholas Stuart Gray

"The Woodcutter's Daughter" reprinted by permission

of Faber and Faber Ltd. from *John Barleycorn* by Alison
Uttley

"The Lord Fish" by Walter de la Mare, reprinted by
permission of the Literary Trustees of Walter de la
Mare and the Society of Authors as their representative

"The Prince with the Nine Sorrows" from *Moonlight and
Fairyland* by Laurence Housman, reprinted by permission of the executors of the Laurence Housman Estate

The Great Quillow by James Thurber, reprinted by permission of Mrs James Thurber

We should like to thank the two librarians (Junior
Books), Margaret Gross and Margaret Hazelden, and my
colleague, Hazel Wilkinson, of the Hertfordshire College
of Higher Education; Mary Junor, Schools Librarian,
Barnet; Veronica Robinson, Senior Children's Librarian
for Camden Libraries; and other librarians, for their
ever-ready help; and, of course, the Children's Books
Editor at Faber and Faber, Phyllis Hunt, without whose
skilful and sensitive guidance this book would not have
seen the light.

The Iron Man

Ted Hughes

(The first three chapters of *The Iron Man*.
There are five chapters in all.)

1

The Coming of the Iron Man

The Iron Man came to the top of the cliff.

How far had he walked? Nobody knows. Where had he come from? Nobody knows. How was he made? Nobody knows.

Taller than a house, the Iron Man stood at the top of the cliff, on the very brink, in the darkness.

The wind sang through his iron fingers. His great iron head, shaped like a dustbin but as big as a bedroom, slowly turned to the right, slowly turned to the left. His iron ears turned, this way, that way. He was hearing the sea. His eyes, like headlamps, glowed white, then red, then infra-red, searching the sea. Never before had the Iron Man seen the sea.

He swayed in the strong wind that pressed against his back. He swayed forward, on the brink of the high cliff.

And his right foot, his enormous iron right foot, lifted – up, out, into space, and the Iron Man stepped forward, off the cliff, into nothingness.

CRRRAAASSSSSSSH!

Down the cliff the Iron Man came toppling, head over heels.

CRASH!

CRASH!

CRASH!

From rock to rock, snag to snag, tumbling slowly. And as he crashed and crashed and crashed

His iron legs fell off.

His iron arms broke off, and the hands broke off the arms.

His great iron ears fell off and his eyes fell out.

His great iron head fell off.

All the separate pieces tumbled, scattered, crashing, bumping, clanging, down on to the rocky beach far below.

A few rocks tumbled with him.

Then

Silence.

Only the sound of the sea, chewing away at the edge of the rocky beach, where the bits and pieces of the Iron Man lay scattered far and wide, silent and unmoving.

Only one of the iron hands, lying beside an old, sand-logged washed-up seaman's boot, waved its fingers for a minute, like a crab on its back. Then it lay still.

While the stars went on wheeling through the sky and the wind went on tugging at the grass on the cliff-top and the sea went on boiling and booming.

Nobody knew the Iron Man had fallen.

Night passed.

Just before dawn, as the darkness grew blue and the shapes of the rocks separated from each other, two seagulls flew crying over the rocks. They landed on a patch of sand. They had two chicks in a nest on the cliff. Now they were searching for food.

One of the seagulls flew up – Aaaaaark! He had seen something. He glided low over the sharp rocks. He landed and picked something up. Something shiny, round and hard. It was one of the Iron Man's eyes. He brought it back to his mate. They both looked at this

strange thing. And the eye looked at them. It rolled from side to side looking first at one gull, then at the other. The gulls, peering at it, thought it was a strange kind of clam, peeping at them from its shell.

Then the other gull flew up, wheeled around and landed and picked something up. Some awkward, heavy thing. The gull flew low and slowly, dragging the heavy thing. Finally, the gull dropped it beside the eye. This new thing had five legs. It moved. The gulls thought it was a strange kind of crab. They thought they had found a strange crab and a strange clam. They did not know they had found the Iron Man's eye and the Iron Man's right hand.

But as soon as the eye and the hand got together the eye looked at the hand. Its light glowed blue. The hand stood up on three fingers and its thumb, and craned its forefinger like a long nose. It felt around. It touched the eye. Gleefully it picked up the eye, and tucked it under its middle finger. The eye peered out, between the forefinger and the thumb. Now the hand could see.

It looked around. Then it darted and jabbed one of the gulls with its stiffly held finger, then darted at the other and jabbed him. The two gulls flew up into the wind with a frightened cry.

Slowly then the hand crept over the stones, searching. It ran forward suddenly, grabbed something and tugged. But the thing was stuck between two rocks.

The thing was one of the Iron Man's arms. At last the hand left the arm and went scuttling hither and thither among the rocks, till it stopped, and touched something gently. This thing was the other hand. This new hand stood up and hooked its finger round the little finger of the hand with the eye, and let itself be led. Now the two hands, the seeing one leading the blind one, walking on their finger-tips, went back together to the arm, and together they tugged it free. The hand with the eye

fastened itself on to the wrist of the arm. The arm stood
up and walked on its hand. The other hand clung on as
before, and this strange trio went searching.

An eye! There it was, blinking at them speechlessly
beside a black and white pebble. The seeing hand fitted
the eye to the blind hand and now both hands could see.
They went running among the rocks. Soon they found a
leg. They jumped on top of the leg and the leg went
hopping over the rocks with the arm swinging from the
hand that clung to the top of the leg. The other hand
clung on top of that hand. The two hands, with their eyes,
guided the leg, twisting it this way and that, as a rider
guides a horse.

Soon they found another leg and the other arm. Now
each hand, with an eye under its palm and an arm dangling from its wrist, rode on a leg separately about the
beach. Hop, hop, hop, they went, peering among the
rocks.

One found an ear and at the same moment the other
found the giant torso. Then the busy hands fitted the legs
to the torso, then they fitted the arms, each fitting the
other, and the torso stood up with legs and arms but no
head. It walked about the beach, holding its eyes up in its
hands, searching for its lost head. At last, there was the
head – eyeless, earless, nested in a heap of red seaweed.
Now in no time the Iron Man had fitted his head back,
and his eyes were in place, and everything in place except
for one ear. He strode about the beach searching for
his lost ear, as the sun rose over the sea and the day
came.

The two gulls sat on their ledge, high on the cliff. They
watched the immense man striding to and fro over the
rocks below. Between them, on the nesting ledge, lay a
great iron ear. The gulls could not eat it. The baby gulls
could not eat it. There it lay on the high ledge.

Far below, the Iron man searched.

At last he stopped, and looked at the sea. Was he thinking the sea had stolen his ear? Perhaps he was thinking the sea had come up, while he lay scattered, and had gone down again with his ear.

He walked towards the sea. He walked into the breakers, and there he stood for a while, the breakers bursting around his knees. Then he walked in deeper, deeper, deeper.

The gulls took off and glided down low over the great iron head that was now moving slowly out through the swell. The eyes blazed red, level with the wavetops, till a big wave covered them and foam spouted over the top of the head. The head still moved out under water. The eyes and the top of the head appeared for a moment in a hollow of the swell. Now the eyes were green. Then the sea covered them and the head.

The gulls circled low over the line of bubbles that went on moving slowly out into the deep sea.

2

The Return of the Iron Man

One evening a farmer's son, a boy called Hogarth, was fishing in a stream that ran down to the sea. It was growing too dark to fish, his hook kept getting caught in weeds and bushes. So he stopped fishing and came up from the stream and stood listening to the owls in the wood farther up the valley, and to the sea behind him. Hush, said the sea. And again, Hush. Hush. Hush.

Suddenly he felt a strange feeling. He felt he was being watched. He felt afraid. He turned and looked up the steep field to the top of the high cliff. Behind that skyline was the sheer rocky cliff and the sea. And on that skyline, just above the edge of it, in the dusk, were two green

lights. What were two green lights doing at the top of the cliff?

Then, as Hogarth watched, a huge dark figure climbed up over the cliff-top. The two lights rose into the sky. They were the giant figure's eyes. A giant black figure, taller than a house, black and towering in the twilight, with green headlamp eyes. The Iron Man! There he stood on the cliff-top, looking inland. Hogarth began to run. He ran and ran. Home. Home. The Iron Man had come back.

So he got home at last and gasping for breath he told his dad. An Iron Man! An Iron Man! A giant!

His father frowned. His mother grew pale. His little sister began to cry.

His father took down his double-barrelled gun. He believed his son. He went out. He locked the door. He got in his car. He drove to the next farm.

But that farmer laughed. He was a fat, red man, with a fat, red-mouthed laugh. When he stopped laughing, his eyes were red too. An Iron Man? Nonsense, he said.

So Hogarth's father got back in his car. Now it was dark and it had begun to rain. He drove to the next farm.

That farmer frowned. He believed. Tomorrow, he said, we must see what he is, this iron man. His feet will have left tracks in the earth.

So Hogarth's father again got back into his car. But as he turned the car in the yard, he saw a strange thing in the headlamps. Half a tractor lay there, just half, chopped clean off, the other half missing. He got out of his car and the other farmer came to look too. The tractor had been bitten off – there were big teeth-marks in the steel.

No explanation! The two men looked at each other. They were puzzled and afraid. What could have bitten the tractor in two? There, in the yard, in the rain, in the night, while they had been talking inside the house.

The farmer ran in and bolted his door.

Hogarth's father jumped into his car and drove off into the night and the rain as fast as he could, homeward.

The rain poured down. Hogarth's father drove hard. The headlights lit up the road and bushes.

Suddenly – two headlamps in a tall treetop at the roadside ahead. Headlamps in a treetop? How?

Hogarth's father slowed, peering up to see what the lights might be, up there in the treetop.

As he slowed, a giant iron foot came down in the middle of the road, a foot as big as a single bed. And the headlamps came down closer. And a giant hand reached down towards the windshield.

The Iron Man!

Hogarth's father put on speed, he aimed his car at the foot.

Crash! He knocked the foot out of the way.

He drove on, faster and faster. And behind him, on the road, a clanging clattering boom went up, as if an iron skyscraper had collapsed. The iron giant, with his foot knocked from under him, had toppled over.

And so Hogarth's father got home safely.

BUT

Next morning all the farmers were shouting with anger. Where were their tractors? Their earth-diggers? Their ploughs? Their harrows? From every farm in the region, all the steel and iron farm machinery had gone. Where to? Who had stolen it all?

There was a clue. Here and there lay half a wheel, or half an axle, or half a mudguard, carved with giant tooth-marks where it had been bitten off. How had it been bitten off? Steel bitten off?

What had happened?

There was another clue.

From farm to farm, over the soft soil of the fields, went giant footprints, each one the size of a single bed.

The farmers, in a frightened, silent, amazed crowd,

followed the footprints. And at every farm the footprints visited, all the metal machinery had disappeared.

Finally, the footprints led back up to the top of the cliff, where the little boy had seen the Iron Man appear the night before, when he was fishing. The footprints led right to the cliff-top.

And all the way down the cliff were torn marks on the rocks, where a huge iron body had slid down. Below, the tide was in. The grey, empty, moving tide. The Iron Man had gone back into the sea.

SO

The furious farmers began to shout. The Iron Man had stolen all their machinery. Had he eaten it? Anyway, he had taken it. It had gone. So what if he came again? What would he take next time? Cows? Houses? People?

They would have to do something.

They couldn't call in the police or the Army, because nobody would believe them about this Iron Monster. They would have to do something for themselves.

So, what did they do?

At the bottom of the hill, below where the Iron Man had come over the high cliff, they dug a deep, enormous hole. A hole wider than a house, and as deep as three trees one on top of the other. It was a colossal hole. A stupendous hole! And the sides of it were sheer as walls.

They pushed all the earth off to one side.

They covered the hole with branches and the branches they covered with straw and the straw with soil, so when they finished the hole looked like a freshly-ploughed field.

Now, on the side of the hole opposite the slope up to the top of the cliff, they put an old rusty lorry. That was the bait. Now they reckoned the Iron Man would come over the top of the cliff out of the sea, and he'd see the old lorry which was painted red, and he'd come down to get

it to chew it up and eat it. But on his way to the lorry he'd be crossing the hole, and the moment he stepped with his great weight on to that soil held up only with straw and branches, he would crash through into the hole and would never get out. They'd find him there in the hole. Then they'd bring the few bulldozers and earth-movers that he hadn't already eaten, and they'd push the pile of earth in on top of him, and bury him for ever in the hole. They were certain now that they'd get him.

Next morning, in great excitement, all the farmers gathered together to go along to examine their trap. They came carefully closer, expecting to see his hands tearing at the edge of the pit. They came carefully closer.

The red lorry stood just as they had left it. The soil lay just as they had left it, undisturbed. Everything was just as they had left it. The Iron Man had not come.

Nor did he come that day.

Next morning, all the farmers came again. Still, every-thing lay just as they had left it.

And so it went on, day after day. Still the Iron Man never came.

Now the farmers began to wonder if he would ever come again. They began to wonder if he had ever come at all. They began to make up explanations of what had happened to their machinery. Nobody likes to believe in an Iron Monster that eats tractors and cars.

Soon, the farmer who owned the red lorry they were using as bait decided that he needed it, and he took it away. So there lay the beautiful deep trap, without any bait. Grass began to grow on the loose soil.

The farmers talked of filling the hole in. After all, you can't leave a giant pit like that, somebody might fall in. Some stranger coming along might just walk over it and fall in.

But they didn't want to fill it in. It had been such hard work digging it. Besides they all had a sneaking fear that

the Iron Man might come again, and that the hole was their only weapon against him.

At last they put up a little notice: "DANGER: KEEP OFF", to warn people away, and they left it at that.

Now the little boy Hogarth had an idea. He thought he could use that hole, to trap a fox. He found a dead hen one day, and threw it out on to the loose soil over the trap. Then towards evening, he climbed a tree nearby, and waited. A long time he waited. A star came out. He could hear the sea.

Then – there, standing at the edge of the hole, was a fox. A big, red fox, looking towards the dead hen. Hogarth stopped breathing. And the fox stood without moving – sniff, sniff, sniff, out towards the hen. But he did not step out on to the trap. Slowly, he walked around the wide patch of raw soil till he got back to where he'd started, sniffing all the time out towards the bird. But he did not step out on to the trap. Was he too smart to walk out there where it was not safe?

But at that moment he stopped sniffing. He turned his head and looked towards the top of the cliff. Hogarth, wondering what the fox had seen, looked towards the top of the cliff.

There, enormous in the blue evening sky, stood the Iron Man, on the brink of the cliff, gazing inland.

In a moment, the fox had vanished.

Now what?

Hogarth carefully quietly hardly breathing climbed slowly down the tree. He must get home and tell his father. But at the bottom of the tree he stopped. He could no longer see the Iron Man against the twilight sky. Had he gone back over the cliff into the sea? Or was he coming down the hill, in the darkness under that high skyline, towards Hogarth and the farms?

The Hogarth understood what was happening. He could hear a strange tearing and creaking sound. The Iron

Man was pulling up the barbed-wire fence that led down the hill. And soon Hogarth could see him, as he came nearer, tearing the wire from the fence posts, rolling it up like spaghetti and eating it. The Iron Man was eating the barbed fencing wire.

But if he went along the fence, eating as he moved, he wouldn't come anywhere near the trap, which was out in the middle of the field. He could spend the whole night wandering about the countryside along the fences, rolling up the wire and eating it, and never would any fence bring him near the trap.

But Hogarth had an idea. In his pocket, among other things, he had a long nail and a knife. He took these out. Did he dare? His idea frightened him. In the silent dusk, he tapped the nail and the knife blade together.

Clink, Clink, Clink!

At the sound of the metal, the Iron Man's hands became still. After a few seconds, he slowly turned his head and the headlamp eyes shone towards Hogarth.

Again, Clink, Clink, Clink! went the nail on the knife.

Slowly, the Iron Man took three strides towards Hogarth, and again stopped. It was now quite dark. The headlamps shone red. Hogarth pressed close to the tree-trunk. Between him and the Iron Man lay the wide lid of the trap.

Clink, Clink, Clink! again he tapped the nail on the knife.

And now the Iron Man was coming. Hogarth could feel the earth shaking under the weight of his footsteps. Was it too late to run? Hogarth stared at the Iron Man, looming, searching towards him for the taste of the metal that had made that inviting sound.

Clink, Clink, Clink! went the nail on the knife. And CRASSSHHH!

The Iron Man vanished.

He was in the pit. The Iron Man had fallen into the pit.

Hogarth went close. The earth was shaking as the Iron Man struggled underground. Hogarth peered over the torn edge of the great pit. Far below, two deep red headlamps glared up at him from the pitch blackness. He could hear the Iron Man's insides grinding down there and it sounded like a big lorry grinding its gears on a steep hill. Hogarth set off. He ran, he ran, home – home with the great news. And as he passed the cottages on the way, and as he turned down the lane towards his father's farm, he was shouting "The Iron Man's in the trap!" and "We've caught the Iron Giant."

When the farmers saw the Iron Man wallowing in their deep pit, they sent up a great cheer. He glared up towards them, his eyes burned from red to purple, from purple to white, from white to fiery whirling black and red, and the cogs inside him ground and screeched, but he could not climb out of the steep-sided pit.

Then under the lights of car headlamps, the farmers brought bulldozers and earth-pushers, and they began to push in on top of the struggling Iron Man all the earth they had dug when they first made the pit and that had been piled off to one side.

The Iron Man roared again as the earth began to fall on him. But soon he roared no more. Soon the pit was full of earth. Soon the Iron Man was buried silent, packed down under all the soil, while the farmers piled the earth over him in a mound and in a hill. They went to and fro over the mound on their new tractors, which they'd bought since the Iron Man ate their old ones, and they packed the earth down hard. Then they all went home talking cheerfully. They were sure they had seen the last of the Iron Man.

Only Hogarth felt suddenly sorry. He felt guilty. It was he after all, who had lured the Iron Man into the pit.

3

What's to be done with the Iron Man?

So the Spring came round the following year, leaves
unfurled from the buds, daffodils speared up from the
soil, and everywhere the grass shook new green points.
The round hill over the Iron Man was covered with new
grass. Before the end of the summer, sheep were grazing
on the fine grass on the lovely hillock. People who had
never heard of the Iron Man saw the green hill as they
drove past on their way to the sea, and they said: "What a
lovely hill! What a perfect place for a picnic!"

So people began to picnic on the top of the hill. Soon,
quite a path was worn up there, by people climbing to eat
their sandwiches and take snaps of each other.

One day, a father, a mother, a little boy and a little girl
stopped their car and climbed the hill for a picnic. They
had never heard of the Iron Man and they thought the hill
had been there for ever.

They spread a tablecloth on the grass. They set down
the plate of sandwiches, a big pie, a roasted chicken, a
bottle of milk, a bowl of tomatoes, a bagful of boiled
eggs, a dish of butter and a loaf of bread, with cheese and
salt and cups. The father got his stove going to boil some
water for tea, and they all lay back on rugs munching
food and waiting for the kettle to boil, under the blue sky.

Suddenly the father said: "That's funny!"

"What is?" asked the mother.

"I felt the ground shake," the father said. "Here, right
beneath us."

"Probably an earthquake in Japan," said the mother.

"An earthquake in Japan?" cried the little boy. "How
could that be?"

So the father began to explain how an earthquake in a

far distant country, that shakes down buildings and emp-
ties lakes, sends a jolt right around the earth. People far
away in other countries feel it as nothing more than a
slight trembling of the ground. An earthquake that
knocks a city flat in South America, might do no more
than shake a picture off a wall in Poland. But as the father
was talking, the mother gave a little gasp, then a yelp.

"The chicken!" she cried. "The cheese! The
tomatoes!"

Everybody sat up. The tablecloth was sagging in the
middle. As they watched the sag got deeper and all the
food fell into it, dragging the tablecloth right down into
the ground. The ground underneath was splitting and the
tablecloth, as they watched, slowly folded and disappeared into the crack, and they were left staring at a
jagged black crack in the ground. The crack grew, it
widened, it lengthened, it ran between them. The mother
and the girl were on one side, and the father and the boy
were on the other side. The little stove toppled into the
growing crack with a clatter and the kettle disappeared.

They could not believe their eyes. They stared at the
widening crack. Then, as they watched, an enormous
iron hand came up through the crack, groping around in
the air, feeling over the grass on either side of the crack. It
nearly touched the little boy, and he rolled over backwards. The mother screamed. "Run to the car," shouted
the father. They all ran. They jumped into the car. They
drove. They did not look back.

So they did not see the great iron head, square like a
bedroom, with red glaring headlamp eyes, and with the
tablecloth, still with the chicken and the cheese, draped
across the top of it, rising out of the top of the hillock, as
the Iron Man freed himself from the pit.

When the farmers realized that the Iron Man had freed
himself they groaned. What could they do now? They
decided to call the Army, who could pound him to bits

with anti-tank guns. But Hogarth had another idea. At first, the farmers would not hear of it, least of all his own father. But at last they agreed. Yes, they would give Hogarth's idea a trial. And if it failed, they would call in the Army.

After spending a night and a day eating all the barbed wire for miles around, as well as hinges he tore off gates and the tin cans he found in ditches, and three new tractors and two cars and a lorry, the Iron Man was resting in a clump of elm trees. There he stood, leaning among the huge branches, almost hidden by the dense leaves, his eyes glowing a soft blue.

The farmers came near, along a lane, in cars so that they could make a quick getaway if things went wrong. They stopped fifty yards from the clump of elm trees. He really was a monster. This was the first time most of them had had a good look at him. His chest was as big as a cattle truck. His arms were like cranes, and he was getting rusty, probably from eating all the old barbed wire.

Now Hogarth walked up towards the Iron Man.

"Hello," he shouted, and stopped. "Hello, Mr Iron Man."

The Iron Man made no move. His eyes did not change.

Then Hogarth picked up a rusty old horseshoe, and knocked it against a stone: Clonk, Clonk, Clonk!

At once, the Iron Man's eyes turned darker blue. Then purple. Then red. And finally white, like a car headlamps. It was the only sign he gave of having heard.

"Mr Iron Man," shouted Hogarth. "We've got all the iron you want, all the food you want, and you can have it for nothing, if only you'll stop eating up the farms."

The Iron Man stood up straight. Slowly he turned, till he was looking directly at Hogarth.

"We're sorry we trapped you and buried you," shouted the little boy. "We promise we'll not deceive you again. Follow us and you can have all the metal you want.

Brass too. Aluminium too. And lots of old chrome. Follow us."

The Iron Man pushed aside the boughs and came into the lane. Hogarth joined the farmers. Slowly they drove back down the lane, and slowly, with all his cogs humming, the Iron Man stepped after them.

They led through the villages. Half the people came out to stare, half ran to shut themselves inside bedrooms and kitchens. Nobody could believe their eyes when they saw the Iron Man marching behind the farmers.

At last they came to the town, and there was a great scrap-metal yard. Everything was there, old cars by the hundred, old trucks, old railway engines, old stoves, old refrigerators, old springs, bedsteads, bicycles, girders, gates, pans – all the scrap iron of the region was piled up there, rusting away.

"There," cried Hogarth. "Eat all you can."

The Iron Man gazed, and his eyes turned red. He kneeled down in the yard, he stretched out on one elbow. He picked up a greasy black stove and chewed it like a toffee. There were delicious crumbs of chrome on it. He followed that with a double-decker bedstead and the brass knobs made his eyes crackle with joy. Never before had the Iron Man eaten such delicacies. As he lay there, a big truck turned into the yard and unloaded a pile of rusty chain. The Iron Man lifted a handful and let it dangle into his mouth – better than any spaghetti.

So there they left him. It was an Iron Man's heaven. The farmers went back to their farms. Hogarth visited the Iron Man every few days. Now the Iron Man's eyes were constantly a happy blue. He was no longer rusty. His body gleamed blue, like a new gun barrel. And he ate, ate, ate, ate – endlessly.

The Squirrel Wife

Philippa Pearce

Once upon a time, long ago, on the edge of a great forest,
there lived two brothers who were swineherds. The elder
brother was very unkind to the younger brother, called
Jack; he made him do all the work and gave him hardly
enough to eat.

Every day in the autumn Jack drove the pigs into the
forest to eat the fallen acorns and the beech-mast and to
rootle in the earth. As he set off, his brother always gave
him the same warning: "Don't take the pigs deep into the
forest, and be sure to bring them home before sunset,
because of the green people."

The green people were the fairy-people who lived in
the heart of the forest; and the forest was their kingdom.
They could be seen only by moonlight. Everyone feared
them.

One autumn evening when Jack was bringing the herd
of pigs out of the forest as usual, he noticed that a wind
was beginning to get up. It whirled the leaves from the
trees and tossed their branches wildly. By the time the
pigs were in their sties and Jack in the cottage which he
shared with his brother, a storm was blowing.

That night, when the two brothers had gone to bed,
they could not sleep for the howling of the wind round
their cottage. In the middle of the storm they heard the

crash of a great tree falling in the distance, from the direction of the forest.

"Did you hear that?" Jack whispered.

"What a fool you are, Jack!" said his brother. "Of course I heard the tree falling."

"But did you hear nothing else?" said Jack. "There it goes again – listen!"

They both listened and, over the howling of the storm, heard a strange voice far off, crying for help.

"There!" said Jack.

"I heard nothing," said his brother.

"But you must have heard it: someone calling from the forest."

"I tell you, I heard nothing. And if there were someone calling, this is not the kind of night to go out helping strangers. Be quiet and go to sleep, or it will be the worse for you."

So Jack held his tongue.

At last the gale blew itself out and then the elder brother fell asleep, but not Jack. As soon as he heard his brother snoring, he crept out of bed and left the cottage. As he went, he stuck his wood-axe into his belt, as protection against wild beasts or any other enemies.

He took the moonlit way that led to the forest. He reached the very edge of the forest, hesitated, and then plunged in. Almost at once he came upon the great tree – a beech tree – whose crashing fall he had heard that night.

The tree lay with its trunk full length upon the ground, its roots torn up into the air and its leaves smashed down into the earth. It was all black and silvery grey in the moonlight; and then Jack noticed a strange greenness where there should have been none.

He looked closely and saw what at first he thought was a child – a green child; but this was a man, perfectly formed in every way, and yet only the height of a child, and green. He was one of the green people.

The green man had been trapped by the fall of the tree, for it had fallen across his legs. He could not move. He stared at Jack, and Jack stared at him; but neither said a word. Jack took the wood-axe from his belt and began to hack him free. When he had done this, Jack expected the green man to escape at once back into the depths of the forest. But the green man lay as before, and Jack saw that one of his legs had been crushed by the fall of the tree.

What was to be done? Jack could not bear to carry the green man home to his cruel brother; nor could he leave him here, where his own people might never find him. Jack looked at the green man, and the green man looked at Jack, and neither said a word; but Jack knew what he must do. Although he was afraid to do it, he must carry the green man back to his own people in the heart of the forest. He picked him up in his arms – he was as light as a child – and began to carry him deeper and deeper into the forest.

At last, in the heart of the forest, Jack came to a clearing where, by moonlight, he saw a company of the green people on horseback. Two of them came to him at once and took the injured man from him, all without a word being spoken on either side.

Then one who was clearly lord of them all beckoned to Jack.

Jack knelt and the lord of the green people said, "Jack, you have done a good night's work and deserve to be paid for it. This is your reward: you shall enjoy the secrets of our forest through your wife."

Jack dared respectfully to point out that he had no wife, nor any thought of one as yet.

"I know that," said the lord of the green people, "just as I know that you are Jack the swineherd, living on the edge of our forest. Now take this gold ring." He took a ring from his finger as he spoke and held it out to Jack. It was a plain gold ring, like a wedding-ring. Jack took it

and thanked him for it; but the lord of the green people
had not finished with Jack. "You will wear this ring upon
your finger," he said, "until the spring comes.

"In spring the squirrels build their dreys in the trees of
our forest and bear their young. At that time you must
climb up to a nest where there is a new-born female
squirrel and put this ring over its left forepaw, like a
bracelet. Then come away."

"But, sir," said Jack, "would not this be a cruel thing to
do? For the young squirrel will grow and the ring will
stay the same size."

The lord of the green people laughed. "Jack, I think
you are sometimes a fool, as your brother says. For this is
a magic ring, that will grow as the wearer grows; and at
the time when squirrels are full grown, you shall find
what you shall find.

"And now, Jack, turn and follow your path home, and
do not look behind you until you are within sight of it."

Jack turned as he was told.

He looked down, and there at his feet was a path, white
in the moonlight, where he could have sworn there had
never been one before. He followed it, without once
looking back, until he came to the very edge of the forest
and within sight of the cottage where he lived. Then he
looked back and saw that there was no path behind him: it
had vanished behind him as he went forward upon it.

Jack got home and back into bed without his brother's
waking, so that his brother never knew what had
happened that night. Nor did he seem to notice the gold
ring that Jack now wore on his finger – perhaps because it
was a fairy ring and invisible to him.

Time passed and time passed, and the time came for
squirrels to build their dreys in the forest.

As he had been told, Jack climbed tree after tree.

He searched for a squirrel to which he might give his
ring. At last he found one – a female, new-born, tiny as a

rat, hairless and blind as yet. He slipped the gold ring over her left forepaw, so that it rested just above it like a bracelet. Then he climbed down the tree and came away.

Time passed and time passed, and autumn came, when squirrels are full grown. Jack was driving the pigs into the forest as usual to eat acorns and beech-mast and rootle in the earth. As he went by a woodland pool that he had often passed before, he saw someone at the edge of it, kneeling. It was a girl, who was staring at her reflection in the water as if in amazement. When she heard Jack's footfall stirring the leaves and twigs on the forest floor, she sprang up at once, more like a wild animal than a woman, and stood facing him.

Jack had never seen her before. She was small for a woman, graceful and exceedingly nimble in her movement. Her hair was brown; her eyes were brown, and what made them remarkable was their strange, wild look of watchfulness.

Jack stared and stared at the strange girl. She smiled at him as though she knew him, and stretched out her left hand towards him. Then he saw that she was wearing a bracelet round the wrist – a bracelet of plain gold, just like a wedding-ring but, of course, much larger.

"Jack," said the girl, "—you are Jack, aren't you? – I am your squirrel-wife."

Then with joy Jack remembered the promise of the lord of the green people. He took the hand she held out towards him, for he knew that already he loved his squirrel-wife, as she loved him. They would live together always, as man and wife. They determined not to go back to Jack's cruel brother, but to settle far from him, within the forest. The forest was the only place for a squirrel-wife.

And there among the trees they would live happily.

So Jack divided the herd of pigs into two equal parts. One half of the herd he beat back towards his brother's

cottage; the other half he took as his rightful share. Then, driving the pigs before them, Jack and his squirrel-wife went farther and farther into the forest.

On and on through the forest they went, until at last they came almost out at the other side – the side of the forest farthest from where Jack had lived with his brother. Here Jack built them a cottage and pigsties and here they settled.

They lived very happily, and they prospered. Jack tended the pigs as before; but now he began also to make tables and chairs and many other things from the different woods of the forest.

His squirrel-wife knew all the trees of the forest: oak, ash, beech, birch and the rest. She could tell him exactly which wood was best for each purpose.

She would set her ear to the tree-trunks, and could tell which tree was sound all through and which was rotten, wholly or in the smallest degree. She could lay her hand upon a tree and tell its age exactly, even before Jack had cut it down and counted its year-rings. She knew where the best blackberries were to be found, and the best mushrooms. She knew where the wild bees stored their honey and – of course – where the squirrels stored their nuts. It was just as the lord of the green people had promised: Jack could enjoy the secrets of the forest through his squirrel-wife.

Jack and his squirrel-wife spent all their time in the forest, except when they took a pigling or a table or a chair to sell in the village just outside. The villagers bought Jack's wares, but at the same time, they distrusted him, because of his wife. They were afraid of the squirrel-wife on account of that strange, watchful look in her eyes. The forest woman, they called her.

Word of Jack and his forest-woman was passed from that village to the next, and so from village to village, until at last it reached Jack's elder brother, far away on the

other side of the forest. He was so enraged to hear of Jack's happiness that he travelled all round the edge of the forest – a journey of many days – until he reached the village where Jack was best known.

There, he spread the story that Jack was a runaway thief.

"He sells you piglings that are by rights my piglings," he said to the villagers. "For this slippery brother of mine disappeared into the forest one day, taking with him half my herd of pigs. He is a thief, and I demand his punishment."

The villagers listened and nodded and said that Jack had seemed an honest man, but then indeed how could any honest man have such a wife as Jack had? So they were willing to believe the falsehoods told them by Jack's brother; and when Jack next came to the village they seized him and threw him into prison.

Their prison was a room with a barred window and a locked door at the top of a tower. The key of the door was given into the charge of Jack's own brother. He had a room at the bottom of the tower to sleep in.

Here he hung the key of Jack's prison from a nail on the wall.

Poor Jack looked out from his prison-window towards the forest; he could see it, but he feared he might never go there freely again. He looked downwards from his window and could see his squirrel-wife, for she stood at the foot of the tower, weeping. The end of the day had come, and the squirrel-wife now turned away from the tower towards the forest, still weeping. Jack called to her to come back; but she would not. "I must go into the forest," she said, "to find the green people."

"Oh, take care!" cried Jack. "What do you mean to ask them?"

"Nothing. I mean only to give back to them my gold bracelet."

"But then you would be a squirrel again!"

"That is what I want; that is what I need to be, if I am to help you."

"Don't go!" cried Jack, shaking the bars of his window in frenzy. "Don't go! Don't go!"

But the squirrel-wife had already gone, leaving Jack in despair.

The sun set. Darkness came, and then moonlight – full moonlight; and Jack was still looking out from his prison-window. Everything was quiet except for the sound of Jack's brother snoring in bed in the room below. Then Jack heard a scrabbling sound in the ivy that grew on the prison-tower. He looked down and saw, by moonshine, a squirrel that was slipping through his brother's open window. The sound of snoring never stopped, but in a moment the squirrel was out again with something glinting between its teeth – a key. Now it was climbing up the ivy – up – up to Jack's window. It slipped in between the bars of the window and dropped the key into the palm of his outstretched hand. Then it leapt upon his shoulder and laid its head against his cheek.

Using this key, Jack unlocked his prison-door and – with the squirrel still on his shoulder – crept out and down the stairway. He could hear his brother's steady snoring as he stole past the door where he slept. He reached the heavy outside door that would let him go free from the tower altogether. He tried it, afraid that he would find it locked; but it was not. He began to ease it open. Its hinges were rusty and stiff and, as the door opened bit by bit, they creaked. At the loudest creak, the snoring stopped. "What is it?" called the sleepy voice of Jack's brother. "Who goes there?" Then fully awake, he shouted:

"The prisoner is escaping! Stop thief, STOP!"

By now Jack was already clear of the tower and running as fast as he could towards the forest, with the

squirrel clinging to his shoulder. After him came his brother; and after his brother came the villagers, roused from their beds and taking up the cry: "Stop thief!"

Jack reached the trees and at once plunged among them, and his brother and all the villagers, forgetting their fear of the forest by moonlight, plunged after him. But, as Jack and his squirrel fled before them deeper and deeper into the forest, the shouting behind them grew fainter. Soon they could hear it no longer.

They went on until at last they came to a moonlit clearing, where a company of the green people was assembled. With his squirrel on his shoulder, Jack went forward.

He knelt humbly before the lord of the green people. The lord was frowning: "You have noisy friends, Jack, who follow you into our forest."

"No friends of mine, sir," said Jack, "but I ask your pardon all the same."

"Is that all you have come to ask us?"

"No, sir," said Jack, but did not dare yet to say more.

The lord of the green people said: "First you came to us and were rewarded handsomely with the gift of a golden ring, that grew in size to a bracelet. Then – this very night – your squirrel-wife came to return that gift to the givers. And now you come back together – Jack and his squirrel who was once a squirrel-wife – to ask something more of us.

"Before you ask, Jack, remember this. Fairy gifts cannot be given twice."

"I do not ask for the ring or for the bracelet again," Jack said, "but I want my squirrel-wife."

The lord of the green people shook his head. "No, Jack. We cannot give you your squirrel-wife a second time. But this we will do for you: you can have either the squirrel on your shoulder or your wife by your side. Which? You must decide."

Jack was bewildered by these words, and hesitated. Then he said, "Sir, a man wants a wife by his side. I choose my wife."

For the first time the lord of the green people smiled. "I think you are not always the fool your brother calls you, Jack. You have chosen wisely. You shall have your wife, and you need fear no harm either from your brother or from the people of the village.

"We shall keep your brother safe with us in the forest until he learns a little wisdom; and we shall send the rest home to their beds. We shall wipe from their minds all memory of the evil they once believed of you both. And now, Jack, turn and follow your path home. You shall find what you shall find."

As once before, Jack turned and followed a fairy path, white in the moonlight. The squirrel was still on his shoulder and, as he went, he grew amazed at its heaviness.

At last he had to stop to rest. Then he looked over his shoulder, and lo and behold! he was carrying not a squirrel at all, but a young woman – his wife.

She slipped down to the ground beside him and he hugged her in his arms. She seemed to be his squirrel-wife, exactly as he had always known her; but now she pressed close to him for protection, shivering as if in dread.

She said, "Dear Jack, I fear the forest – I don't know how I could ever have wished to live here. I have one thing to beg of you. When we get home, let us gather the herd of pigs and all your tools and our household goods, and let us take them out of the forest and settle in the village. We must live like other people, because now I am like other women."

Looking into her eyes, Jack could no longer see that strange watchfulness that had made her seem like a wild creature. It had vanished altogether. Then he knew that she was no longer partly squirrel and partly woman – a

squirrel-wife; she was all woman now, according to the choice he had made before the lord of the green people.

"Dear wife," said Jack, "we shall do just as you wish."

So they moved all their belongings and settled in the village just outside the forest. The villagers welcomed them, for they had lost all memory of Jack and his wife as they had once been. Jack herded pigs and made tables and chairs as before; his wife cooked and cleaned and minded the babies that were born, but she had lost her knowledge of the secrets of the forest.

Nor did she wish to go into the forest again: for she said that the tall trees made her afraid, even by daylight.

By moonlight, nobody would go into the forest, because of the green people.

So Jack and his wife lived happily on the edge of the forest and had children and grandchildren and great-grandchildren.

As for Jack's elder brother, the green people kept him as their servant for a thousand years, until he should learn a little wisdom.

The Clumber Pup

Eleanor Farjeon

1

When Joe Jolly's father died, his fortunes were almost at their lowest ebb. Not quite, for he had at least the chair he sat in. But the hut the Jollys lived in was not theirs; it was lent to them, as part wages, by the Lord of the Manor whose wood John Jolly chopped. For the rest, he got three shillings every Friday. Even the axe he chopped with was not Mr Jolly's own.

Joe grew up in the woods with little education beyond the use of his hands, and a love of animals; and much in the same way he loved his father, whom he often helped with the chopping, though neither the Lord of the Manor nor his Steward knew of his existence.

Old Mr Jolly was taken ill of a Thursday evening, when last week's wages were spent. He sat down in his old chair and said, "Joe, I see a better world ahead of me." Next day he couldn't get up, so Joe did a man's day's work, and at the end of it went to the Steward for his father's shillings. The Steward asked, "Who may you be?" and Joe replied, "John Jolly's son."

"And why doesn't John Jolly come himself?"

"He's sick."

"And who'll do his work till he's well?"

"I will," said Joe.

The Steward counted out the three shillings, and left it at that. In the back of his mind was the thought that if, by the grace of God, John Jolly died, he might put in his place an old uncle of his wife's who was considered by the Steward both a nuisance and an expense, as he was obliged to keep him under his own roof. But John Jolly lasted a month, during which time Joe tended him like a woman, and did all his work besides. As three shillings did not go far, with sickness in the house, he sold up their sticks, bit by bit, to get his father extra little comforts. By the fourth Thursday everything was sold but the chair and his mother's brass wedding-ring. John Jolly lay at peace under the grass, and Joe, for the first time in his life, considered his future.

He did not consider it for long; here he was, at the age of eighteen, a fine upstanding young chap, as limber as a squirrel, with a skin like the red tan on a pine tree, and no trade to his hands except the power to chop wood. So he decided to put in for his father's job.

When he went as usual on the Friday evening for his pay, he said to the Steward, "Dad'll not be cutting timber for you any more."

"How's that?" asked the Steward, hoping for the best.

"He's gone to a better world," explained Joe.

"Ah!" said the Steward. "Then the post of Lord's Woodcutter falls vacant after fifty years."

"I'd like to put in for it," said Joe.

But the Steward's chance to rid himself of his uncle had come; so he pursed his lips, scratched his nose, shook his head, and said, "It wants a man of experience." Then he counted out three shillings, wished Joe well, and sent him away.

Joe was not one for arguing; he knew he was experienced by craft, but not by years, and if the Steward thought one way, it was no manner of use thinking

another. He went back to the hut, looked at his father's chair, and thought, "Well, I can't take it with me, and I don't want to sell it, and I'd never chop it for firewood, and the next woodcutter will want something to sit on, and over and above that it'll like to stay where it has always been, as much as I should do. But it can't be helped, good-bye to you, old chair!" And so, with three shillings and a brass ring in his pocket, Joe left the only home that he had ever known.

<h1 style="text-align:center">2</h1>

It was quite a new experience for Joe to be walking along a highroad many miles from his dwelling. Loving his wood better than most things, he had seldom seen reason to go out of it; but within forty hours of his father's death he was strolling through the world, with a bright eye and a quick ear for anything he might see and hear. Not minding which way he turned, he told himself to follow the first sound he heard. He had no sooner cocked his ear than he heard, very faint and distant, the familiar tapping of the axe-stroke on the tree. It was so far away that it might have come from another world. However, Joe heard it clear enough, and let it lead him on his way.

About noontime on the Saturday he heard a sound far more disturbing, the whining of a dog in distress. Joe quickened his pace, and turning the end of a lane he found himself in view of a village pond. A group of youths stood around it, one of whom had a puppy in his hands, which he was trying to hold under water; but the puppy's mother, a beautiful Clumber spaniel, was whining and worrying him so that half his attention had to be given to kicking her off, while the rest of the youths looked on, taking neither side, amused by the contest between the boy and the dog. As Joe appeared on the scene, the

puppy-drowner lost patience, and, with a final kick at the spaniel, was about to toss the puppy into the middle of the pond. But before he could do so, Joe caught his arm, and said, "None o' that!"

The youth turned on him roughly, but seeing somebody both taller and stronger than himself, instead of looking fierce looked sulky, and said:

"Why not? Puppies were born to be drowned, weren't they?"

"Not where I am," said Joe, "and you shan't drown this one."

"Will you buy it?" asked the youth.

"What do you want for it?" asked Joe.

"What have you got?" asked the youth.

"Three shillings," said Joe.

"Agreed!" said the youth. He handed the Clumber Pup to Joe, snatched the three shillings, and ran off, followed by the other lads, who were shouting with laughter, he who had taken the money laughing louder than any. The spaniel stood on her hind legs, placed her forepaws against Joe's chest, and licked the hands that held her pup so gently.

Joe looked into her melting brown eyes and said, "I'll see to your baby, lass; run you after your master."

One of the boys then bawled over his shoulder, "He's not her master! 'Tis a strange dog he found with the pup on father's straw rick this morning!" And with a last guffaw of triumph over the simpleton who had parted with his money for nothing, they scampered out of sight.

"Well," said Joe, "it's no such bad bargain that's got me a fine little pup and a beautiful bitch to boot. So now you can both join my fortunes, mother and child together."

He cuddled the pup inside his jacket, and as it settled there he knew, with a pang of joy, that this dog was *his* dog as no other ever could be again. He resumed his road

with an empty pocket, and the Clumber spaniel running at his heels.

3

As Joe had no money, he had to walk hungry for the best part of the day. Towards evening, when the tapping of the distant axe which had never ceased to call him had become very near, he came to a wood. It was the first he had struck since leaving his own green forest, and he entered its shade with delight, feeling himself at home again. He had not been walking long when he heard the sound of mewing, a mew as tiny as the squeak of his pup. Following the sound, he soon found a scrap of a kitten, as gold as sunlight dappling a running stream, with eyes as clear as swung honey. It trembled on its four tottering legs, and was evidently pleased when Joe stooped and picked it up; he could almost hide it from sight by shutting his big fingers over its morsel of a body, soft as down. It was very cold, so he buttoned it under his jacket alongside the pup, where it lay purring with bliss.

The night was advancing; and now the sound of the axe hewing timber, which to Joe was better than music, was within a hundred yards of him. He stood still to listen to it for sheer pleasure. All of a sudden came the crash of a tree, followed by a groan. Now he stood still no longer, but hastened to the scene of the accident. Under the fallen tree a man lay pinned, an old man in shape so like his father that in the dusk Joe almost took him for John Jolly himself. But how could that be? Running to him, he saw that this old woodcutter merely resembled his father as one old man will resemble another, when they are much of a size, and have followed the same calling for a lifetime.

"Are you hurt badly?" asked Joe.

"I can't rightly tell till I'm unpinned," said the old man.

A great limb of the tree lay across the woodcutter's right arm. Joe found the old man's axe, and chopped him free. Then he felt the limb tenderly and skilfully, and found that it was broken; but he had too often set the broken legs and wings of hares and jays not to know what to do. In a few minutes he had made the old man comfortable, and lifting him from the ground asked where he might take him.

"My hut's not fifty steps from here," said the old man. Under his direction, Joe bore him there. It was just such a dwelling as he was used to, but rather better furnished. A narrow bed with a gay coverlet stood in one corner, and on this Joe laid the old man down. Then, without asking questions, he set about brightening the fire, boiling the kettle, and preparing the old man's supper. He looked in the cupboard and on the shelf for food and crocks, and in no time had the teapot steaming, and the bread-and-dripping spread, while the old man lay and watched him with eyes as shrewd as a weasel's.

As soon as the sick man's meal was ready, Joe undid his jacket and took out the pup and the kitten. The Clumber spaniel settled herself by the hearth and suckled them both; and her eyes, following Joe's actions, were as bright as those of the old man.

Then Joe said, "Where might I find water and scraps for the bitch?"

"There's a pump outside, and a bone on the shelf," said the old man.

Joe found the bone, and fetched a pan of water, and set them beside the spaniel.

"Now," said the old man, "fetch cup and plate for yourself."

This Joe did, and ate his bread and drank his tea with the relish of hunger.

"If you care to stretch out on the hearth," said the old man, "you're welcome to sleep here; further, if you will

stay till my arm is mended, you can take care of my job
for me."

"What is your job?" asked Joe.

"That of King's Woodcutter."

"And how do you know I'm fit for it?"

"Didn't I see you handle the axe, when you chopped
me free?" said the old man. "I've no doubt as to your
fitness. But in the morning you must go and tell the King
you are doing my work."

4

Joe slept sound on the hearth-rug, and was up betimes.
He saw to the old man, the animals, and the hut; and,
when all was in order, asked his way to the King's palace.
The old man told him it was in the heart of the city, which
lay three miles due north; and he advised Joe to take with
him the royal axe, with the crown burned into the handle,
as a sign that his tale was true. So Joe set out upon this
new adventure.

At the end of the first mile, hearing a tiny mewing, he
looked behind him and saw that the honey-coloured
kitten had followed him; not wishing to go back, he
buttoned the pretty creature under his jacket again, and
pursued his way. The end of the second mile brought him
out of the forest, and at the end of the third he saw for the
first time the capital city of the country he lived in. As he
drew near, amazed at the sight of so many houses and
shops and churches, towers, temples, and turrets, domes,
spires, and weathercocks, he saw that the whole place was
in a commotion. The streets were packed with people
running about, or stooping and crawling, as they poked
their noses into every corner, grating, and cranny. At the
gates a tall sentinel barred Joe's way, demanding, "What
is your business?"

"Does that matter?" asked Joe.

"Not at all," said the sentinel, "for whatever it may be I have strict orders to let nobody in and nobody out."

"Very well," said Joe, supposing that this was the way it was in cities; whereas in the woods you came and went as you pleased. But as he turned to go the sentinel caught him by the shoulder, and cried: "How come you to be handling the royal axe?"

Joe told his story briefly, and the sentinel opened the gates. "Your business is the King's business," he said, "therefore you *must* come in. If anybody questions you, show him the axe, and it will be as good as a passport."

Nobody questioned Joe's right to be in the city, however, all being much too concerned with their peeping and poking and prying; the nearer Joe approached to the palace, the greater became the fuss; and on arrival he found the palace in such a state of confusion, with nobles and pages running hither and thither and wringing their hands in despair, that once more he passed unheeded through the courtyards and corridors, until he reached the throne-room itself. Here he found nobody at all but a lovely girl in tears. In her white dress, with her lemon-coloured hair, she reminded Joe of his Clumber Pup. He could not bear to see her in trouble, so he approached her and said, "If it's a hurt, show me, and perhaps I can heal it."

The girl checked her sobs enough to answer, "It is a very bad hurt indeed!"

"Whereabouts?" asked Joe.

"In my heart," said she.

"That's a hard place," said Joe. "How did it happen?"

"I have lost my kitten," said the girl, and began to cry again.

"I will give you my kitten in its place," said Joe.

"I only want *my* kitten."

"This is a very pretty kitten, picked up in the woods overnight," said Joe. "She's marked like the flower in oak, and her eyes are as gold as honey." And he took it out of his jacket.

"That is *my* kitten!" cried the girl. She stopped crying again, and caught the little ball of gold fluff from his hands, and kissed it many times. Then she ran and pulled a gold chain that rang a golden bell hanging in the middle of the hall. Instantly the room appeared to overflow with people, as everyone, from the kitchen boy to the King, came running to see what had happened. For the bell was only rung on great occasions.

The Princess, for it was no other, stood up on the throne, holding up her kitten in full view, and cried, "This boy has found my Honey!" The joy was overwhelming; the news ran like wildfire from the throne-room to the courtyard, and from the courtyard to the streets. In five minutes, everybody had returned to his business, the city gates were opened, and the King was asking Joe Jolly what he would like for a reward.

Joe would rather have liked to ask for the Princess, for she would have matched so nicely with his Clumber Pup; her hair was just the colour of his ears, and her soft brown eyes were looking at him as meltingly as any spaniel's. But of course she was out of the question, so he answered, "I should like the Royal Woodman's job, till the Royal Woodman is whole again."

"That won't be in *your* lifetime," said the King; a remark that puzzled Joe greatly, but he was too diffident to ask the King what he meant, for Kings, he supposed, had the right to talk as they pleased, even in riddles.

"Hand me that axe," said the King, "which I see is the royal axe, and kneel down on both knees and bow your head."

Joe hoped the King was not going to cut his head off, for any reason or none; but he obeyed, knelt down, and

felt himself touched between the shoulder-blades with the axe head. "Rise, Royal Woodman!" commanded the King. "Come once a month to the Forester's Lodge for orders, and let it be your first care to cut the choicest firing daily for the Princess's chamber."

No order could have pleased Joe better; he pulled his forelock, with a smile at the Princess, but she had turned away, and with her nose in her kitten's fur was whispering things into its ear. So he pulled his forelock again to the King, returned on his traces, and found all in the hut as he had left it.

"Well?" asked the old man.

"Very well, indeed," said Joe Jolly. "The kitten was the kitten of the Princess, in consequence of which the King has made me Royal Woodman till you are whole again."

"Did he say so?" asked the old man, with a curious smile.

"It's how I understood it," said Joe.

"Then so we will leave it," said the old man. "And since we are to bide together for a bit, you shall call me Daddy, for once I had a son who was a good son to me, and for his sake I like the ring of the word."

5

Daddy took longer to heal than Joe would have supposed possible. Month after month went by, and the fracture in his arm would not set; moreover, he seemed to have been so shaken by the accident, that he never left his bed. Gradually Joe grew accustomed to stretching out on the hearth without thinking that it would soon be for the last time; the new job turned into an old one, and the days mounted until a year had passed. The Clumber Pup was now a dog as beautiful as his Mother, but Joe continued to think of him as the Pup, if only to mark the difference

between them. The old dog lay mostly indoors by the hearth, or out of doors in the sun; but the Clumber Pup followed Joe daily to his work, and was the joy and delight of his heart. Since the day of his appointment Joe had stuck to the woods, and gone no nearer to the city than the Lodge of the King's Forester on the outskirts of the trees. He put in an appearance early in the morning on the first day of each month, and more often than not found the Forester chatting with a pretty chambermaid from the palace, whose name was Betty, and who evidently fancied a stroll in the morning dew before the duties of the day.

When she had gone, the Forester gave Joe his orders for the month; and wherever he might be cutting, he had each day to bind the special faggot of firing for the room of the Princess. He made the faggot of the sweetest-smelling wood he could find, and with it he always bound up a little posy of whatever the season might offer. In spring there were the primroses and violets; in summer, harebells, wild rose, and honeysuckle; in autumn the brightest leaves and berries; and even winter had her aconites.

On Joe's nineteenth birthday, which fell on the First of June, he went as usual to the Forester's Lodge, and there found Betty in her striped silk frock, gabbling away a little faster than her habit.

"Yes," she was saying, "that's how it is, and no other! There's something she wants, and nobody knows what, for she won't say. Sometimes she mopes, and sometimes she sings, sometimes she pouts and sometimes smiles, as changeable as the quarters of the year, and she won't tell her father, she won't tell her mother, she won't tell her nanny, and she won't tell *me!* And the doctor says if she don't get it soon, whatever it may be, she'll fall into a decline and die of longing."

"What's to be the end of it?" asked the Forester.

"Why, this; the King says that whoever can find out what the Princess is thinking, and give her what she wants, shall have whatever *he* wants, no matter whatso! On the last day of the month there's to be an Assembly at the palace, so that everybody can offer his opinion, and – Oh la! there's the eight o'clock bell ringing! Don't keep me gossiping any longer, or I'll be sure to be dismissed!"

The Forester kept her just long enough to give her a kiss, for which she boxed his ears, and then ran off as fast as her heels could carry her. The Forester laughed and said, "That's something like a wench!" and turned to Joe and gave him his orders for the month. Joe went back, his head so full of them, except for one corner that was full of being sorry for the Princess, that for some time he did not miss his Clumber Pup. But it was no longer gambolling about him, and even when he whistled did not come bounding and bouncing as usual; a thing any dog that loves his master must do when he hears the whistle, whether he wants to or not. So by then the pup must have got a long way off.

However, half through the morning he appeared, in the highest spirits, where Joe was working; though when they got home that evening he would not touch his supper. This would have worried Joe, if the pup had not been so unusually boisterous.

That night Joe had a curious dream, as he lay stretched on the rug before the dying fire: one of those dreams we get when we are half awake, that seem to take place outside instead of inside us. In this dream, Joe saw, as plain as if he was waking, his Clumber Pup lying nose to nose with the spaniel his mother, who lay with her head sunk flat on the floor between her two silky paws, and opened one beautiful brown eye to look at her child. And in his dream Joe seemed to hear how dogs make known their thoughts to each other, and the talk went this way between them. The spaniel said:

"What's the matter, son? Off your feed?"

"Not me, mother! I've had my fill today!"

"Where, then?"

"In the King's yard."

"What were you doing in the King's yard?"

"Meeting a friend of mine."

"What sort of a friend?"

"A cat."

"Be ashamed of yourself!"

"Not me, mother! It was my foster-sister."

"Oh, *that* cat."

"Yes, the Princess's cat."

"What is she like now?"

"Gold as honey."

"Does she spit?"

"Yes, secrets."

"What secrets?"

"She tells me what the Princess is thinking."

"How does she know?"

"The Princess cuddles her into her neck, and tells her in her ear."

"Whose neck and whose ear?"

"The Princess's neck and the cat's ear."

"Well, what is the Princess thinking?"

"She's thinking it's time she had a love-letter."

"Oh," said the spaniel, and suddenly went to sleep; and Joe's own sleep must have deepened, for he dreamed no more.

But in the morning he remembered his dream, and it seemed so real that he fell to puzzling. Was it a dream after all? His puzzle showed in his eyes, and Daddy from his couch asked, "What's bothering you?"

"A dream I had," said Joe. "I don't know whether to act on it or not."

"Would it be a good thing to act on it?" asked Daddy.

"It might save a damsel from a decline."

"And would it be a bad thing to act on it?"

"Not that *I* can see," said Joe.

"Then act on it," said Daddy.

So before he went to work that morning, Joe sat down and wrote a love-letter. He was not very good at writing, so he did not make it a long one, and therefore made it as much to the point as he could.

He wrote:

> "MY LOVE!
> "I love you because you are lovely like my Pup.
> "JOE JOLLY."

It was rather straggly and blotted by the time he had folded it, but it was quite readable, which, after what is in it, is the best thing about a love-letter; so Joe, quite satisfied, took it with him to his work, and put it inside a bunch of pink campions which he tied to the Princess's faggot. Then he thought no more about the matter till the First of July, when, going to the Forester's, he found Betty taking her leave with these words:

"So that's the end of it, thanks be! for when the folk came yesterday to say in Assembly what they thought she wanted, the Princess just laughed at them all and said, 'No need to guess, because I've got it!' but what it was she still wouldn't say; not that it matters, since now she's as gay as a lark, and the doctor comes no more."

6

Another year went by in peace and content. The work was good, the dogs thrived, the hut was comfortable, and there was always enough to eat; though, as Daddy still lay on the bed, Joe still lay on the floor. And on the First of June, his twentieth birthday, he went once more through the wood with the pup at his heels, to find Betty before

him at the Forester's Lodge. Who wouldn't, thought Joe, be glad to be out at such an hour, with the birds singing in the leaves, and the dew on the flowers in the grass? But today Betty looked less glad than usual as she gabbled the news.

"Yes!" she was saying, "there we are, just where we were a year ago, and it's all to do again. And she's no more help now than she was then; there's only one thing she wants in the world, what, nobody knows! though her father asks what, and her mother asks what, and her nanny asks what, and *I* ask what! The doctor comes daily to change her physic, all to no purpose, and he says if she doesn't get it soon she'll die of longing. So the last day of the month there's to be another Assembly, to say what the Princess wants, since she won't say herself, and he who gives it her shall have anything he names, no matter whatso, and – Bless me, Forester, there's the eight o'clock bell! Out upon you, keeping me here a-talking and a-talking when it's time for the Princess's chocolate!"

Off she ran, but not before the Forester had given her a hearty kiss, for which she smacked his face; and he only wagged his head saying, "An excellent wench!" Joe took his orders, and went away very much troubled. If the Princess wanted a second love-letter, he couldn't think of anything else to say; yet the first one had plainly ceased to serve her purpose. In his bother, he failed once more to observe the absence of the Clumber Pup. Later in the day he turned up, barking and jumping and wagging his tail, so that Joe had to throw down his axe and have a rough and tumble before he would be satisfied. Yet that night he never touched his supper at all, a thing that had only happened once before, just a twelve-month since, now Joe came to think of it. It brought it all back so strong to him, that as he lay on the mat before the fire and dozed off into his first sleep, he even dreamed that he heard the spaniel and her pup talking as they had talked a year ago.

"Now, pup, what's wrong that you can't gnaw your bone? Don't tell me you've distemper!"

"Not me, mother! I'm fed full of King's meat."

"Where did you get King's meat?"

"In the King's kitchen."

"What were you doing in the King's kitchen, then?"

"Calling on a friend."

"What friend, indeed?"

"A cat."

"Go drown yourself!"

"What for, mother? It was your foster-daughter."

"Ah, *that* one! How's she grown?"

"Gold as honey."

"But spits, no doubt?"

"Yes, secrets."

"Still what the Princess is thinking?"

"Still. The Princess tells her what she tells no other."

"And what's she thinking now?"

"That it is time she had a ring."

"Oh," said the spaniel. Her ear flopped over her eye, and she was asleep; and Joe's dream passed out of being.

But in the morning it revived in his mind, as clear as if it had happened. And had it not? He could not decide; and Daddy from his bed asked, "What's the puzzle?"

"A funny sort of dream I had last night. I don't know whether to do aught about it, or naught."

"If you did aught, what then?"

"It might save a damsel's life."

"And if naught?"

"She might die."

"I say, do aught," said Daddy.

So when he had bound the day's faggots for the Princess, Joe slipped his mother's brass wedding ring over the stems of a wild-rose posy, and tied it carefully among the branches. Then, having done his best, he dismissed it

from his thoughts, until a month later he heard Betty chattering volubly on the Forester's doorstep:

"Yes, clouds will pass on the darkest day, and butter come after the longest churning, and yesterday at the Assembly, before anybody could so much as open his mouth, the Princess laughed as happy as a child, and said, 'Don't put yourself to the trouble of guessing, for what I wanted I now have!' Never a word more, so we're still all at sea, but there, no matter; doctor's stopped coming, King and Queen stopped worrying, and the Princess goes singing all over the shop!"

7

Alas! a year later, on Joe's twenty-first birthday, the chambermaid had her sorry tale to tell again. That morning, when he reached the Lodge, she was relating, full of woe:

"Eat she won't and sleep she won't! She's white as a new pillow-slip! She weeps in corners, and stares at the sky, and says, 'no thank you' to all our offers; but sits by the hour with her honey cat in her arms, while doctor tears his hair, her father is distracted, her mother is distraught, and her nanny says nothing but 'Lawks-a-mussy me!' Even *I* can't get out of her what she wants. But this much I do know, if she doesn't get it soon, they'll be digging her green grave. The King has ordered another Assembly on the last day of the month, and whoever can give her what *she* wants may have whatever *he* wants, no matter whatso! Eight o'clock, eight o'clock, there goes eight o'clock, and me oughting to be at my work: give over gossiping, Forester, do!"

Away she started, but the Forester pulled her back to give her a kiss, for which she tugged his hair and ran; and he nodded his head remarking, "What a wench!" and

gave Joe his orders. But the thought of the Princess's
green grave was such a grief to Joe that he did not observe
the absence of the Clumber Pup till he was well at work.
After a bit, the pup sneaked up, with his tail between his
legs. Nothing Joe could do put him in spirits, and Joe
being out of spirits himself it was not a happy day. They
both went home depressed that night, and neither of
them touched his supper. As Joe stretched out on the
hearth, Daddy, who noticed everything, said, "Off your
feed?"

"Yes, somehow," replied Joe; and fell into an uneasy
sleep, in which he thought he heard the spaniel repeat the
question to her son.

"Off your feed, pup? What's up? A canker in your
ear?"

"Something like it, mother."

"No doubt you've been overeating again at the
palace."

"Not a bone. Not a scrap. I just went there to see a
friend."

"Oh, you've a friend there?"

"A cat."

"Give yourself a bad name, and hang yourself!"

"Why, mother? It was our honey cat."

"Our honey cat! How is she?"

"Gold as honey."

"Spits, though, I fear."

"Only secrets."

"Whose secrets?"

"The Princess's."

"And what does the Princess want now?"

"She wants me."

"You! What does she know of you?"

"The honey cat took me to her boudoir."

"The minx! I disown her! You in a boudoir, a kennel
dog like you!"

The spaniel put her paws over her eyes, and Joe heard no more talking in his fitful dreams.

But were they dreams, he asked himself in the morning, or had he been awake? Dream or no dream, he had a hole in his heart and Daddy could not but be aware of it.

"What is it, son?" he asked.

"I had a dream last night that's left me torn two ways."

"If you went one way, what then?"

"There might be no need to dig a green grave."

"And if you went the other?"

Joe fondled the Clumber Pup's lemon ears, and said, "That way might break my heart."

"Should we dig *your* grave then?"

"I expect I'd get over it."

"You'd not be the first," said Daddy, "to go through life with a mended heart; but once a grave is digged, it's digged."

"All right," said Joe.

He went out to his work, whistling to his pup to follow him, and when the day was done he made for the Princess a better faggot than he had ever made before, and tied his pup to it. The Clumber looked at him with mournful eyes, and tried to follow Joe home, dragging the faggot behind him. But Joe Jolly said, "Stay there!" and went away quickly through the forest.

8

That was the saddest month Joe ever lived through. He tried to be cheerful for Daddy's sake and the spaniel's, but Daddy himself was extra quiet, the spaniel moped for her pup, and Joe had to bear his own broken heart. On the last day of the month, when June was at her zenith, and the forest was rich with sunshine, Daddy said, "Joe, a man

can't work all the year round all his lifetime. Take a holiday!"

"What would I do with it?" asked Joe.

"Go to the city and see the sights."

Then it occurred to Joe that among the sights of the city was his own sweet pup. The mere thought of looking into his brown eyes and hearing his gay excited bark again made Joe's heart as light as a feather. He decided to follow Daddy's advice; his work was well in hand, and he could spare the day.

So off he set, and once out of the forest was amazed at the crowds on the road, until he remembered that this was the day of the Assembly. He allowed himself to be swept along on the stream towards the palace; for everybody had a right there on this day, and there, if anywhere, he would see his pup. It was with an eager heart he passed, for the second time, under the royal gateway, and entered the throne-room with the rest of the crowd.

The court was all assembled; from the middle of the crush, Joe could just manage to see the heads of the King and Queen, and the tops of the soldiers' pikes. A trumpet sounded, and a herald cried for silence. When this was obtained, he shouted:

"If any man present knows what the Princess wants, let him say so!"

But before a word could be spoken, the voice of the Princess called out, as gay as sunshine in the leaves, "There is no need, for what I want I have!"

"What is it?" asked the King.

"Who gave it to you?" asked the Queen.

"I will neither say what it is nor who gave it to me," said the Princess. "Let everybody go."

The herald blew his trumpet and dismissed the crowd. As it dispersed, Joe was left standing in the middle of the floor, in view of the great double throne, with the Princess seated at the King's feet, the honey cat in her arms,

and crouched against her knee the Clumber Pup.
Suddenly there was a yelp of joy, the pup leapt into the
air, bounded across the floor, placed his gleaming paws
on Joe's two shoulders, and licked his face, whining and
barking as though his heart would burst. Joe hugged him,
and wept.

Then what a commotion in court! Everybody asked,
"What is it? Who is it? What is happening?" The Princess
rose, looking over the head of her honey cat, half smiling
and half crying, and the King demanded, "Who are
you?"

"I'm your Royal Woodman," said Joe.

"Why, so I remember! But the dog goes to you as to his
master."

"He was his master," said the Princess, "but now I am.
This boy gave him to me, because what I wanted was the
Clumber Pup."

"Then I can at last make good my word!" said the
King. He beckoned Joe nearer. "What do you want,
Woodman? Name it, and it is yours."

The Princess looked at Joe, and he looked at the Princess, with her white dress and her lemon-coloured locks.
But he knew he must not ask for what he wanted most.
So he put it out of his mind, and said, "I would be glad of
an extra mattress, so that I could lie on it instead of on the
floor."

"You shall have the best in the kingdom," said the
King.

But the Princess cried quickly, "He must have something besides, for last year he also gave me what I
wanted!" And she held up the old brass wedding-ring.

The King, being as good as his word, turned again to
Joe, and asked, "What else do you want?"

Joe clasped the Clumber Pup to his heart, but of course
he could not ask for it, for the Princess would die of
longing if he took his dog away. So he put the thought

from him, and said, "When I came to this place, I left behind me, in my dwelling far away, my father's old chair. I should like to have that chair to sit in of a night, if it was doing nobody a bad turn."

The King smiled graciously, and said, "The chair shall be brought to you this very night, and in its place we will leave the best chair in the kingdom."

He made a sign that the audience was ended, but the Princess cried still quicker than before, "No, father! he must ask for a third thing, because two years ago he gave me this." And she pulled out of her dress the old blotted love-letter, which was now older and more blotted than ever. The King took it from her, opened it curiously, and read aloud for all the court to hear:

"MY LOVE!
"I love you because you are lovely like my Pup.
"JOE JOLLY."

The Princess hid her face in her honey cat.
"Are you Joe Jolly?" asked the King.
"Yes, sir," said Joe.
"Did you write this?"
"Yes, sir."
"And is it true?"

Joe looked from his white pup, with its lemon head, to the white-robed Princess with her lemon hair, and said for the third time, "Yes, sir."

"Then," said the King, "you must ask for the thing you want most in the world."

Joe looked longingly at the Clumber Pup, and kissed it hard between the eyes. Then he looked at the Princess, but she wouldn't look at him. He had to say something, and at last said slowly, "As I can't have my pup, I'll have the honey cat."

"Oh!" cried the Princess quickly, "you can't have my cat without me!"

"Then," said Joe, quicker still, "you can't have my dog without me!"

"So let it be!" said the King. "One half of the year you shall live in the Woodman's hut, and the other half in the palace; and wherever you live, the dog and the cat must live with you."

That very evening Joe Jolly took his bride back to the hut, the honey cat purring in her arms like an aeroplane, and the Clumber Pup leaping round them, being a happy nuisance. A bright fire burned on the hearth, supper was spread on the table, a soft mattress lay on the bed, and by the fire stood old John Jolly's armchair. But the Clumber spaniel had disappeared for ever, and Daddy was gone too. When Joe came to inquire about him, he was told that the old Royal Woodman had died a month before Joe Jolly had come that way, and that the post had been left vacant till the right man appeared to fill it.

The Charmed Life

E. Nesbit

There was once a Prince whose father failed in business and lost everything he had in the world – crown, kingdom, money, jewels, and friends. This was because he was so fond of machinery that he was always making working models of things he invented, and so had no time to attend to the duties that Kings are engaged for. So he lost his situation. There is a King in French history who was fond of machinery, particularly clock-work, and he lost everything too, even his head. The King in this story kept his head, however, and when he wasn't allowed to make laws any more, he was quite content to go on making machines. And as his machines were a great deal better than his laws had ever been, he soon got a nice little business together, and was able to buy a house in another kingdom, and settle down comfortably with his wife and son. The house was one of those delightful villas called after Queen Anne (the one whose death is still so often mentioned and so justly deplored), with stained glass to the front door, and coloured tiles on the front-garden path, and gables where there was never need of gables, and nice geraniums and calceolarias in the front garden, and pretty red brick on the front of the house. The back of the house was yellow brick, because that did not show so much.

Here the King and Queen and the Prince lived very pleasantly. The Queen snipped the dead geraniums off with a pair of gold scissors, and did fancy-work for bazaars. The Prince went to the Red-Coat School, and the King worked up his business. In due time the Prince was apprenticed to his father's trade: and a very industrious apprentice he was, and never had anything to do with the idle apprentices who play pitch and toss on tombstones, as you see in Mr Hogarth's picture.

When the Prince was twenty-one his mother called him to her. She put down the blotting-book she was embroidering for the School Bazaar in a tasteful pattern of stocks and nasturtiums, and said:

"My dear son, you have had the usual coming-of-age presents – silver cigar-case and match-box; a handsome set of brushes with your initials on the back; a Gladstone bag, also richly initialled; the complete works of Dickens and Thackeray; a Swan fountain-pen mounted in gold; and the heartfelt blessing of your father and mother. But there is still one more present for you."

"You are too good, mamma," said the Prince, fingering the nasturtium-coloured silks.

"Don't fidget," said the Queen, "and listen to me. When you were a baby a fairy, who was your godmother, gave you a most valuable present – a Charmed Life. As long as you keep it safely, nothing can harm you."

"How delightful!" said the Prince. "Why, mamma, you might have let me go to sea when I wanted to. It would have been quite safe."

"Yes, my dear," said the Queen, "but it's best to be careful. I have taken care of your life all these years, but now you are old enough to take care of it for yourself. Let me advise you to keep it in a safe place. You should never carry valuables about on your person."

And then she handed the Charmed Life over to him, and he took it and kissed her, and thanked her and then

went away and hid it. He took a brick out of the wall of
the villa, and hid his Life behind it. The bricks in the walls
of these Queen Anne villas generally come out quite
easily.

Now, the father of the Prince had been King of
Bohemia, so, of course, the Prince was called Florizel,
which is their family name; but when the King went
into business he went in as Rex Bloomsbury, and his
great patent Lightning Lift Company called itself
R. Bloomsbury and Co., so that the Prince was
known as F. Bloomsbury, which was as near as the
King dared go to 'Florizel, Prince of Bohemia'. His
mother, I am sorry to say, called him Florrie till he was
quite grown up.

Now, the King of the country where Florizel lived was
a very go-ahead sort of man, and as soon as he heard that
there were such things as lifts – which was not for a long
time, because no one ever lets a King know anything if it
can be helped – he ordered one of the very, very best for
his palace. Next day a card was brought in by one of
the palace footmen. It had on it: 'Mr. F. Bloomsbury,
R. Bloomsbury and Co.'

"Show him in," said the King.

"Good-morning, sire," said Florizel, bowing with that
perfect grace which is proper to Princes.

"Good-morning, young man," said the King. "About
this lift, now."

"Yes, sire. May I ask how much your Majesty is prepared to . . ."

"Oh, never mind price," said the King; "it all comes
out of the taxes."

"I should think, then, that Class A . . . our special
Argentinella design – white satin cushions, woodwork
overlaid with ivory and inset with pearls, opals, and
silver."

"Gold," said the King shortly.

"Not with pearls and ivory," said Florizel firmly. He had excellent taste. "The gold pattern – we call it the Anriradia – is inlaid with sapphires, emeralds, and black diamonds."

"I'll have the gold pattern," said the King; "but you might run up a little special lift for the Princess's apartments. I dare say she'd like that Argentinella pattern – 'Simple and girlish', I see it says in your circular."

So Florizel booked the order, and the gold and sapphire and emerald lift was made and fixed, and all the Court was so delighted that it spent its whole time in going up and down in it, and there had to be new blue satin cushions within a week.

Then the Prince superintended the fixing of the Princess's lift – the Argentinella design – and the Princess Candida herself came to look on at the works; and she and Florizel met, and their eyes met, and their hands met, because his caught hers, and dragged her back, just in time to save her from being crushed by a heavy steel bar that was being lowered into its place.

"Why, you've saved my life," said the Princess.

But Florizel could say nothing. His heart was beating too fast, and it seemed to be beating in his throat, and not in its proper place behind his waistcoat.

"Who are you?" said the Princess.

"I'm an engineer," said the Prince.

"Oh dear!" said the Princess, "I thought you were a Prince. I'm sure you look more like a Prince than any Prince *I've* ever seen."

"I wish I was a Prince," said Florizel; "but I never wished it till three minutes ago."

The Princess smiled, and then she frowned, and then she went away.

Florizel went straight back to the office, where his father, Mr Rex Bloomsbury, was busy at his knee-hole writing-table.

He spent the morning at the office, and the afternoon in the workshop.

"Father," he said, "I don't know what ever will become of me. I wish I was a Prince!"

The King and Queen of Bohemia had never let their son know that he was a Prince; for what is the use of being a Prince if there's never going to be a kingdom for you?

Now, the King, who was called R. Bloomsbury, Esq., looked at his son over his spectacles and said:

"Why?"

"Because I've been and gone and fallen head over ears in love with the Princess Candida."

The father rubbed his nose thoughtfully with his fountain pen.

"Humph!" he said; "you've fixed your choice high."

"Choice!" cried the Prince distractedly. "There wasn't much choice about it. She just looked at me, and there I was, don't you know? I didn't *want* to fall in love like this. Oh, father, it hurts most awfully! What ever shall I do?"

After a long pause, full of thought, his father replied:

"Bear it, I suppose."

"But I *can't* bear it – at least, not unless I can see her every day. Nothing else in the world matters in the least."

"Dear me!" said his father.

"Couldn't I disguise myself as a Prince, and try to make her like me a little?"

"The disguise you suggest is quite beyond our means at present."

"Then I'll disguise myself as a lift attendant," said Florizel.

And what is more, he did it. His father did not interfere. He believed in letting young people manage their own love affairs.

So then when the lift was finished, and the Princess and her ladies crowded round to make the first ascent in it,

there was Florizel dressed in white satin knee-breeches,
and coat with mother-o'-pearl buttons. He had silver
buckles to his shoes, and a tiny opal breast-pin on the
lappet of his coat, where the white flower goes at wed-
dings.

When the Princess saw him she said:

"Now, none of you girls are to go in the lift at all,
mind! It's *my* lift. You can use the other one, or go up the
mother-of-pearl staircase, as usual."

Then she stepped into the lift, and the silver doors
clicked, and the lift went up, just carrying her and
him.

She had put on a white silky gown, to match the new
lift, and she, too, had silver buckles on her shoes, and a
string of pearls round her throat, and a silver chain set
with opals in her dark hair; and she had a bunch of
jasmine flowers at her neck. As the lift went out of sight
the youngest lady-in-waiting whispered:

"What a pretty pair! Why, they're made for each other!
What a pity he's a lift-man. He looks exactly like a
Prince."

"Hold your tongue, silly!" said the eldest lady-in-
waiting, and she slapped her.

The Princess went up and down in the lift all the
morning, and when at last she had to step out of it because
the palace luncheon-bell had rung three times, and the
roast peacock was getting cold, the eldest lady-in-waiting
noticed that the Lift-man had a jasmine flower fastened to
his coat with a little opal pin.

The eldest lady-in-waiting kept a sharp eye on the
Princess, but after the first day the Princess only seemed
to go up and down in the lift when it was really necessary,
and then she always took the youngest lady-in-waiting
with her; so that though the Lift-man always had a flower
in his buttonhole, there was no reason to suppose it had
not been given him by his mother.

"I suppose I'm a silly, suspicious little thing," said the eldest lady-in-waiting. "Of course, it was the lift that amused her, just at first. How *could* a Princess be interested in a lift-man?"

Now, when people are in love, and want to be quite certain that they are loved in return, they will take any risks to find out what they want to know. But as soon as they are *quite sure*, they begin to be careful.

And after those seventy-five ups and downs in the lift, on the first day, the Princess no longer had any doubt that she was beloved by the Lift-man. Not that he had said a word about it, but she was a clever Princess, and she had seen how he picked up the jasmine flower she let fall, and kissed it when she pretended she wasn't looking and he pretended he didn't know she was. Of course, she had been in love with him ever since they met, and their eyes met, and their hands. She told herself it was because he had saved her life, but that wasn't the real reason at all.

So, being quite sure, she began to be careful.

"Since he really loves me he'll find a way to tell me so, right out. It's his part, not mine, to make everything possible," she said.

As for Florizel, he was quite happy. He saw her every day, and every day when he took his place in his lift there was a fresh jasmine flower lying on the satin cushion. And he pinned it into his buttonhole and wore it there all day, and thought of his lady, and of how that first wonderful day she had dropped a jasmine flower, and how he had picked it up when she pretended she was not looking, and he was pretending that he did not know she was. But all the same he wanted to know exactly how that jasmine flower came there every day, and whose hand brought it. It might be the youngest lady-in-waiting, but Florizel didn't think so.

So he went to the palace one morning bright and early, much earlier than usual, and there was no jasmine flower.

Then he hid behind one of the white velvet window-curtains of the corridor and waited. And, presently, who should come stealing along on the tips of her pink toes – so as to make no noise at all – but the Princess herself, fresh as the morning in a white muslin frock with a silver ribbon round her waist, and a bunch of jasmine at her neck. She took one of the jasmine flowers and kissed it and laid it on the white satin seat of the lift, and when she stepped back there was the Lift-man.

"Oh!" said Candida, and blushed like a child that is caught in mischief.

"Oh!" said Florizel, and he picked up the jasmine and kissed it many times.

"Why do you do that?" said the Princess.

"Because you did," said the Prince. "I saw you. Do you want to go on pretending any more?"

The Princess did not know what to say, so she said nothing.

Florizel came and stood quite close to her.

"I used to wish I was a Prince," he said, "but I don't know now. I'd rather be an engineer. If I'd been a Prince I should never have seen you."

"I don't want you to be a bit different," said the Princess. And she stopped to smell the jasmine in his buttonhole.

"So we're betrothed," said Florizel.

"Are we?" said Candida.

"Aren't we?" he said.

"Well, yes, I suppose we are," said she.

"Very well, then," said Florizel, and he kissed the Princess.

"You're sure you don't mind marrying an engineer?" he said, when she had kissed him back.

"Of course not," said the Princess.

"Then I'll buy the ring," said he, and kissed her again.

Then she gave him the rest of the jasmine, with a kiss

for each star, and he gave her a keepsake in return, and they parted.

"My heart is yours," said Florizel, "and my life is in your hands."

"My life is yours," said she, "and my heart is in your heart."

Now, I am sorry to say that somebody had been listening all the time behind another curtain, and when the Princess had gone to breakfast and the Lift-man had gone down in his lift, this somebody came out and said, "Aha!"

It was a wicked, disagreeable, snub-nosed page-boy, who would have liked to marry the Princess himself. He had really no chance, and never could have had, because his father was only a rich brewer. But he felt himself to be much superior to a lift-man. And he was the kind of boy who always sneaks if he has half a chance. So he went and told the King that he had seen the Princess kissing the Lift-man in the morning all bright and early.

The King said he was a lying hound, and put him in prison at once for mentioning such a thing – which served him right.

Then the King thought it best to find out for himself whether the snub-nosed page-boy had spoken the truth.

So he watched in the morning all bright and early, and he saw the Princess come stealing along on the tips of her little pink toes, and the lift (Argentinella design) came up, and the Lift-man in it. And the Princess gave him kissed jasmine to put in his buttonhole.

So the King jumped out on them and startled them dreadfully. And Florizel was locked up in prison, and the Princess was locked up in her room with only the eldest lady-in-waiting to keep her company. And the Princess cried all day and all night. And she managed to hide the keepsake the Prince had given her. She hid it in a little

book of verses. And the eldest lady saw her do it. Florizel was condemned to be executed for having wanted to marry someone so much above him in station. But when the axe fell on his neck the axe flew to pieces, and the neck was not hurt at all. So they sent for another axe and tried again. And again the axe splintered and flew. And when they picked up the bits of the axe they had all turned to leaves of poetry books.

So they put off the execution till next day.

The gaoler told the snub-nosed page all about it when he took him his dinner of green water and mouldering crusts.

"Couldn't do the trick!" said the gaoler. "Two axes broke off short and the bits turned to rubbish. The executioner says the rascal has a Charmed Life."

"Of course he has," said the page, sniffing at the crusts with his snub-nose. "I know all about that, but I shan't tell unless the King gives me a free pardon and something fit to eat. Roast pork and onion stuffing, I think. And you can tell him so."

So the gaoler told the King. And the King gave the snub-nosed page the pardon and the pork, and then the page said:

"He has a Charmed Life. I heard him tell the Princess so. And what is more, he gave it to her to keep. And she said she'd hide it in a safe place!"

Then the King told the eldest lady-in-waiting to watch, and she did watch, and saw the Princess take Florizel's Charmed Life and hide it in a bunch of jasmine. So she took the jasmine and gave it to the King, and he burnt it. But the Princess had not left the Life in the jasmine.

Then they tried to hang Florizel, because, of course, he had an ordinary life as well as a charmed one, and the King wished him to be without any life at all.

Thousands of people crowded to see the presumptuous

Lift-man hanged, and the execution lasted the whole morning, and seven brand new ropes were wasted one after the other, and they all left off being ropes and turned into long wreaths of jasmine, which broke into bits rather than hang such a handsome Lift-man.

The King was furious. But he was not too furious to see that the Princess must have taken the Charmed Life out from the jasmine flowers, and put it somewhere else, when the eldest lady-in-waiting was not looking.

And it turned out afterwards that the Princess had held Florizel's life in her hand all the time the execution was going on. The eldest lady-in-waiting was clever, but was not so clever as the Princess.

The next morning the eldest lady brought the Princess's silver mirror to the King.

"The Charmed Life is in that, your Majesty," she said. "I saw the Princess put it in."

And so she had, but she had not seen the Princess take it out again almost directly afterwards.

The King smashed the looking-glass, and gave orders that poor Florizel was to be drowned in the palace fishpond.

So they tied big stones to his hands and feet and threw him in. And the stones changed to corks and held him up, and he swam to land, and when they arrested him as he landed they found that on each of the corks there was a beautiful painting of Candida's face, as she saw it every morning in her mirror.

Now, the King and Queen of Bohemia, Florizel's father and mother, had gone to Margate for a fortnight's holiday.

"We will have a thorough holiday," said the King; "we will forget the world, and not even look at a newspaper."

But on the third day they both got tired of forgetting

the world, and each of them secretly bought a newspaper and read it on the beach, and each rushed back and met the other on the steps of the boarding-house where they were staying. And the Queen began to cry, and the King took her in his arms on the doorstep, to the horror of the other boarders, who were looking out of the windows at them; and then they rushed off to the railway station, leaving behind them their luggage and the astonished boarders, and took a special train to town. Because the King had read in his newspaper, and the Queen in hers, that the Lift-man was being executed every morning from nine to twelve; and though, so far, none of the executions had ended fatally, yet at any moment the Prince's Charmed Life might be taken, and then there would be an end of the daily executions – a very terrible end.

Arrived at the capital, the poor Queen of Bohemia got into a hansom with the King, and they were driven to the palace. The palace-yard was crowded.

"What is the matter?" the King of Bohemia asked.

"It's that Lift-man," said a bystander, with spectacles and a straw hat; "he has as many lives as a cat. They tried boiling oil this morning, and the oil turned into white-rose leaves, and the fire under it turned to a white-rose bush. And now the King has sent for Princess Candida, and is going to have it out with her. The whole thing has been most exciting."

"I should think so," said the Lift-man's father.

He gave his arm to his wife, and they managed to squeeze through to the great council hall, where the King of that country sat on his gold throne, surrounded by lords-in-waiting, judges in wigs, and other people in other things.

Florizel was there loaded with chains, and standing in a very noble attitude at one corner of the throne steps. At the other stood the Princess, looking across at her lover.

"Now," said the King, "I am tired of diplomacy and tact, and the eldest lady-in-waiting is less of a Sherlock Holmes than I thought her, so let us be straightforward and honest. Have you got a Charmed Life?"

"I haven't exactly got it," said Florizel. "My life is not my own now."

"Did he give it to you?" the King asked his daughter.

"I cannot tell a lie, father," said the Princess, just as though her name had been George Washington instead of Candida; "he did give it to me."

"What have you done with it?"

"I have hidden it in different places. I have saved it; he saved mine once."

"Where is it?" asked her father, "as you so justly observe you cannot tell a lie."

"If I tell you," said the Princess, "will you give your Royal word that the execution you have ordered for this morning shall be really the last? You can destroy the object that I have hidden his Charmed Life in, and then you can destroy him. But you must promise me not to ask me to hide his Life in any new place, because I am tired of hide-and-seek."

All the judges and lords-in-waiting and people felt really sorry for the Princess, for they thought that all these executions had turned her brain.

"I gave you my Royal word," said the King upon his throne. "I won't ask you to hide his Life any more. Indeed, I was against the practice from the first. Now, where have you hidden his Life?"

"In my heart," said the Princess, brave and clear, so that everyone heard her in the big hall. "You can't take his Life without taking mine, and if you take mine you may as well take his, for he won't care to go on living without me."

She sprang across the throne steps to Florizel, and his fetters jangled as she threw her arms around him.

"Dear me!" said the King, rubbing his nose with his sceptre; "this is very awkward."

But the father and mother of Florizel had wriggled and wormed their way through the crowd to a front place, and now the father spoke.

"Your Majesty, allow me. Perhaps I can assist your decision."

"Oh, all right," said the King upon his throne; "go ahead. I'm struck all of a heap."

"You see before you," said the King of Bohemia, "one known to the world of science and of business as R. Bloomsbury, inventor and patenter of many mechanical novelties – among others the Patent Lightning Lift – now formed into a company of which I am chairman. The young Lift-man – whose fetters are most clumsily designed, if you will pardon my saying so – is my son."

"Of course he's somebody's son," said the King upon his throne.

"Well, he happens to be mine, and I gather that you do not think him a good enough match for your daughter."

"Without wishing to hurt your feelings ..." began Candida's father.

"Exactly. Well, know, O King on your throne, and everyone else, that this young Lift-man is no other than Florizel, Prince of Bohemia. I am the King of Bohemia, and this is my Queen."

As he spoke he took his crown out of his pocket and put it on. His wife took off her bonnet and got her crown out of her reticule and put that on, and Florizel's crown was handed to the Princess, who fitted it on for him, because his hands were awkward with chains.

"Your most convincing explanation alters everything," said the King upon his throne, and he came down to meet the visitors. "Bless you, my children! Strike off his chains, can't you? I hope there's no ill-feeling,

Florizel," he added, turning to the Prince. "Will half an hour from now suit you for the wedding?"

So they were married, and they still live very happily. They will live as long as is good for them, and when Candida dies Florizel will die too, because she still carries his Life in her heart.

The Young Man with Music in his Fingers

Diana Ross

Once upon a time there was a young man who went out into the world to seek his fortune with nothing but a pleasant face, good health, and a kind heart.

He had not gone far before he came to a forest and heard such a clamour of birds, as if all the birds of the air were gathered together in that one place and making a noise.

When he went into the forest to see what was afoot he found a Jenny Wren caught fast in a snare, and all her friends and relations, and even her casual acquaintances sitting round her on the branches of trees and bushes, weeping and wailing and scolding and screeching, which may have consoled her, but was of little practical value.

The youth, however, took pity on her and at once set her free. And now there was such a sweet sound of rejoicing and whistling and cooing, you would have thought that all the springs for a hundred years were being celebrated all at once.

And Jenny Wren flew up on the young man's shoulder, and thanking him prettily for his timely aid told him that she in return would give him a gift.

"Only blow upon your fingers," she said, "and you shall make such music as if all the flutes in the world were being played by skilled musicians."

So the youth put up his fingers and blew upon them, and sure enough, it was just as Jenny Wren had said. There was the sweet sound of flutes in that forest as if all the musicians in the world were blowing on their flutes at a king's banquet.

So the youth thanked Jenny Wren and was glad to see how gaily now she flew away, and on he went well pleased at his accomplishment.

He went on with his travels and at last he came to the sea, and was walking on the shore wondering how he should go farther when he suddenly noticed a flashing of silver among the dark rocks and heard the sound of splashing water, and hurrying over to where it was he saw a fine fish which had been left high and dry in a small rock pool, and the tide had gone back and left it.

He saw how desperately it was flapping about under the hot noon sun and he was sorry for it, so he caught it in his hands and carried it from the shallow pool and threw it once more into the deep water of the sea, and was glad to see the splendid shining of its scales as it plunged proudly down into the deep water.

But before it disappeared it swam close to the rock on which he was standing.

"Twang upon your fingers," said the fish, "and you shall make the music of harps, as if all the waters of the world were running sweetly down to the sea."

So the youth twanged upon his fingers and it was just as the fish had said, and there was the noise of harps playing as if all the harps in the world were being plucked by skilled musicians.

So he thanked the fish and went on his way well pleased with this new accomplishment.

Well, he found a boat by the sea and he crossed over it in the boat and came to a strange land.

He went ashore and found a savage wilderness, and he

began to journey through it, and dreary and desolate he found it.

Now as he was going forward he suddenly heard a great roaring, and the tall grass through which he went trembled and bent low before the sound.

So terrible was the roaring that at first he was afraid, but he was a bold youth and did not like to go back, so on he went and came to a pit cunningly dug in the ground, and a young lion had fallen into it, and its mother and father and three young brothers were standing round, looking into the pit and bewailing its fate with their terrible cries.

Now, he might well have been more frightened than before, but his pity for the poor beasts quite overcame his fear, and climbing down into the pit he lifted up the young lion in his arms and put it once more at its mother's side. Then climbing out again he rejoiced to see how gaily it ran about and how proudly the parents tossed their great heads with joy.

He was about to continue on his way when the lion approached him and said:

"For restoring our son to safety I will give you a gift. Only clap your hands together and the noise will be as if all the drummers of all the armies in the world were beating on their drums."

So the youth did as the lion said and clapped his hands, and at once, such a tattooing and drumming and rub-a-dub dubbing, as if a thousand thousand drummer boys were let loose with their drums to make as much noise as they could for the king's coronation.

So here was the youth with yet another talent, and on he went well pleased with himself as well he might be.

Then he passed out of the wilderness and came among men, and went through villages and cultivated land, and saw a town in the distance where the king of that country lived. He was hurrying to reach it before nightfall when

he heard a wailing coming from a field at the side of the
road, and he found lying under the bushes a tiny child,
quite exhausted and scarcely breathing.

So he picked it up and carried it into the next village,
which he found in a state of great confusion, for the child
had strayed from its mother's side in the harvest field and
for three days and nights had been lost, and everyone had
joined in the search, but with no result, and they had all
despaired of ever seeing it again.

Well, as you can imagine, they were all rejoiced to see
him approaching, the child in his arms, and its parents
made him stay by them for the night, and nothing they
could do was too much for them. And in the morning, as
he was about to set forth, the mother said:

"I will give you a gift for bringing me back my child. If
ever you open you mouth to sing the sound shall be like a
choir of sweet singers singing at a festival in honour of the
king."

And the young man opened his mouth and sang, and
the sound was even as she had said. So he thanked her for
her gift and went rejoicing on his way towards the city.

Now as he drew near the city gates he noticed all the
people going in, and he saw a tiny hovel just beside the
gates, and an old woman sitting there, her cat by her side.
And as the people went by she greeted each one, and
asked them where they were going and where they had
come from, and how they fared and what was their
business.

But such a miserable old thing she seemed that most of
those who passed took no notice of her, a few cursed her,
many told her rudely they were about their own business,
and not one of them gave her a civil answer or returned
her greeting.

But when the young man came by and she hailed him,
he returned her a good morrow, and told her where he
came from, and how he was seeking his fortune, and as

for how he fared, he fared well and wished the same to her. And he stooped and tickled the cat under its chin, and it shut its eyes and purred.

"You are a polite young man," said the old woman, "and that is a rare thing hereabouts. As for me, I am a Wise Woman, and if you will lodge in my house I can help you to come by the fortune you seek."

So he thanked her and went in, and then she told him that so many people were coming into the city because the king's only daughter had come of age to marry, and at noon this day heralds at the gate of the palace would declare the conditions of her choice.

So at noon that day the young man went with many others and stood at the gates of the palace. And as the hour struck the princess herself appeared on a golden throne set up in the courtyard of the palace, and at her side were heralds in scarlet and gold who blew loud blasts on their trumpets and cried in a loud voice:

"Listen to me, all you people, and then you shall hear of that which must be done.

"The Princess will marry no-one until she is properly crowned. And the crown with which she wishes to be crowned is thus.

"It shall be fashioned of the lightning snapped from the fingers of the Mad Man of the Sky.

"It shall be set with the seven rubies which shine among the scales of the Old Serpent of the Earth and the seven green emeralds that hang in the hair of the Ancient Maiden of the Sea.

"If this you cannot bring to her, then she will have none of you, but will live and die a maiden, and the country at her death will be left without a ruler, and woe betide the people if that day should come!"

And again they blew on their trumpets, and the people began to murmur, and soon there was a great noise of talk, some rejoicing that all men were free to try to win

the maiden. "For," said these, "one man is as good as another, and you or I are as likely to win the treasures with which to fashion her crown as anyone else."

But though they spoke so hopefully, they didn't seem very clear as to how they should set about it.

And the rest of the people, and most of the old ones among them, bewailed these hard conditions, and were full of foreboding.

"Be sure," these said, "the land will be left without a ruler, and then you may be certain there will be trouble and wars, and no peace anywhere, and injustice and evil. And all were better dead."

But the young man when he heard what the heralds had said was well enough pleased. No sooner had he seen the Princess where she sat on her throne than he had no thought beside than to marry her.

"And if the conditions are hard," he thought, "my rivals will be all the fewer."

So he went back quickly to the Wise Woman and told her all about it, and asked her how he might find the Old Serpent of the Earth, for he thought he would come to him more easily than to either of the others. "And I may as well start by succeeding, even if in the end I fail."

So the Wise Woman told him how he should find the lair of the Old Serpent, in the side of a dark mountain at the farthest ends of the earth.

"But beware," she said, "how you approach him. For he is old and terrible, and has moreover not slept these thousand thousand years. And this, as you can imagine, has not improved his temper. And if you approach him, you do so at your own risk, for I would not go near him. No! Not for all the rubies in the world."

"Oh! well," said the youth, "but you are not wooing a maiden, and that makes all the difference, as everyone knows."

And he thanked her for her directions, and away he went just as she had told him.

He travelled without ceasing for seven days and seven nights, and then he came to the dark mountain at the farthest ends of the earth, and here it was the Old Serpent had his lair.

So he boldly went up the face of the mountain till he came to the entrance of a dark cavern, and very dark and dismal it looked, and he feared going into that place, knowing what he would find there.

But then he bethought himself of his accomplishments.

"I have heard," he thought, "that serpents have a liking for sweet sounds. I will play to him the sweet music of flutes, and if that fails to please him I am a lost man."

So he sat down at the grisly entrance of the cave and he blew on his fingers, and he blew and blew, and such sweet music was made as if all the flutes in the world were blown upon softly by skilled musicians, and the extreme sweetness of the noise sounded strange in that grim place.

Then as he played he felt the earth begin to shake beneath him.

"Ah! here is the old one bestirring himself," he said, and grew pale, as well he might.

But he went on blowing on his fingers, and soon, from the dark recesses of the cavern, he saw the great serpent uprearing its golden scales set with precious stones glowing dimly in the dark, and he saw its shining eyes, cold and bright as diamonds, and his hands and feet grew clammy and cold, and his mouth dry as he met its hard unwinking stare.

But still he blew upon his fingers and made soft music, and at last the huge serpent began to swing and sway. And as it uncoiled itself and reared itself up in that vast cavern the whole mountain shook, and the whole world

with it, for it had not so bestirred itself for a million years and more.

"Who are you?" it said at last. "It is well for you that you make sweet music, for had you disturbed me otherwise, you would not have long regretted it."

"I am come," said the youth, "to ask you a favour. Give me the seven red rubies set in the scales of your head. For the maiden I want to marry must have them in her crown, or she will not marry, but will live and die a maid."

"You are brave," said the serpent, "to come asking favours of me. But only go on playing the music you were making for seven days and seven nights without ceasing and then I will sleep. And that I have not done for a thousand thousand years, and for that I will gladly give you the jewels you are seeking."

So the youth set himself down and for seven days and seven nights he blew on his fingers without ceasing, and all that time the rocky wilderness echoed and re-echoed to the sweet sound of flutes, and the Old Serpent coiled itself up, and its hard, unwinking eyes were closed, and such a deep peace fell on the place and on the whole earth people marvelled and wondered what it could mean.

At the end of that time the youth stopped playing, and on the instant the Old Serpent was awake.

Then the serpent let the youth approach, and he took the seven red rubies from the other bright jewels set in the scales of its head, and wrapping them up in his kerchief and tying it to his belt the young man thanked the serpent and turned his back on that lonely place, and though he came out unharmed he was not sorry to be gone.

"I have not heard such music since the stars took up their station in the sky", it said. And it sighed, and it was as if the earth shook itself and was awake.

Then he made his way back to the city, and the Wise Woman at the gate, and he told her all that had happened

and gave her the jewels to look after while he went seeking the others, and asked her how he should come to the Ancient Maiden of the Sea, to get the seven green emeralds the princess wanted for her crown.

So the Wise Woman told him how he must go to the edge of the sea, and unless he could win her to come up to him he would never hold speech with her, for she sat in her palace ten thousand fathoms deep in the middle of the sea, and so hated the light and the sounds and sight of men that she had not come to the surface for a hundred thousand years.

"And if," said the Wise Woman, "you manage to rouse her now, even so, I would not change places with you. For she has only to stir a finger and all the waters of the world will rise up and engulf you. And I would not risk that for all the jewels in her hair!"

"Oh! well," said the youth, "but you are not wooing a maiden. And that, as I said before, makes all the difference."

So he listened carefully to her directions and thanked her for her help, and away he went, his spirits high.

For seven days and seven nights he travelled without ceasing and then he came to the shore of the deepest ocean and he saw how it spread out before him to the far edge of the sky.

Remembering how the Ancient Maiden of the Sea hated the light, he sat down on a rock to await the coming of darkness, and blessed his luck that it was a moonless night.

At the very darkest hour of midnight, by the pale light of the stars, he made his way out on to a rock which jutted far into the sea, and there he sat down on the glistening seaweed and began to twang upon his fingers and to make the sweet noise of harps playing as if all the harps in the world were being plucked by skilled musicians.

It was not long before he saw the water begin to shake,

and he felt afraid, as well he might all alone by the edge of the sea and only the Ancient Maiden coming to keep him company.

But he did not falter, but kept twanging on his fingers, and in the dim starlight, he saw the surface of the sea begin to heave and break, and the cold light of phosphorus flickering in the depths, and then out of the sea rose up the Ancient Maiden, her skin pale and white and glistening with drops of water, and her face beautiful and terrible, the face of a young maiden but old with the wisdom of ages, and her eyes were dark and unfathomable with no light in their darkness, and her long green hair floated all around her like trailing seaweed on the surface of the water.

"Who are you?" she said. "For a hundred thousand years no-one has disturbed me. And I so hate man and his works and ways that I set myself down in the deepest part of the sea to avoid him. And now, you, with the sweet music you make, as if all the waters of the world were flowing sweetly down to the sea, have drawn me up from my silence and darkness to the light of the stars and the sound of your music."

So then he told her why he had come and what he was seeking, and indeed he could see the faint glimmer of the gems set in the darkness of her hair.

"Play to me again," she said, "but speak no more, for your voice is as the voice of all men, harsh to my ears. But for the sake of your music I will give you what you ask."

So he sat there on the wet rock and twanged on his fingers and made her music all through the night until the stars grew pale and the sky grew light at the edge of the sea, and the Sea Maiden shuddered and cried to him to be still.

"Play no more," she said, "for the sweetness of the sounds holds me, but I fear the light and dare not stay."

And she plucked the seven green stones from her hair and threw them up on to the rock, and plunged swiftly down into the deep salt water, and he saw the flash of her white body and the floating strands of her hair and the foam white where she had plunged away, and then she was gone.

So he took the seven green emeralds where they lay on the rock and wrapped them in his kerchief and tied them to his belt and turned his back on the sea and made his way as soon as he could back to the city and the Wise Woman at the gate.

He told her all that had happened and gave her the seven green emeralds, to put with the seven red rubies until he should bring the gold in which they must be set. And he asked her how he should find the Mad Man of the Sky, in the snapping of whose fingers was the lightning which must furnish the gold for the maiden's crown.

The Wise Woman told him how he should find him, but warned him that if he did so he would certainly regret it.

"For the Mad Man of the Sky has sudden fits of violence, and when these fits are on him the sky is filled with hurricanes and tempests, and thunderbolts hurtle through the air, and woe betide anyone who should be near him at such a time. And besides these fits of violence the Mad Man of the Sky is proud. So proud that he despises man and his puny ways and sits high up among the clouds and laughs at our antics, and blows with his breath to torment us with fierce winds, and spits upon us so that the rivers and seas are flooded and overflow their limits, and he claps his hands together so that thunder and lightning shall strike terror into the small hearts of men. And as for me," she concluded, "I would not go to that one. No! Not for all the gold in creation."

"Oh! well," said the youth. "But you know, I go to

win a maiden, and there's the difference, as I have said before."

So he said good-bye to the Wise Woman and thanked her for her directions, and away he went travelling for seven days and seven nights without ceasing.

At the end of that time he came to the edge of the sky and stood there, the immense distances of air before him.

Well, certainly it seemed improbable that his voice, however loud he shouted, should reach to the farthest limit of that expanse of space and bring the Mad Man of the Sky to have speech with him.

So then he bethought himself of his third talent, and he began to clap his hands together. And then, such a noise of beating drums the sky shook with the volume of the sound, and the very farthest corners of space were filled with the drumming, and the sky echoed and re-echoed to the music he made.

He had not been clapping long when he saw huge clouds come rolling together, and in the midst of them the vast shape of him he was seeking, and he felt himself small and afraid before him as well he might.

But he went on clapping and the drumming never ceased, and at last the Mad Man of the Sky saw him and said:

"For twice ten thousand years I have sat in my cloudy fastness and have held myself aloof from the small affairs of men, and have despised them and their works and have held no truck with them. But who are you to make music I myself might be glad to make, and why do you come and brave the thunderbolts I hold in the palm of my hand, and the sharp lightning I can flash from the snapping of my fingers?"

"It is that very lightning I have come for," said the youth, "for without I make her a crown of it I shall never win the maiden on whom my heart is set."

"Well," said the Mad Man of the Sky. "You are a bold

youth, and I like such a one. But you cannot have my golden lightning merely for the asking. But if you can earn it honestly, you shall have as much as you wish for.

"When I let out my winds from the cave in which they are kept, I do so, telling them to return to me as soon as they hear the rolling of my thunder, so." And the Mad Man of the Sky clapped his hands, clap, clap, clap, clap, first fast and then slow, and at once there was a rolling of thunder all round the sky and such a sudden rushing of winds past the youth where he was standing, his clothes were well nigh torn from his back and he himself bowled over.

"You see," said the Mad Man, laughing, "they are afraid to disobey me." And he clapped his hands together again with a great bang just to hurry up the loiterers.

"But this is how it is," he went on, and his face grew dark and gloomy and his hands trembled.

"A hundred thousand years ago a little wind went out together with some others, a little wind, the fairest of all the winds who haunt the caverns of space. It went out with the others, but it did not return. I made my thunder go rumbling round the sky, till heaven and earth were so filled with the sound that people thought it was the end of Time and fell on their knees with terror and began to pray.

"But still that little wind did not return, and when I questioned the others, they said this wind on going out had laughed and said, 'If I do not hear the summons to return I cannot be said to have disobeyed the summons. I will go so far that not even our master's loudest thundering can reach me, and then I shall be free to dance and whistle and sing for ever and ever.' And away it had fled so swiftly that by the time I thundered to bring them all home again it had gone so far into space that thunder as I might it did not hear me, and I have not seen it since.

"Now, if you with your drumming can reach the ears

of that wind and bring it home, then my lightning shall be yours and my thanks into the bargain."

Well, that was an admission to win from so proud and surly an old creature!

So then the youth began to clap his hands, first gently and slowly, CLAP CLAP CLAP, and there was the noise of rolling drums that set the air vibrating.

Then louder he clapped and faster, and the rolling of the drums grew and grew, BANG BANG BANG – RUB DUB A DUB DUB, the whole of space and beyond was filled with the sound of the drumming, DUM DURRA DRUMM DRUMM – BOOM BEROOM BOOM, till even the Mad Man of the Sky began to roll his eyes and twitch his fingers.

And the young man clapped and clapped, and suddenly his hair was stirred by a soft warm wind, and the sweet cool air blew on his cheek, and the Mad Man of the Sky burst out laughing and clapped his hands, and then what a noise there was with the two of them at it together!

So then the young man stopped his clapping, and the Mad Man of the Sky held out his hands as if he were holding something.

"See," he cried, "my little wind has come home again. Ah! you little villain, you thought you could cheat even me!" And he laughed again with delight and stroked it and spoke to it fondly, like a father, though the young man could see nothing there.

"Well, now indeed you shall have what you ask for," said the Mad Man of the Sky. And with that he snapped his fingers, and a sharp flash of forked lightning came suddenly forth, so bright the young man was blinded, but he snatched at the brightness as it went by and caught it fast and thrust it quickly into his kerchief, which he tied at his belt. Then he thanked the Mad Man of the Sky and turned back to the earth and the dwellings of men, and now he went gaily, for his task was nearly accomplished.

When he got back to the city he went to the Wise
Woman at the gate.

"See," he said, "now I have the gold and the emeralds
and the rubies. All that remains to be done is to fashion
the crown, and that will soon be done."

So he took the gold from his kerchief to work it into
shape. But here was a pretty pass! He no sooner shook it
free from the kerchief than his eyes were so dazzled by the
light that he could see nothing, and as for doing fine work
on it he might as well throw it on the dung heap for all the
good he could make of it!

While he was standing in dismay, not knowing what to
do, his eyes turned away from it, the Wise Woman came
up to him.

"Do not despair," she said, "but wrap it up again in
your kerchief and take it to the blind smith who lives
alone in the wilderness. If you can please him, he will do
it, and no man better, although his eyes are blind. For
your gold is so bright that no other man could do it save
only he who has no sight in his eyes to be dazzled by it."

So the young man wrapped up the gold again and took
the emeralds and rubies, and he found out the place where
the blind smith was working, in a lonely place far away in
a wilderness, for he was a sorrowful man and shunned
company.

When he came there he found the blind smith sitting
outside the cave in which he lived and worked.

"I have found you at last," cried the youth, "and right
glad am I to have done so. For if you can fashion me a
crown set with these emeralds and rubies I shall win such
a maiden to wife as no man had before or since."

"I can do anything if I will, but I won't," said the smith,
sitting still and scowling. "What do I care if you win you
a maiden or no? I have lost the sight of my eyes and the
world is a dark place to me, and why should I make it fair
for another?"

"Have you no pleasures left?" said the youth.

"Aye," said the smith. "Now that I am blind I take pleasure through my ears, and the sound of sweet singing can make me forget my sorrows. But the birds are afraid to come near me, frightened by the noise I make at my work, and as for men, if there be sweet singers among them they take good care to keep their own distance."

"I will sing you a song," said the youth, and he opened his mouth to sing, and at once the wilderness was filled with the sound of a choir of sweet singers singing in honour of the king.

When he had done, the blind smith got up and held out his hand for the gold and never said a word.

But the young man gave it to him and the emeralds and rubies also, and he turned away from the brightness which suddenly shone out into the cave and only listened to the roaring of the fire when the smith used the bellows, and the tap tap tapping as he worked at the metal.

All night long the smith was working, and in the morning he cried to the young man:

"You sang sweetly, and I carry the sound still in my ears. Take the crown I have fashioned and good luck to you and your maiden."

And the young man came and took the crown, and though the brightness made him blink he could see that it was beautiful.

So he thanked the smith, and again sang him a song, and away he went, whistling and singing to himself, he was so light of heart.

When he came again to the Wise Woman she tidied him up and gave him her blessing, and hiding the crown in his kerchief he boldly went to the gates of the palace.

"I am come to claim the king's daughter," he said, "and I have the crown here in my kerchief."

The gatekeeper looked at him sourly.

"As like as not," he said. "They all say the same thing.

There are already ninety and nine of you young men and each one with the crown in his kerchief and each will win the maiden, they have no doubt of that! Well, come along in, and to-night you shall spend in feasting, and to-morrow you shall present yourselves. For the princess has said that when a hundred of you are come there shall be a showing of crowns, and if none of you have the right one, bad luck to all of you."

So the youth went in, and that night was feasted and entertained with the ninety and nine other young men, and they looked at him disdainfully, in his poor clothes, for they were all rich and fine, and had a need to be, seeing that to produce a crown they had been about buying the finest gold and rubies and emeralds they could lay their hands on, hoping that the maiden would not notice that these were not the jewels and gold she had asked for.

Well, the very next day the suitors were led into the great hall of the palace and the princess sat high upon her throne, and her mother and father at her side, and you may be sure there was no-one in the world more beauti-ful.

Then one by one the young men came forward and put their crowns on the steps of her throne, and there was such a shining of golden crowns, each one worked more gorgeously than the last, you would have thought that nothing could have been more magnificent.

But when the ninety-ninth crown was set at her feet the maiden's face was sad, for well she knew the crown she had asked for was not among these.

Then forward came the youth and undid his kerchief and all in the great court of the palace hid their eyes, for the shining of that crown had the sharpness of lightning, and the red of those rubies was like the heart of the fire, and the green of those emeralds like the cold green light of icebergs floating on the waters of polar seas.

And when the maiden saw it she smiled at the youth,

and bade him come up and put the crown on her head. And this was strange. For of all that company he and she were the only two who could look on the crown and not be blinded by its splendour, and now that he could look upon it, he saw that the blind smith had worked well, and no crown before or since was so finely made as this.

So then they were married and the young man took his place on the throne beside the Princess, and all the people of the land rejoiced, for now they need not fear one day to be without a ruler.

And the young man caused a little house to be built in the fairest part of the palace grounds, and this he gave to the Wise Woman, that she should live there in comfort with her cat till the end of her days. And the maiden, after her wedding, gave her bright crown to the Wise Woman that she should hide it away in some secret place, for it was too rare and too bright to be seen at all times by all men.

And as for the celebration of the wedding, nothing could be finer! For the young man himself made all the music, blowing and twanging on his fingers, clapping his hands together and singing, so it seemed that all the flutes and harps and drums in the world were playing together in concert, and choirs of sweet singers were singing in chorus, till the oldest feet were dancing and the saddest hearts laughing.

The Good Little Girl

F. Anstey

Her name was Priscilla Prodgers, and she was a very good little girl indeed. So good was she, in fact, that she could not help being aware of it herself, and that is a stage to which very many quite excellent persons never succeed in attaining. She was only just a child, it is true, but she had read a great many beautiful story-books, and so she knew what a powerful reforming influence a childish and innocent remark, or a youthful example or a happy combination of both, can exert over grown-up people. And early in life – she was but eleven at the date of this history – early in life she had seen clearly that her mission was to reform her family and relatives generally. This was a heavy task for one so young, particularly in Priscilla's case, for, besides a father, mother, brother, and sister, in whom she could not but discern many and serious failings, she possessed an aunt who was addicted to insincerity, two female cousins whose selfishness and unamiability were painful to witness, and a male cousin who talked slang and was so worldly that he habitually went about in yellow boots! Nevertheless Priscilla did not flinch, although, for some reason, her earnest and unremitting efforts had hitherto failed to produce any deep impression. At times she thought this was owing to the fact that she tried to reform all her family together,

and that her best plan would be to take each one separately, and devote her whole energies to improving that
person alone. But then she never could make up her mind
which member of the family to begin with. It is small
wonder that she often felt a little disheartened, but even
that was a cheering symptom, for in the books it is
generally just when the little heroine becomes most dis-
couraged that the seemingly impenitent relative exhibits
the first sign of softening.

So Priscilla persevered: sometimes with merely a
shocked glance of disapproval, which she had practised
before the looking-glass until she could do it perfectly;
sometimes with some tender, tactful little hint. "Don't
you think, dear papa," she would say softly, on a Saturday morning, "don't you *think* you could write your
newspaper article on some *other* day – is it a work of *real*
necessity?" Or she would ask her mother, who was certainly fond of wearing pretty things: "How much bread
for poor starving people would the price of your new
bonnet buy, Mother? I should *so* like to work it out on my
little slate!"

Then she would remind her brother Alick that it would
be so much better if, instead of wasting his time in playing with silly little tin soldiers, he would try to learn as
much as he could before he was sent to school; while she
was never tired of quoting to her sister Betty the line: "Be
good, sweet maid, and let who will be clever!" which
Betty, quite unjustly, interpreted to mean that Priscilla
thought but poorly of her sister's intellectual capacity.
Once when, as a great treat, the children were allowed to
read *Ivanhoe* aloud, Priscilla declined to participate until
she had conscientiously read up the whole Norman
period in her English history; and on another occasion
she cried bitterly on hearing that her mother had arranged
for them to learn dancing, and even endured bread and
water for an entire day rather than consent to acquire an

accomplishment which she feared, from what she had read, would prove a snare. On the second day – well, there was roast beef and Yorkshire pudding for dinner, and Priscilla yielded; but she made the resolution – and kept it too – that, if she went to the dancing class, she would firmly refuse to take the slightest pains to learn a single step.

I only mention all these traits to show that Priscilla really was an unusually good child, which makes it the more sad and strange that her family should have profited so little by her example. She was neither loved nor respected as she ought to have been, I am grieved to say. Her papa, when he was not angry, made the cruellest fun of her mild reproofs; her mother continued to spend money on dresses and bonnets, and even allowed the maid to say that her mistress was "not at home", when she was merely unwilling to receive visitors. Alick and Betty too only grew more exasperated when Priscilla urged them to keep their tempers, and altogether she could not help feeling how wasted and thrown away she was in such a circle.

But she never quite lost heart; her papa was a literary man and wrote tales, some of which she feared were not as true as they affected to be, while he invariably neglected to insert a moral in any of them; frequently she dropped little remarks before him with apparent carelessness, in the hope that he might put them in print – but he never did; she never could recognize herself as a character in any of his stories, and so at last she gave up reading them at all!

But one morning she came more near to giving up in utter despair than ever before. Only the previous day she had been so hopeful! Her father had really seemed to be beginning to appreciate his little daughter, and had presented her with sixpence in the new coinage to put in her money-box. This had emboldened her to such a

degree that, happening on the following morning to hear him ejaculate "Confound it!" she had, pressing one hand to her beating heart and laying the other hand softly upon his shoulder (which is the proper attitude on these occasions), reminded him that such an expression was scarcely less reprehensible than actual bad language. Upon which her hard-hearted papa had told her, almost sharply, *"not to be a little prig!"*

Priscilla forgave him, of course, and freely, because he was her father and it was her duty to bear with him; but she felt the injustice deeply, for all that. Then, when she went up into the nursery, Alick and Betty made a frantic uproar, merely because she insisted on teaching them the moves in chess, when they perversely wanted to play Halma! So, feeling baffled and sick at heart, she had put on her hat and run out all alone to a quiet lane near her home, where she could soothe her troubled mind by thinking over the ingratitude and lack of appreciation with which her efforts were met.

She had not gone very far up the lane when she saw, seated on a bench, a bent old woman in a poke-bonnet with a crutch-handled stick in her hands, and this old woman Priscilla (who was very quick of observation) instantly guessed to be a fairy – in which, as it fell out, she was perfectly right.

"Good day, my pretty child!" croaked the old dame.

"Good day to you, ma'am!" answered Priscilla politely (for she knew that it was not only right but prudent to be civil to fairies, particularly when they take the form of old women). "But, if you please, you musn't call me pretty – because I am not. At least," she added, for she prided herself upon her truthfulness, "not exactly pretty. And I should hate to be always thinking about my looks, like poor Milly – she's our housemaid, you know – and I so often have to tell her that she did not make her *own* face."

"I don't alarm you, I see," said the old crone; "but possibly you are not aware that you're talking to a fairy?"

'Oh yes I am – but I'm not a bit afraid, because, you see, fairies can only hurt *bad* children."

"Ah, and you're a good little child – that's not difficult to see!"

"They don't see it at home!" said Priscilla, with a sad little sigh, "or they would listen more when I tell them of things they oughtn't to do."

"And what things do they do that they oughtn't to, my child – if you don't mind telling me?"

"Oh, I don't mind in the *least*!" Priscilla hastened to assure her; and then she told the old woman all her family's faults, and the trial it was to bear with them and go on trying to induce them to mend their ways. "And papa is getting worse than ever," she concluded dolefully; "only fancy, this very morning, he called me a little prig!"

"Tut, tut!" said the fairy sympathetically. "Deary, deary me! So he called you *that*, did he? – 'a little prig!' And *you*, too! Ah, the world's coming to a pretty pass! I suppose, now, your papa and the rest of them have got it into their heads that you are too young and too inexperienced to set up as their adviser – is that it?"

"I'm afraid so," admitted Priscilla; "but we musn't blame them," she added gently, "we must remember that they don't know any better – musn't we, ma'am?"

"You sweet child!" said the old lady, with enthusiasm; "I must see if I can't do something to help you, though I'm not the fairy I used to be – still, there are tricks I can manage still, if I'm put to it. What you want is something that will prove to them that they ought to pay more attention to you, eh? – something there can be no possible mistake about?"

"Yes!" cried Priscilla eagerly, "and – and – how would it be if you changed them into something else, just to *show*

them, and then I could ask for them to be transformed
back again, you know?"

"What an ingenious little thing you are!" exclaimed the
fairy; "but let us see – if you came home and found your
cruel papa doing duty as the family hatstand, or strutting
about as a Cochin China fowl—"

"Oh *yes*; and I'd feed him every day, till he was sorry?"
interrupted the warm-hearted little girl impulsively.

"Ah, but you're so hasty, my dear. Who would write all
the clever articles and tales to earn bread and meat for you
all? – fowls can't use a pen. No, we must find a prettier
trick than that – there *was* one I seem to remember, long,
long ago, performing for a good little ill-used girl, just
like you, my dearie, just like you! Now what was it?
Some gift I gave her whenever she opened her lips—"

"Why, *I* remember – how funny that you should have
forgotten! Whenever she opened her lips, roses and
diamonds and rubies fell out. That would be the very
thing! Then they'd *have* to attend to me! Oh, do be a kind
old fairy and give me a gift like that, do do!"

"No, don't be so impetuous! You forget that this is not
the time of year for roses, and, as for jewels, well, I don't
think I can be very far wrong in supposing that you open
your lips pretty frequently in the course of the day?"

"Alick does call me a 'nag'," said Priscilla; "but that's
wrong, because I never speak without having something
to say. I don't think people ought to – it may do so *much*
harm; mayn't it?"

"Undoubtedly. But, anyhow, if we made it *every* time
you opened your lips, you would soon ruin me in
precious stones, that's plain! No, I think we had better say
that the jewels shall only drop when you are saying
something you wish to be particularly improving – how
will that do?"

"Very nicely indeed ma'am, thank you," said Priscilla,
"because, you see, it comes to just the same thing."

"Ah well, try to be as economical of your good things as you can – remember that in these hard times a poor old fairy's riches are not as inexhaustible as they used to be."

"And jewels really will drop out?"

"Whenever they are wanted to 'point a moral and adorn a tale,'" said the old woman (who, for a fairy, was particularly well read). "There, run along home, do, and scatter your pearls before your relations."

It need scarcely be said that Priscilla was only too willing to obey; she ran all the way home with a light heart, eager to exhibit her wonderful gift. "How surprised they will be!" she was thinking. "If it had been Betty, instead of me, I suppose she would have come back talking toads! It would have been a good lesson for her – but still, toads are nasty things, and it would have been rather unpleasant for the rest of us. I think I won't tell Betty *where* I met the fairy."

She came in and took her place demurely at the family luncheon, which was the children's dinner; they were all seated already, including her father, who had got through most of his writing in the course of the morning.

"Now make haste and eat your dinner, Priscilla," said her mother, "or it will be quite cold."

"I always let it get a little cold, Mother," replied the good little girl, "so that I mayn't come to think too much about eating, you know."

As she uttered this remark, she felt a jewel producing itself in some mysterious way from the tip of her tongue, and saw it fall with a clatter into her plate. "I'll pretend not to notice anything," she thought.

"Hallo!" exclaimed Alick, pausing in the act of mastication. "I say – *Prissie!*"

"If you ask Mother, I'm sure she will tell you that it is most ill-mannered to speak with your mouth full," said Priscilla, her speech greatly impeded by an immense emerald.

"I like that!" exclaimed her rude brother; "who's speaking with their mouth full *now*?"

"'*Their*' is not grammar, dear," was Priscilla's only reply to this taunt, as she delicately ejected a pearl, "you should say *her* mouth full." For Priscilla's grammar was as good as her principles.

"But really, Priscilla, dear," said her mother, who felt some embarrassment at so novel an experience as being obliged to find fault with her little daughter, "you should not eat sweets just before dinner, and – couldn't you get rid of them in some other manner?"

"Sweets!" cried Priscilla, considerably annoyed at being so misunderstood. "They are not *sweets*, Mother. Look!" And she offered to submit one for inspection.

"If I may venture to express an opinion," observed her father, "I would rather that a child of mine should suck sweets than coloured beads, and in either case I object to having them prominently forced upon my notice at meal-times. But I dare say I'm wrong. I generally am."

"Papa is quite right, dear," said her mother, "it *is* such a dangerous habit – suppose you were to swallow one, you know! Put them in the fire, like a good girl, and go on with your dinner."

Priscilla rose without a word, her cheeks crimsoning, and dropped the pearl, ruby, and emerald, with great accuracy into the very centre of the fire. This done, she returned to her seat, and went on with her dinner in silence, though her feelings prevented her from eating very much.

"If they choose to think my pearls are only beads, or jujubes, or acidulated drops," she said to herself bitterly, "I won't waste any more on them, that's all! I won't open my lips again, except to say quite ordinary things – *so there!*"

If Priscilla had not been such a good little girl, you might almost have thought she was in a temper; but she

was not – her feelings were wounded, that was all, which is quite a different thing.

That afternoon, her Aunt Margarine, Mrs Hoyle, came to call. She was the aunt whom we have already mentioned as being given to insincerity; she was not well off, and had a tendency to flatter people; but Priscilla was fond of her notwithstanding, and she had never detected her in any insincerity towards herself. She was sent into the drawing-room to entertain her aunt until her mother was ready to come down, and her aunt, as usual, overwhelmed her with affectionate admiration. "How pretty and well you are looking, my pet!" she began, "and oh, what a beautiful frock you have on!"

"The little silkworms wore it before I did, Aunt," said Priscilla modestly.

"How sweet of you to say so! But they never looked half so well in it, I'll be bound – Why, my child, you've dropped a stone out of a brooch or something. Look – on the carpet there!"

"Oh," said Priscilla carelessly, "it was out of my mouth, not out of a brooch – I never wear jewellery. I think jewellery makes people grow so conceited; don't you, Aunt Margarine?"

"Yes, indeed, dearest – indeed you are *so* right!" said her aunt (who wore a cameo-brooch as large as a tart upon her cloak), "and – surely that can't be a *diamond* in your lap?"

"Oh yes it is. I met a fairy this morning in the lane, and so . . ." and here Priscilla proceeded to narrate her wonderful experience. "I thought it might perhaps make papa and mamma value me a little more than they do," she said wistfully, as she finished her story, "but they don't take the least notice; they made me put the jewels on the fire – they did, really!"

"What blindness!" cried her aunt; "how *can* people shut their eyes to such treasure? And – and may I just have

one look? What, you really don't want them? – I may keep
them for my very own? You precious love! Ah, I know a
humble home where you would be appreciated at you
proper worth. What would I not give for my poor
naughty Belle and Cathie to have the advantage of seeing
more of such a cousin!'

"I don't know whether I could do them much good,"
said Priscilla, "but I would try my best."

"I am sure you would!" said Aunt Margarine, "and
now, dearest sweet, I am going to ask your dear mamma
to spare you to us for just a little while; we must both beg
very hard."

"I'll go and tell nurse to pack my things now, and then I
can go away with you," said the little girl.

When her mother heard of the invitation, she
consented quite willingly. "To tell you the truth,
Margarine," she said, "I shall be very glad for the child
to have a change. She seems a little unhappy at home
with us, and she behaved most unlike her usual self at
lunch; it *can't* be natural for a child of her age to chew
large glass beads. Did your Cathie and Belle ever do
such a thing?"

"Never," said Aunt Margarine, coughing. "It is a habit
that certainly ought to be checked, and I promise you, my
dear Lucy, that if you will only trust Priscilla to me, I will
take away anything of that kind the very moment I find
it. And I do think, poor as we are, we shall manage to
make her feel at home. We are all so fond of your sweet
Priscilla!"

So the end of it was that Priscilla went to stay with her
aunt that very afternoon, and her family bore the parting
with the greatest composure.

"I can't give you nice food, or a pretty bedroom to
sleep in such as you have at home," said her kind aunt.
"We are very plain people, my pet; but at least we can
promise you a warm welcome."

"Oh, Auntie," protested Priscilla, "you musn't think I mind a little hardship! Why, if beds weren't hard and food not nicely cooked now and then, we should soon grow too luxurious to do our duty, and that would be so very bad for us!"

"Oh, what *beauties!*" cried her aunt involuntarily, as she stooped to recover several sparkling gems from the floor of the cab. "I mean – it's better to pick them up, dear, don't you think? They might get in people's *way*, you know. What a blessing you will be in our simple home! I want you to do all you can to instruct your cousins; don't be afraid of telling them of any faults you may happen to see. Poor Cathie and Belle, I fear they are very far from being all they should be!" and Aunt Margarine heaved a sigh.

"Never mind, Auntie; they will be better in time, I am sure. *I* wasn't *always* a good girl."

Priscilla thoroughly enjoyed the first few days of her visit; even her aunt was only too grateful for instruction, and begged that Priscilla would tell her, quite candidly, of any shortcoming she might notice. And Priscilla, very kindly and considerately, always *did* tell her. Belle and Catherine were less docile, and she saw that it would take her some time to win their esteem and affection; but this was just what Priscilla liked: it was the usual experience of the heroines in the books, and much more interesting, too, than conquering her cousins' hearts at once.

Still, both Catherine and Belle persistently hardened their hearts against their gentle little cousin in the unkindest way; they would scarcely speak to her, and chose to make a grievance out of the fact that one or other of them was obliged, by their mother's strict orders, to be constantly in attendance upon her, in order to pick up and bring Mrs Hoyle all the jewels that Priscilla scattered in profusion wherever she went.

"If you would only carry a plate about with you,

Priscilla," complained Belle one day, "you could catch
the jewels in that."

"But I don't *want* to catch the jewels, dear Belle," said
Priscilla, with a playful but very sweet smile; "if other
people prize such things, that is not my fault, is it? *Jewels*
do not make people any happier, Belle!"

"I should think not!" exclaimed Belle. "I am sure my
back perfectly aches with stooping, and so does Cathie's.
There! that big topaz has just gone and rolled under the
sideboard, and mother will be *so* angry if I don't get it out!
I believe you do it on purpose!"

"Ah, you will know me better some day, dear," was
the gentle response.

"Well, at all events, I think you might be naughty just
now and then, Prissie, and give Cathie and me a half-
holiday."

"I would do anything else to please you, dear, but not
that; you must not ask me to do what is impossible."

Alas! not even this angelic behaviour, not even the
loving admonitions, the tender rebukes, the shocked
reproaches that fell, accompanied by perfect cascades of
jewels, from the lips of our pattern little Priscilla, succeeded in removing the utterly unfounded prejudices of
her cousins, though it was some consolation to feel that
she was gradually acquiring a most beneficial influence
over her aunt, who called Priscilla "her little conscience".
For, you see, Priscilla's conscience had so little to do on
her own account that it was always at the service of other
people, and indeed quite enjoyed being useful, as was
only natural to a conscientious conscience which felt that
it could never have been created to be idle.

Very soon another responsibility was added to little
Priscilla's burdens. Her cousin Dick, the worldly one
with the yellow boots, came home after his annual
holiday, which, as he was the junior clerk in a large bank,
he was obliged to take rather late in the year. She had

looked forward to his return with some excitement. Dick, she knew, was frivolous and reckless in his habits – he went to the theatre occasionally and frequently spent an evening in playing billiards and smoking cigars at a friend's house. There would be real credit in reforming poor cousin Dick.

He was not long, of course, in hearing of Priscilla's marvellous endowment, and upon the first occasion they were alone together treated her with respect and admiration which he had very certainly never shown her before.

"You're wonderful, Prissie!" he said; "I'd no idea you had it in you!"

"Nor had I, Dick, but it shows that even a little girl can do something."

"I should rather think so! and – and the way you look – as grave as a judge all the time! Prissie, I wish you'd tell me how you manage it – I wouldn't tell a soul."

"But I don't know, Dick. I only talk and the jewels come – that is all."

"You artful little girl! You can keep a secret, I see, but so can I. And you might tell me how you do the trick. What put you up to the dodge? I'm to be trusted, I assure you."

"Dick, you can't – you musn't – think there is any trickery about it! How can you believe I could be such a wicked little girl as to play tricks? It was an old fairy that gave me the gift. I'm sure I don't know why – unless she thought that I was a good child and deserved to be encouraged."

"By Jove!" cried Dick, "I never knew you were half such fun!"

"I am not fun, Dick. I think fun is generally very vulgar, and oh, I wish you wouldn't say 'By Jove!' Surely you know he was a heathen god!"

"I seem to have heard of him in some such capacity," said Dick. "I say, Prissie, what a ripping big ruby!"

"Ah, Dick, Dick, you are like the others! I'm afraid you think more of the jewels than any words I may say – and yet *jewels* are common enough!"

"They seem to be with you. Pearls, too, and such fine ones! Here, Priscilla, take them; they're your property."

Priscilla put her hands behind her. "No, indeed, Dick, they are of no use to me. Keep them, please; they may help to remind you of what I have said."

"It's awfully kind of you," said Dick, looking really touched. "Then – since you put it in that way – thanks, I will, Priscilla. I'll have them made into a horse-shoe pin."

"You musn't let it make you too fond of dress, then," said Priscilla; "but I'm afraid you're that already, Dick."

"A diamond!" he cried. "Go on, Priscilla, I'm listening – pitch into me, it will do me a *lot* of good!"

But Priscilla thought it wisest to say no more just then.

That night after Priscilla and Cathie and Belle had gone to bed, Dick and his mother sat talking until a late hour.

"Is dear little cousin Priscilla to be a permanency in this establishment?" began her cousin, stifling a yawn, for there had been a rather copious flow of precious stones during the evening.

"Well, I shall keep her with us as long as I can," said Mrs Hoyle, "she's such a darling, and they don't seem to want her at home. I'm sure, limited as my means are, I'm most happy to have such a visitor."

"She seems to pay her way – only her way is a trifle trying at times, isn't it? She lectured me for half an hour on end without a single check!"

"Are you sure you picked them all up, dear boy?"

"Got a few of the best in my waistcoat pocket now. I'm afraid I scrunched a pearl or two, though: they were all over the place, you know. I suppose you've been collecting too, Mater?"

"I picked up one or two," said his mother; "I should

think I must have nearly enough now to fill a bandbox. And that brings me to what I wanted to consult you about, Richard. How are we to dispose of them? She has given them all to me."

"You haven't done anything with them yet, then?"

"How could I? I have been obliged to stay at home: I've been so afraid of letting that precious child go out of my sight for a single hour, for fear some unscrupulous persons might get hold of her. I thought that perhaps, when you came home, you would dispose of the jewels for me."

"But, Mater," protested Dick, "I can't go about asking who'll buy a whole bandbox full of jewels!"

"Oh, very well, then; I suppose we must go on living this hugger-mugger life when we have the means of being as rich as princes, just because you are too lazy and selfish to take a little trouble!"

"I know something about these things," said Dick. "I know a fellow who's a diamond merchant, and it's not so easy to sell a lot of valuable stones as you seem to imagine, Mother. And then Priscilla really overdoes it, you know – why, if she goes on like this, she'll make diamonds as cheap as currants!"

"*I* should have thought that was a reason for selling them as soon as possible; but I'm only a woman, and of course *my* opinion is worth nothing! Still, you might take some of the biggest to your friend, and accept whatever he'll give you for them – there are plenty more, you needn't haggle over the price."

"He'd want to know all about them, and what should I say? I can't tell him a cousin of mine produces them whenever she feels disposed?"

"You could say they have been in the family for some time, and you are obliged to part with them; I don't ask you to tell a falsehood, Richard."

"Well, to tell you the honest truth," said Dick, "I'd

rather have nothing to do with it. I'm not proud, but I shouldn't like it to get about among our fellows at the bank that I went about hawking diamonds.''

"But you stupid, undutiful boy, don't you see that you could leave the bank – you need never do anything any more – we should all live rich and happy somewhere in the country, if we could only sell those jewels! And you won't do that one little thing!''

"Well,'' said Dick, "I'll think over it. I'll see what I can do.''

And his mother knew that it was perfectly useless to urge him any further; for, on some things, Dick was as obstinate as a mule, and, in others, far too easy-going and careless ever to succeed in life. He had promised to think over it, and she had to be contented with that.

On the evening following this conversation cousin Dick entered the sitting-room the moment after his return from the city, and found his mother to all appearances alone.

"What a dear sweet little guileless angel cousin Priscilla is, to be sure!'' was his first remark.

"Then you *have* sold some of the stones!'' cried Aunt Margarine. "Sit down, like a good boy, and tell me all about it.''

"Well,'' said Dick, "I took the finest diamonds and rubies and pearls that escaped from that saint-like child last night in the course of some extremely disparaging comments on my character and pursuits – I took those jewels to Faycett and Rosewater's in New Bond Street – you know the shop on the right-hand side as you go up—''

"Oh, go on, Dick; go on – never mind *where* it is – how much did you get for them?''

"I'm coming to that; keep cool, dear mamma. Well, I went in, and I saw the manager, and I said: 'I want you to make these up into a horse-shoe scarf-pin for me.'''

"You said that! You never tried to sell one? Oh, Dick, you are too provoking!"

"Hold on, Mater; I haven't done yet. So the manager – a very gentlemanly person, rather thin on the top of the head – not that that affects his business capacities; for, after all—"

"Dick, do you want to drive me frantic?"

"I can't conceive any domestic occurrence which would be more distressing or generally inconvenient, Mother dear. You do interrupt a fellow so! I forget where I was now – oh, the manager, ah yes! Well, the manager said: 'We shall be happy to have the stones made in any design you may select' – jewellery, by the way, seems to exercise a most refining influence upon the manners: this man had the deportment of a duke – 'you may select,' he said; 'but of course I need not tell you that none of these stones are genuine.'"

"Not genuine!" cried Aunt Margarine excitedly. "They must be – he was lying!"

"West End jewellers never lie," said Dick; "but naturally, when he said that, I told him I should like to have some proof of his assertion. 'Will you take the risk of testing?' said he. 'Test away, my dear man!' said I. So he brought a little wheel near the emerald – 'whizz!' and away went the emerald! Then he let a drop of something fall on the ruby – and it fizzled up for all the world like pink champagne. 'Go on, don't mind *me*!' I told him, so he touched the diamond with an electric wire – 'phit!' and there was only something that looked like the ash of a shocking bad cigar. Then the pearls – and they popped like so many air-balloons. 'Are you satisfied?' he asked.

"'Oh, perfectly,' said I, 'you needn't trouble about the horse-shoe pin now. Good evening,' and so I came away, after thanking him for his very amusing scientific experiments."

"And do you believe that the jewels are all shams, Dick? Do you really?"

"I think it so probable that nothing on earth will induce me to offer a single one for sale. I should never hear the last of it at the bank. No, Mater, dear little Priscilla's sparkling conversation may be unspeakably precious from a moral point of view, but it has no commercial value. Those jewels are bogus – shams, every stone of them!"

Now all this time our heroine had been sitting unperceived in a corner behind a window curtain, reading *The Wide, Wide World*, a work which she was never weary of perusing. Some children would have come forward earlier, but Priscilla was never a forward child, and she remained as quiet as a little mouse up to the moment when she could control her feelings no longer.

"It isn't true!" she cried passionately, bursting out of her retreat and confronting her cousin. "It's cruel and unkind to say my jewels are shams! They are real – they are, they *are*!"

"Hallo, Prissie!" said her abandoned cousin. "So you combine jewel-dropping with eavesdropping, eh?"

"How dare you!" cried Aunt Margarine, almost beside herself. "You odious little prying minx, setting up to teach your elders and your betters with your cut-and-dried priggish maxims! When I think how I have petted and indulged you all this time, and borne with the abominable litter you left in every room you entered – and now to find you are only a little, conceited, hypocritical impostor – oh, *why* haven't I words to express my contempt for such conduct – why am I dumb at such a moment as this?"

"Come, Mother," said her son soothingly, "that's not such a bad beginning; I should call it fairly fluent and expressive, myself."

"Be quiet, Dick! I'm speaking to this wicked child, who has obtained our love and sympathy and attention

on false pretences, for which she ought to be put in prison
– yes, in *prison*, for such a heartless trick on relatives who
can ill afford to be so cruelly disappointed!"

"But, Aunt!" expostulated poor Priscilla, "you always
said you only kept the jewels as souvenirs, and that it did
you so much good to hear me talk!"

"Don't argue with *me*, miss! If I had known the stones
were wretched tawdry imitations, do you imagine for an
instant—?"

"Now, Mother," said Dick, "be fair – they were
uncommonly good imitations, you must admit that!"

"Indeed, indeed I thought they were real – the fairy
never told me!"

"After all," said Dick, "it's not Priscilla's fault. She
can't help it if the stones aren't real, and she made up for
quality by quantity anyhow; didn't you, Prissie?"

"Hold your tongue, Richard; she *could* help it – she
knew all the time, and she's a hateful, sanctimonious little
stuck-up viper, and so I tell her to her face!"

Priscilla could scarcely believe that kind, indulgent,
smooth-spoken Aunt Margarine could be addressing
such words to her; it frightened her so much that she did
not dare to answer, and just then Cathie and Belle came
into the room.

"Oh, Mother," they began penitently, "we're *so* sorry,
but we couldn't find dear Prissie anywhere, so we haven't
picked up anything the whole afternoon!"

"Ah, my poor darlings, you shall never be your
cousin's slaves any more. Don't go near her – she's a
naughty deceitful wretch; her jewels are false, my sweet
loves, false! She has imposed upon us all; she does not
deserve to associate with you!"

"I always said Prissie's jewels looked like the things
you get in crackers!" said Belle, tossing her head.

"Now we shall have a little rest, I hope," chimed in
Cathie.

"I shall send her home to her parents this very night," declared Aunt Margarine. "She shall not stay here to pervert our happy household with her miserable *gew-gaws!*"

Here Priscilla found her tongue. "Do you think I *want* to stay?" she said proudly. "I see now that you only wanted to have me here because – because of the horrid jewels, and I never knew they were false, and I let you have them all, every one, you know I did; and I wanted you to mind what I said and not trouble about picking them up, but you *would* do it! And now you all turn round upon me like this! What have I done to be treated so? What have I done?"

"Bravo, Prissie!" cried Dick. "Mother, if you ask me, I think it serves us all jolly well right, and it's a downright shame to bullrag poor Prissie in this way!"

"I *don't* ask you," retorted his mother sharply; "so you will kindly keep your opinions to yourself."

"Tra-la-la!" sang rude Dick, "we are a united family – we are, we are, we *are!*" – a vulgar refrain he had picked up at one of the burlesque theatres he was only too fond of frequenting.

But Priscilla came to him and held her hand out quite gratefully and humbly. "Thank you, Dick," she said; "*you* are kind, at all events. And I am sorry you couldn't have your horse-shoe pin!"

"Oh, *hang* the horse-shoe pin!" exclaimed Dick, and poor Priscilla was so thoroughly cast down that she quite forgot to reprove him.

She was not sent home that night after all, for Dick protested against it in such strong terms that even Aunt Margarine saw that she must give way; but early on the following morning Priscilla quitted her Aunt's house, leaving her belongings to be sent on after her.

She had not far to walk, and it so happened that her way led through the identical lane in which she had met

the fairy. Wonderful to relate, there, on the very same bench, and in precisely the same attitude, sat the old lady, peering out from under her poke-bonnet, and resting her knotty old hands on her crutch-handled stick!

Priscilla walked past with her head in the air pretending not to notice her, for she considered that the fairy had played her a most malicious and ill-natured trick.

"Heyday!" said the old lady (it is only fairies who can permit themselves such old-fashioned expressions nowadays). "Heyday, why, here's my good little girl again! Isn't she going to speak to me?"

"No, she's not," said Priscilla – but she found herself compelled to stop, notwithstanding.

"Why, what's all this about? You're not going to sulk with me, my dear, are you?"

"I think you're a very cruel, bad, unkind old woman for deceiving me like this!"

"Goodness me! Why, didn't the jewels come, after all?"

"Yes – they came, only they were all horrid artificial ones – and it is a shame, it *is*!" cried poor Priscilla from her bursting heart.

"Artificial, were they? That really is very odd! Can you account for that at all, now?"

"Of course I can't! You told me that they would drop out whenever I said anything to improve people – and I was *always* saying *something* improving! Aunt had a bandbox in her room quite full of them."

"Ah, you've been very industrious, evidently; it's unfortunate your jewels should all have been artificial – most unfortunate. I don't know how to explain it, unless—" and here the old lady looked up queerly from under her white eyelashes – "unless your goodness was artificial too?"

"How do you mean?" asked Priscilla, feeling strangely uncomfortable. "I'm sure I've never done anything the

least bit naughty – how can my goodness possibly be artificial?"

"Ah, that I can't explain; but I think (I only say I *think*, mind) that a little girl so young as you must have some faults hidden about her somewhere, and that perhaps on the whole she would be better employed in trying to find them out and cure them before she attempted to correct those of other people. And I'm sure it can't be good for any child to be always seeing herself in a little picture, just as she likes to fancy other people see her. But of course, my dear, you never made such a mistake as that!"

Priscilla turned very red, and began to scrape one of her feet against the other; she was thinking, and her thoughts were not at all pleasant ones.

"Oh, fairy," she said at last, "I'm afraid that's just what I *did* do. I was always thinking how good I was and putting everybody – papa, mamma, Alick, Betty, Aunt Margarine, Cathie, Belle and even poor cousin Dick – right! I have been a horrid little hateful prig, and that's why all the jewels were rubbish. But, oh, shall I have to go on talking sham diamonds and things all the rest of my life?"

"That," said the fairy, "depends entirely on yourself. You have the remedy in your own hands – or lips."

"Ah, you mean I needn't talk at all? But I must – sometimes. I couldn't bear to be dumb as long as I lived – and it would look so odd, too!"

"I never said you were not to open your lips at all. But can't you try to talk simply and naturally – not like little girls or boys in any story-books whatever – not to 'show off' or improve people; only as a girl would talk who remembers that, after all, her elders are quite as likely as she is to know what they ought or ought not to do and say?"

"I shall forget sometimes, I know I shall!" said Priscilla disconsolately.

"If you do, there will be something to remind you, you know. And by and by, perhaps, as you grow up, you may, quite by accident, say something sincere and noble and true – and then a jewel will fall which will really be of value!"

"No!" cried Priscilla, "no, *please*! Oh, fairy, let me off that. If I *must* drop them, let them be false ones to punish me – not real. I don't want to be rewarded any more for being good – if I ever am really good!"

"Come," said the fairy, with a much pleasanter smile, "you are not a hopeless case, at all events. It shall be as you wish, then, and perhaps it will be the wisest arrangement for all parties. Now rush away home, and see how little use you can make of your fairy gift."

Priscilla found her family still at breakfast.

"Why," observed her father, raising his eyebrows as she entered the door, "here's our little monitor (or is it *monitress*, eh, Priscilla?) back again. Children, we shall all have to mind our p's and q's – and indeed, our alphabet, now."

"I'm sure," said her mother, kissing her fondly, "Priscilla knows we're all delighted to have her home!"

"*I'm* not," said Alick, with a boy's engaging candour.

"Nor am I," added Betty; "it's been ever so much nicer at home while she's been away!"

Priscilla burst into tears as she hid her face upon her mother's protecting shoulder. "It's true!" she sobbed, "I don't deserve that you should be glad to see me – I've been hateful and horrid, I know – but, oh, if you'll only forgive me and love me and put up with me a little, I'll try not to preach and be a prig any more – I will truly!"

And at this her father called her to his side and embraced her with a fervour he had not shown for a very long time.

*   *   *

I should not like to go so far as to assert that no imitation diamond, ruby, pearl, or emerald ever proceeded from Priscilla's lips again. Habits are not cured in a day, and fairies – however old they may be – are still fairies; so it *did* occasionally happen that a mock jewel made an unwelcome appearance after one of Priscilla's more unguarded utterances. But she was always frightfully ashamed and abashed by such an accident, and buried the imitation stones immediately in a corner of the garden. And as time went on the jewels grew smaller and smaller, and frequently dissolved upon her tongue, leaving a faintly bitter taste, until at last they ceased altogether, and Priscilla became as pleasant and unaffected a girl as she who may now be finishing this history.

Aunt Margarine never sent back the contents of that bandbox; she kept the biggest stones and had a brooch made of them, while, as she never mentioned that they were false, no one out of the family ever so much as suspected it.

But, for all that, she always declared that her niece Priscilla had bitterly disappointed her expectations – which was perhaps the truest thing that Aunt Margarine ever said.

Where the Wind Blows

Helen Cresswell

1

The Old Man of the Stile

Once upon a time there was a mill that stood beside a lazy river called Slow. Some days it was a fat, solid, contented mill, planted firmly in the buttercups and with sails rolling idly in the air. But if the wind blew, the mill sneezed and stirred and soon it was wide awake and a-clatter. The sails creaked and picked up speed, they turned till the air was filled with the rushing of the wind at work.

In the mill lived a little girl called Kirstine with her grandfather who was the miller. He was round and comfortable as a new-baked loaf and had lived so long in the dusty mill that his skin and hair were soft and powdery with flour. He had a marmalade cat called Marigold to catch the mice. In the meadows round the mill were fat slow-moving cows, jigsawed brown and white and with tasselled tails.

Kirstine loved the mill and the river and all the slow lazy world that wound and stretched about her. She helped her grandfather in the mill and sewed the bursting sacks of flour with stout thread or swept the floors and polished all the knobs.

But sometimes on the days when the mill was fast asleep and the long hours ticked by in a drowsy sun, she

would wish suddenly that the world would change and
that she was far away. She wished the mill would shiver
and turn to splinters and the earth rock and the fat cows
go tumbledown to the river nose over tail.

"That's because you are bored," the miller nodded
when Kirstine told him one day. "Always have something to put your hand to and the world will go well
enough. You spend too long by the river dreaming."

And that was true, for Kirstine loved to see the
moorhens sail and nod in passing as they went. Or she
would drop a pebble in the river and watch the water curl,
or lie for hours to see the fish go by.

One morning Kirstine woke just at dawn. Outside the
cock, stiff as stone, arched and sang. The dew dripped
from the gates and the cold air glittered.

Tiptoe Kirstine ran from the mill, stealing an apple
from the barrel as she went.

"I shan't be home till dinner," she told the yawning
Marigold. "The wind is away and the mill is fast asleep.
You may lie all day licking your paws for all the good it
will do you, but I am off to the river to find adventure."

Her legs were wet as she waded through long grasses
to reach the place where she lay to watch the river. She
sniffed the night smells of the river and nettles and icy
fern and root.

"Good day, Kirstine," came a deep dark voice. "Are
you off to the river again?"

It was the Old Man of the Stile. In tattered leathers he
sat on the stile, century in and century out, and watched
the world and the weather. His eyes were pale and green
as a sour apple, and filled with secrets to the brim.

"Yes, Old Man of the Stile," said Kirstine, dropping a
curtsey. "I always go to the river on days when the mill
stops turning. It is so quiet in the granary, and so still. I
like things to move and sparkle as the river does. Sometimes, on days like this, I think I should like to run away."

"Where to?" asked the Old Man of the Stile. He sat hunched, chin on his drawn-up knees, brown and jagged as a piece of bark.

"I don't know," said Kirstine. She tossed her apple high in the air and caught it. "I don't care. Anywhere in the whole wide world."

"That's easy enough to say," remarked the Old Man.

Kirstine was silent and a little ashamed.

"Easy enough to do, too," he said after a little while. "Easy enough. The hard thing is to sit on a stile, and go neither this way nor that."

His pale green eyes flickered. He stretched out a lean hand and plucked a grass. Slowly he raised it to his mouth and nibbled it. He seemed to have forgotten she was there at all.

"Have you seen the wild geese?" he asked suddenly.

Kirstine nodded.

"Many times," she said. "I often wish that I could follow them when they clap by with their necks stretched forward."

"Do you know where they go?" asked the Old Man of the Stile.

"No," replied Kirstine. "No one knows. They are like the wind and go where they please."

"No map and no compass," nodded the Old Man. "They go on journeys and never know the endings."

"I want to go on a journey," said Kirstine impatiently.

"Anywhere in the wide world," mused the Old Man of the Stile. Still he nibbled the sweet grass. "Is that what you want? Away from the mill, away from your grandfather? You might be afraid."

"Perhaps I might," she said stoutly, "but I want to go."

The Old Man sat staring at the river.

"Come back tomorrow," he said at last. "You may have till tomorrow to make up your mind. But if you go on this journey, it must be without knowing the end.

You must be still, like a leaf in the wind, and go where it takes you, whether you will or no."

Kirstine stared into the sour green eyes.

"I will come back tomorrow," she said. "Then I will give you my answer."

The Old Man shook himself and with a twist flung a line down into the water ready to fish till the sun dropped. Kirstine was left looking at his hunched shoulders.

"Good day, Old Man of the Stile," she said loudly, and went on her way, never expecting an answer.

2

Kirstine Decides

At dinner-time Kirstine went back to the mill. It was very hot and the meadow slept in the sun. The cows lay umbrella'd in the shade and bees fumbled in the clover.

She pushed the creaking door of the mill and went in. There it was shadowy cool and so still that she went on tiptoes. Marigold slept in a patch of sunlight.

Kirstine shouted suddenly:

"Grandfather! Grandfather!"

There was no reply. The clocks ticked and the pan on the hob simmered.

Kirstine ran to the cupboard and fetched the yellow bowls and banged them on the table. She clattered the spoons and Marigold woke, frightened, and ran out of doors. Kirstine burst out singing as loud as she could, and did not hear the miller come downstairs.

"What's the matter?" he asked, tapping her shoulder. "Why are you making so much noise? I was having a nap when I heard the din. Is something wrong?"

"Yes!" cried Kirstine. "The wind is asleep and the mill is asleep and you are asleep! I wish I lived where the winds

are always blowing! I don't like a world where everything is sleeping!"

"Oh, is that all?" said Grandfather, still yawning.
"You'll learn in time, that is the way life goes. Tomorrow
the wind may blow and things may be different."

"Tomorrow!" cried Kirstine impatiently. "But what
of today?"

"It's a good enough day," said the miller. "Where's the
dinner?"

Kirstine put down her wooden spoon very carefully
and turned to her grandfather.

"I'm going away tomorrow," she said.

"Going away?" said Grandfather. "Where to? What
for?"

"I don't know where I'm going," said Kirstine, "and I
don't really know why, except that I'm tired of spending
todays wishing for tomorrows when the wind may
blow."

"Dear me," said Grandfather, "what a strange child
you are to be sure. What did you say was for dinner?"

But a strange thing was happening. Grandfather's
voice sounded faint and far away, and Kirstine did not
hear what he said at all. She was listening to another
voice, so near and clear that it startled her, saying "Go
where the wind blows, Kirstine, go where the wind
blows."

It was as if she were a thousand miles away, hung in
space, and time stopped still. Then suddenly she was back
in the dim mill kitchen, with the clock ticking loudly on
the wall and her grandfather's voice was saying:

"What did you say was for dinner?"

Kirstine smiled suddenly and brilliantly.

"Here, Grandfather," she replied, handing his bowl.
And she tucked her legs under the wooden table and ate
her dinner, still smiling, as if the whole familiar world of
the mill was unreal and far away, because just for a

moment she had glimpsed another world, one where the wind was always blowing.

After dinner she climbed to her own room and began to pack the few belongings she would need for her journey. That night before she went to bed she found Grandfather sitting on the wooden bench outside the mill and watching the stars as he always did. Above him the sails of the mill were moveless in the quiet air and silver edged with moonlight. It was as if they had been sleeping for centuries. There was such a silence and a stillness as Kirstine had never known before.

"Grandfather," she said softly, "I have come to say good-bye. Tomorrow at dawn I shall start on my journey."

Grandfather slowly turned his head to look at her. He did not speak for a long while, biding his time as he always did.

"Go, then, Kirstine," he nodded at last. "The wind and the world are tugging you away. But you will come back and find your old grandfather and his lazy mill just the same as the day you left them. Nothing will have changed."

"Except me," said Kirstine. "I shall have changed."

"When you are as old as me," said Grandfather, "you will be content to let the world go as it pleases. You will be glad that on some days the wind blows and on others it sleeps. My mill and I have grown old together, and we take things as they are. Go, Kirstine, and come back to us when you are ready."

Kirstine kissed her grandfather and stole upstairs to her room to fall asleep gazing at the stars.

Next day she woke with the gay cock who stretched and yawned and split the glittering air. And the whole meadow was afire with sun and water in tiny licking tongues and the sky was huger than Kirstine had ever known it.

"I'm going somewhere today in the wide world," she said with delight as she swiftly tied her bundle and tip-toed down the creaking telltale stairs.

"Good-bye, Marigold, lazy puss. Or will you come with me on my journey?"

But Marigold merely tilted an eyelid and blinked an almond eye, and Kirstine went out of the mill alone.

It was another day without a feather of wind and Kirstine ran and jumped with excitement till the dew whirled round her in a fine spray and she tasted it cold on her lips and even her arms and neck were stinging wet.

She could see the Old Man of the Stile waiting, hunched and wise, hugging himself in his tattered leathers as an owl sinks in its down.

"I'm going, Old Man of the Stile," she called, even before she reached him. The words came spilling out and her legs tumbled eagerly towards him.

"I've made up my mind! I'm going!"

3

The Wicker Boat

The Old Man of the Stile was not at all excited. He sat on a stile for that very reason.

"If you have made up your mind, Kirstine," he said, "you had better get started at once."

He took from his pocket a curious whistle carved from a cane and blew on it, one or two notes, not very loud, but sad and lingering. He put it back in his pocket and they both waited.

"Like a leaf in the wind, remember, Kirstine," warned the Old Man. "You must go wherever they take you, whether you will or no."

"They?" began Kirstine, wondering.

But then there was a sound of wild wings beating and a rush of air and wind in that still place. And suddenly Kirstine could feel the wind, although it was not there, and then she saw the geese, seven of them, necks green and eager, wings urgent. And she could have cried aloud with longing and delight. The geese went in a circle overhead, restless and glinting, chafing to be gone. The Old Man pointed a long finger towards the river.

Floating under the willows was a small boat made of wicker and lined with green. Trailing from the prow were two long streamers of plaited rushes, and on the side was the name 'The Wicker Boat'.

"Mine?" asked Kirstine, scarcely daring to hope.

"Yours," nodded the Old Man of the Stile. Without moving from his perch he leaned forward and with a hooked stick caught the boat and brought it in to the bank.

"Climb in," he commanded.

Kirstine obeyed, and putting her basket and box beside her, sat on the wide seat, rocking gently on the stream and hearing the sound of the geese crying, impatient to be off.

Kirstine looked up and the jutting face of the Old Man of the Stile loomed over her. His sour green eyes were narrowed so that all of a sudden she shivered because she could feel magic as she had felt it yesterday in the dim mill kitchen.

"Remember two things, Kirstine," said the Old Man. "The first is that you may turn back whenever you please. You have only to tell the boat to stop three times, and the boat will turn. Do you understand?"

Kirstine nodded.

"The second," went on the Old Man, "is that you may not speak to the wild geese, nor they to you, except in dreams."

"Only in dreams," repeated Kirstine, wondering at the strangeness of it. "I will remember."

"Go, then," said the Old Man of the Stile. "Farewell, Kirstine. I hope you will find what you are looking for."

Then with a push of his long stick he sent the boat forward into midstream and Kirstine's journey had begun. She turned to wave but the Old Man was already casting out his line ready to fish all day till the sun dropped.

The boat drifted down the stream and Kirstine saw the jigsawed cows in the meadow and the old mill with its ivy coat and still sails. Above her willows fell in waterfalls of sunlit green and soft fronds touched her cheek and neck and the sun-flecked water dazzled her till she was all a-dream and dizzied.

She lay on her back and trailed her hand and wrist in the cold water and watched through half-closed eyes the sun in golden strands among the grasses. All the time she could hear faintly the crying of the geese, but although she scanned the sky to east and west there was no sign of them.

"But they are there," she told herself. "For don't I hear them, and did not the Old Man of the Stile promise that they would be near?"

She knew, too, that magic was round her all the time, for the boat was moving strongly and surely as if it were rowed by invisible oars. At noon when the sun hung overhead she fell asleep and on waking she found a little basket full of cakes and fruit, which she ate hungrily.

Still there was no wind, but still the little wicker boat sailed steadily on. Now she was in a deep forest in a chill, tunnelling gloom, and the water was a depthless green and the song of birds echoed in the high trees.

As night drew on Kirstine noticed that the wicker boat was moving more and more slowly as if it were tired and seeking rest. Till at last it came to a stop among the spearing reeds and Kirstine tied it to a willow with the long plaited ropes.

She lay on her back and looked right up to a huge sky prickling with stars, and saw for a moment the wild geese with moonlight whitening their backs, ringing above her. Then she fell asleep.

4

The Land Where the Sun is Always Shining

When Kirstine woke it was dawn and cold. Dew trembled on the fringes of her shawl, and she sat up, shaking it. There was food again in the little basket and she gobbled it quickly, eager to be off. She untied the long green plaits and the wicker boat moved away.

"Today the wind may blow," she told herself.

By the time the sun was fully up she was out of the forest. Suddenly the world spilled with golden light and Kirstine shaded her eyes, so long accustomed to the green gloom. Blinking she looked about her.

On either side lay meadows waist-high in grass, very hot and still. In the distance Kirstine could see the roofs of a village.

"I want to go and look," she said aloud.

Straight away the wicker boat glided to the bank and stopped. So Kirstine stepped ashore and skipped a little way, delighted to have her toes on the warm earth again. The flowers and trees were bent with blossom and fruit and the air was crowded with drifting seeds and pollen and the hum of bees.

As she drew near the village she began to see people. Their hats tilted against the sun, they were sunburnt and whistled softly as they went. They moved slowly, like people who are not really going anywhere at all. They smiled at Kirstine, slow contented smiles. Under the trees they lay in groups, toes turned up, eyes shut. The trees

were hunchbacked under the weight of fruit and the air was drowsy with the scent of ripeness, of oranges, lemons and plump grapes.

In the village it was silent. The sun beat down hammer hard on bare streets and cobbles. Pigeons slept under the shadowy eaves and cats dreamed in dark doorways. Then Kirstine saw a man sitting on a bench, knee-deep in tumbling blue flowers, eyes squeezed tight shut. She went up.

"Good morning," she said loudly. There was no reply.

"Good morning," she shouted. The pigeons whirred with alarm and flew in a white blur. One eye opened, then the other.

"Of course," said the man drowsily.

He looked as if he were going to sleep again so Kirstine said quickly:

"What is this place? And why is everyone so sleepy and contented?"

"This is the land where the sun is always shining," the man replied. "We open our palms and fruit drops into them. We sleep by day and dance by night. Why should we not be happy?"

"Does the wind ever blow?" asked Kirstine.

"The wind?" said the man. "Never."

And with that he closed his eyes and was asleep again. The heads of the blue flowers knocked against his knees.

Kirstine ran back to the river. The people watched her whirling legs.

"Stay, Kirstine, stay with us," they called lazily, but she took no notice.

Pell-mell she stamped through the flowers and fallen fruit, straining her ears for the crying of the geese. The tangling grass caught at her legs as she passed as if to keep her.

"This is not what I am looking for!" she cried. And as she spoke she heard again the calling geese and thought she felt a cool breath of wind go over her hot cheeks. Then she had reached the river and she stepped swiftly into the wicker boat and cast off.

The boat moved away, but it seemed to Kirstine that now it was moving more slowly and dipping more deeply into the water. As they went she looked over her shoulder for a last glimpse of the land where the sun is always shining. Only then did she see the boy.

He was lying curled in the bow of the boat, fast asleep, his cheek resting on his folded hands. As if he could feel her gaze he suddenly opened his eyes and the next minute was bolt upright, rocking the wicker boat.

"Oh!" he said. "Is this your boat?"

"Who are you?" asked Kirstine. "How did you get here?"

"I'm Peter," he answered, "and I'm running away from the land where the sun is always shining. I meant to sail away in this boat, but I must have fallen asleep. I'm sorry now. I didn't know it was your boat."

"Where are you going?" asked Kirstine.

"I don't know. I want to find my father. He is a painter," he added proudly.

"My grandfather is a miller," Kirstine told him. "I live with him. Where does your father live?"

"I don't know," replied Peter sadly. "He went away a long time ago. He said that the land where the sun is always shining was lazy and dull, and he wanted to go where the wind was always blowing."

"That is where I am going!" cried Kirstine in astonishment. "So perhaps we shall find him after all."

"But how do you know where to go?" asked Peter. "No one knows where the winds go."

So Kirstine told him the whole story of how she had longed to go on a journey and how the Old Man of the

Stile had helped her. And then she told him of the wild geese and their search for the world's end, and Peter listened with eyes like moons.

When she had finished he was silent for a little while.

"And may I really go with you, Kirstine?" he asked.

"Of course," she cried. "And listen, I will speak to the geese in my dreams and tell them about your father. They go on so many journeys by day and by night, and hear so many secrets as they go. Perhaps they will help you and bring you where he lives."

So the two of them decided that this was best. And they gladly sailed away from the land where the sun is always shining, and longed for the night to come, and the wild geese.

5

The Marshes

The sun fell behind a hill. The wicker boat was idling and the first star came out. Peter and Kirstine looked at each other and smiled, sitting very still. A fish jumped and plopped in the calm water and the rings widened.

Faint and far away came the call of wild geese in flight.

"Surely," said Kirstine, "I am not dreaming yet?"

"No," whispered Peter, "I can hear them too."

The beat of wings came nearer and lifting her eyes she saw the shadow of the geese on the sky, flying two by two with their leader before them. Twice they circled, thrice, and then down they flung like stones to the darkening river.

And as they came Kirstine cried aloud, for in the last glow of light she saw that they were linked in pairs with a fine silver chain and waiting to be harnessed to the boat. So Kirstine stooped and lifted from the water the drip-

ping ropes and fastened them securely, while the geese cried and paddled the water and yearned forward with their long necks.

Almost believing she was dreaming Kirstine sat again on the little bench, huddling close to Peter for fear and wonder. And with a great glad shout the geese rose into the air, two by two with their leader before, and the wicker boat smoothly took the tides of air and they were afloat in the sky.

Up and up they soared until Peter and Kirstine could see the river spilt silver beneath them and fields of corn bleached white under the moon. They brushed the tops of the high trees and the boat rolled and staggered until Kirstine and Peter were pitched from side to side, gasping and clutching passing boughs like handfuls of silver straw.

The geese were silent now and nothing could be heard beyond the thunder of their wings. And listening and watching she could never have told you where the watching ended and the dream began, for the night went like a shadow over the sun and it was morning.

"Peter! Peter!" cried Kirstine, shaking him. He blinked, woke and sat up.

"Look," whispered Kirstine, pointing round them. "Look where we are."

The thinning mist shone yellow with early sun. Round them on every side were marshes, grey, flat, reflecting sky. A world without corners it lay. Curlew and piper, heron and gull were there, and the air was filled with their hungry cries.

But best of all there was a freshness, a taste of salt on the tongue and a blowing air, hardly a wind at all, but promising the wind. Kirstine threw back her head and sucked it in in great long gulps.

"Peter!" she cried, "I can smell the sea and feel the wind!"

And Peter too threw out his chest and breathed mightily.

The wicker boat was threading the vast, bare flats, puddled with blue now that the day was growing brighter. Gulls were following with scissor-sharp cries and diving. Kirstine could see the seven geese far away out at the very rim of the marsh.

And suddenly, right through the pale shafting sunlight the rain came, long and soft and slanting on their faces. The rustling sigh of the shower went over the marsh and stilled the birds, piper, curlew, and heron picking fish.

Just as a rainbow began to arch they heard a loud shout, "Ahoy!", and looking up, saw a hut where a hut had never been before.

"The marsh was empty," thought Kirstine, "and now there is a hut. This is magic." And she felt it, too, in her bones.

The wicker boat moved towards the hut and Peter and Kirstine saw a thin brown man who waited for them by the door.

"You must come in," he told them, "out of the rain. I will tie up your boat for you."

So they climbed out and gratefully entered the hut. Inside it was shadowy and the bitter smoke of a wood fire stung their eyes. There were shelves of books, shelves of bottles and piles of ropes and sailing tackle.

"Look," whispered Peter, nudging Kirstine, "Birds!"

There were several cages made of cane and in each was a bird, drooping. The man entered and told them to sit by the fire while he made some hot soup.

"My name is Jan," he told them.

"Why do you keep birds in cages?" asked Peter boldly. "They look so sad and drooping."

"That is because they are hurt," Jan told him. And as he stirred the soup and cut the loaf, he told them of his work out there alone on the bare marsh. He told how each day

he took his boat, the *Puffin*, and went searching the flats for birds that were hurt with broken wing or leg, and brought them here to get well.

"And then there are the travellers," he went on. "I give them food and shelter when it is cold or wet, just as I am doing now."

Kirstine went to the cages and put her hands through the bars, stroking the soft feathers of a curlew, who looked at her with soft golden eyes. And while she did so, Jan took out a pipe made from a reed and began to play. All the sadness of the marshes was in his music. It was made of birds crying and quiet sounds of water. As he played Kirstine stared at the eyes of the curlew and the spell of the marshes was on her.

When the music died away at last Kirstine heard Jan's voice saying softly:

"You must stay, Kirstine, here on the marshes. Stay, stay."

And then she heard her own voice, as if it were a long way off, saying, "Yes, I will stay. I will stay."

6

A Spell Breaks

Kirstine's sleep that night was dreamless. When she woke the rain and mist had gone. The marsh glittered in the sun, the birds wheeled and speared and the song of the reed pipe still ran in her head.

"I will stay, I will stay," she sang as she picked her barefoot way. She had forgotten the words of the Old Man of the Stile, and to the wind and the wild geese she gave never a thought. She was under the spell of the grey marshes and skimmed the salt flats lightly as a bird.

"Jan!" she called, seeing him stoop to his yellow painted boat. "Wait, Jan!"

"Where is your friend?" he asked, straightening his back.

"Fast asleep in the hut," replied Kirstine. "I couldn't wait for him to wake. I wanted to be out here and to help you. This is a good life, I think I shall like it."

Jan looked at her and smiled.

"Will you, Kirstine?" was all he said, and a faint cold breath of wind went over her and then was gone.

There was a shout in the distance and Peter came running, flying in leaps over narrow creeks and puddles.

"I woke and found you gone," he panted. "I thought you had gone on without me, Kirstine. But then I saw the wicker boat still tied to the post and I knew you were somewhere near. Are we going out to find birds today? May we help you, Jan?"

He too had forgotten his search for his father and the place where the wind is always blowing.

So all three of them climbed into the *Puffin* and Jan dipped his oars lightly and steered them through the maze of creeks and gullies between banks and reeds and little islands where the birds nested and flocked in storms of feathers. It was all water and sky and a clear, rinsed light.

Suddenly Jan stopped rowing and pointed a finger.

"What is it?" asked Kirstine, leaning forward eagerly. "Ah, now I see it. Poor thing. See, Peter, his wing is broken."

A curlew not far off was vainly beating his good wing and uttering shrill cries.

"How will you capture him?" asked Peter curiously. "He could escape if he wanted to."

For reply Jan drew from his pocket the reed pipe that he had played the night before. He played on it then, a strange music like the wind in the reeds and the sob of

water in a creek. The curlew with the wounded wing
stood perfectly still, his head tilted delicately as if he were
sipping the music, tasting it on his thin tongue.

"Look, Peter," whispered Kirstine, "look at the other
birds."

And Peter saw that they, too, stood still as stone,
enchanted by the music of the reed pipe.

Still playing, Jan stepped from the boat and lifting the
wounded curlew gently under his arm turned again and
the music stopped.

For a moment there was a hush, a holding of the breath.
Then life ran back through the spellbound birds. The
heron dipped his spindle leg again in pools and the gull
blinked his polished eye, and every bird stretched and
spread his feathers.

In the boat Jan passed the curlew carefully to Kirstine,
who cradled it in her arms and with delight stroked the
soft down of its head and neck. The bird trembled a little
and lay very still. Jan smiled over her head. The water
sucked gently at the dipping oars.

Then the spell broke. A stir ran over the marsh like the
first gust of a storm. The birds grew restless and took to
the air in great, searching circles. Still Kirstine bent over
the curlew and neither saw nor heard them.

Like giants the wild geese were striding the marsh.
They filled the air with harsh cries and the waters
trembled under them.

Kirstine lifted her head for the first time. As she did so,
she saw the skein of geese go over and felt the wind cold
on her face. She forgot the wounded curlew and her wish
to stay on the marshes. She thought only of the geese and
their journey to the world's end.

"I must go," she said. "The geese are calling me. Peter,
we must go."

He nodded. Without a word Jan lifted the oars and
drew the boat back to the hut where the wicker boat was

waiting on the grey waters. As Peter and Kirstine clambered aboard, Jan took out the reed pipe and played again. But this time Kirstine was deaf to its spell. She was listening to the crying of the geese and untied the green plaits with eager fingers.

Sadly Jan placed the pipe in his pocket.

"So I shall be alone, after all," he said. "Good-bye, Kirstine, good-bye, Peter. I had hoped you would stay, but I see you must go."

As they waved good-bye he turned and, with the wounded curlew cradled in his arms, disappeared.

"Where is he?" asked Peter, amazed. "And where are his boat and hut?"

"Gone," said Kirstine, "I don't think they were ever really there at all. But for all that, if the wild geese had not come for us we might have stayed, and never reached the place where the wind is always blowing."

7

The Marsh Lights

That evening at sunset the wicker boat did not glide to the bank for rest as usual. Fire spilt from the sky to the water, the sun dropped, darkness came, and still Peter and Kirstine were being carried through the cornerless marshes.

It was very quiet. Water splashed now and then on the sides of the boat. Sometimes a single bird would cry out in its sleep.

"Look!" whispered Peter, catching Kirstine's arm. "What is that?"

It was a light moving, bobbing away out on the marshes.

"See," said Kirstine, "there are hundreds of them!"

The whole marsh seemed suddenly alive with moving lights, and here and there wide glows of blue or green swelled out and then burst like bubbles. There were soft explosions of yellow light and it whirled in shreds and splinters.

"Come Kirstine, come Peter," voices came, whispering and hissing. "Come, come with us!"

A soft orange light hovered in front of Kirstine and then danced off as if beckoning her to follow.

"Look, Peter," cried Kirstine, delighted. "Let us stop the boat and follow them!"

"No," cried Peter, holding her back. "Don't you see, Kirstine, they are Jack o' Lanterns and Will o' the Wisps. They vanish into the air if you follow them, and leave you lost and alone."

A pale yellow blossom floated by and Kirstine snatched at it so that she almost lost her balance. Her fingers plucked at empty air.

"Come, Kirstine, come, come," came the whispers, and the lights crowded nearer, jostling and weaving.

"They're so beautiful," cried Kirstine, "I wish I could run and catch them and play with them. Listen, how they call me. See how they throng to meet me. Help me to stop the boat, Peter. Wicker Boat, stop!"

But the boat went quietly on.

"Wicker boat, stop, I command you!" cried Kirstine, stamping her foot so that the boat nearly overturned and the thronging lights let out a high, tangled laughter and burned more brightly.

"Please, Kirstine, do not stop the boat," begged Peter. "Don't you see that the boat doesn't want you to leave? It's trying to save you from being led away by the Jack o' Lanterns and Will o' the Wisps. Come away, Kirstine, come away, please!"

But Kirstine hardly heard him. She saw only the light falling thickly now in golden flakes and the smouldering

of the dark greens and blues, and she longed to reach them. She stretched out her hands to touch them as they rained past her, and thought she felt their warmth and softness on her cheeks.

"I must go, I must!" she cried again.

"Kirstine, listen!" Peter held her arm. "Twice you have told the Wicker Boat to stop. If you call the third time, we shall be lost. The spell will be broken and we shall never reach the land where the wind is always blowing. We shall be left alone on the wide marsh and the lights will fade and die away and all will be lost."

An emerald star with a blue halo floated before her.

"Kirstine, Kirstine," came a sweet whisper. "Leave the boat and come with me."

"Ah!" breathed Kirstine. "How beautiful! I'll come! I will!"

"Where are the wild geese?" cried Peter desperately. "Oh help us, help-us!"

The green star glowed and sucked the darkness in. Kirstine's eyes were fixed on it.

The wind came in a cold rush and on it came the calls of wild geese in flight, drowning the whispers of the marshes. And the wind blew the lights out as it went. They leaned and swayed, pulled out thin like candle flames, and went out.

The green star before Kirstine's eyes trembled and flickered and she heard a voice saying:

"Choose, Kirstine, choose quickly. The lights of the marsh or the wild geese. Choose, choose!"

And Kirstine felt the cold wind washing her face and hair and cried aloud with all her might:

"I choose the wind and the world's end!"

And the star cracked end to end, and fell, though there was no splash as it tumbled to the dark water. The wind ebbed and went away over the rim of the marsh. It was pitch dark and still as stone.

Kirstine and Peter without a word lay in their blankets side by side and went to sleep, quickly and soundly, as if they had been told to, and were obeying a voice that they never even heard.

8

Where the Wind Blows

Kirstine and Peter dreamed. They went with sleep into a world of ice and snow, into the huge silence of frost. It was as if they stood at the centre of the world for no path lay in any direction. The snow lay printless all around them.

The wild geese came into the chalky sky and they flew silently, they uttered no cry. The seven geese alighted on a single bough. It creaked and the cold air rang.

"Kirstine," said the leader, "you have journeyed well. Three times have you been tempted to turn aside, to forget the land where the wind is always blowing. Three times you have chosen well."

"And you, Peter," the bird continued, "you have deserved to find your father, and we will bring you to him, never fear."

"Thank you," said Peter, and his breath smoked.

"After that we seek the world's end, where only we and the wind may go. Farewell!"

The seven geese took the air and ice splintered from their feathers in silver needles. Peter and Kirstine were left standing at the centre of the spokeless wheel of snow.

Then it was morning and there they lay in the wicker boat. And the moment Kirstine raised her head she felt the wind blowing at last, cold and strong and salty. She saw that the trees were pitching and the grass leaned and shivered. The water pursed and wrinkled.

"Kirstine!" cried Peter, waving his arms. "We're nearly there! We must be!"

Kirstine tightened her shawl round her shoulders.

"The river is widening," she said eagerly. "We must be near the sea."

As she spoke they rounded a bend and suddenly in front of them was the sea itself, grey-green and restless, shouldering the land. They could see a village on the cliffs above them and beneath it a harbour full of bobbing boats. Black-headed gulls were riding the wind, scooping and soaring. Everything moved and glittered and sang in the blowing air.

"The wind! The wind!" chanted Kirstine joyfully, and her cheeks were whipped into redness.

The wicker boat sailed in by the harbour wall and the wind dropped a little and the sun burned strongly. On the quay were fishermen busy with baskets of fish. All the people laughed and sang and the golden weather-cock on the stone steeple whirled and flashed in the wind. And the wind was always blowing and making movement; boats bounced and the clouds ran along the sky, shawls flapped and the waves slapped on the barnacled wall of the quay.

Kirstine squeezed her hands tight together and almost laughed aloud because it was so careless and so beautiful.

As the wicker boat drew to the side willing hands pulled on the green ropes to make her fast to a rusty iron ring. Kirstine and Peter stepped up on to the quayside and for a moment the ground came up and the world went steeply sideways, making them dizzy. The crowd drew round, eager and excited.

"Who are you?" they cried. "Where are you from?"

"I'm looking for my father," said Peter. "And Kirstine is going to the world's end."

Kirstine stood shyly by and people nearby nodded and winked at her delightedly.

"It's Mr John's boy," they said to each other. And "Look at that – come sailing in right out of the blue!"

A tall man with a brown face and shiny oilskins told them where Mr John lived.

"Cuttle Cottage, Cuttle Hill," he told them. "Right up at the top, next the sky."

Peter and Kirstine thanked him and went on along the gusty quay. It seemed to Kirstine that the whole place was alive, even to the rough grey stones under her feet. An old fiddler was playing tunes while his rags streamed about him and barefoot children danced to his music. Laughing women walked swiftly by, baskets balanced on their heads and spray showering about them.

Kirstine and Peter started up a steep cobbled street of nudging cottages. Up and up they climbed, and the higher they went the harder the wind blew, plucking their clothes and filling their mouths with air as cold as water. Right at the very top was a leaning yellow house, blown sideways by a century of wind.

"Father!" called Peter, pushing open the door.

They went inside and a gust blew in with them, scattering papers about the room and swinging the hanging lantern.

"Father!" cried Peter again. He banged the door shut, so that it seemed suddenly very quiet and still. No one came.

"He's painting," said Peter. "Every day he used to paint till the sun went down. We'll find him."

Out they went and up to the cliffs. They called to each other but were deafened by the thunder of the wind and waves. Then they saw him, at his easel, sheltered behind a huge, whitish boulder.

"Father!" cried Peter. And Mr John flung down his brush and ran to meet him, his thin face shining.

"You've come!" he cried.

Then they sat behind the chalky stone and Kirstine and

Peter told him of their travels, of the wild geese and the marshes and the Jack o' Lanterns. He seemed to listen, but by and by his eyes began to wander, back to his canvas and the wet, shining paints. His fingers began to twitch, and in the end he got up without a word and began his painting, as if he had forgotten they were there at all.

A white mist was rolling in from the sea when at last he put down his brushes. They walked back over the cliffs watching the lights come out below them one by one, decorating the dusk.

Kirstine had never felt so tired in her whole life. She ached where the wind had hammered her from head to foot. At Cuttle Cottage there was hot stew by the swaying lamplight and a steep climb up rickety stairs and then at last a slow sinking into a deep bed of feathers, sleeping even as she sank.

9

World's End

Next morning Kirstine woke early and lay for a moment wondering where she was. She was used to feeling the movement of the wicker boat and seeing a tangle of leaves about her. Now she was lying on a bed and above her were beams decorated with cobwebs and lobster pots. A stuffed sea-gull stood on each bed post. Seeing the birds made Kirstine remember the wild geese. She jumped up. She had not seen them since they had spoken to her in the dream, and she ran to the window and threw it open.

A cold gust of wind blew in. Dawn was breaking over the sea and the gulls were waking and walking on the shingle or screaming from the chimney pots of the cottages below. As she watched the seven geese came into

the hyacinth sky, lit with sun and cutting the morning like arrows. They flew down and alighted on the black rotting wood of the jetty.

"Soon they will be gone," thought Kirstine, "off to the world's end. I must say good-bye."

She turned to the tumbled bed and seized her shawl and leather shoes. She ran down the curving stairs and through the painter's tackle and sleeping pictures and out into the empty street. A window banged open above her and first Peter's head appeared, then Mr John's.

"Kirstine," cried Peter, "where are you going? Wait!"

"I'm going to see the wild geese go," said Kirstine. "And then I must go too. Grandfather will be waiting for me."

"But you've only been here a day," said Mr John. "I thought you wanted to live where the wind is always blowing?"

"I did," said Kirstine. "But now I'm here and it's the end of the journey. Today the wild geese will fly to the world's end and the adventure will be over."

"Just for a day, Kirstine," pleaded Peter.

The wind whipped round her legs and curled her shawl around her. On it came the calls of the geese far out at sea.

"I can't," she said. She remembered the words of the Old Man of the Stile. "You must go where they take you, whether you will or no."

"I must go, Peter," she cried. "But I shall see you again one day, I know I shall. I'll come myself, now that I know the way. I shan't need the wild geese next time. Good-bye, Peter. Good-bye, Mr John!"

And she began to run pell-mell in case she should change her mind, past the church with its whirling cock, past the lobster-pots and window-boxes of geraniums, past the shell gardens and rows of cockles down to the gusty quay. The wicker boat lay knocking against the sea wall and Kirstine untied the green plaits for the last time

and climbed down. Straight away the boat moved off, strongly and surely threading the crowded harbour until it reached the outer wall and the open sea.

And the wind blew, every minute it blew more strongly until Kirstine felt as if it were blowing through her very bones, blowing through her fingertips, elbows, feet. She could see the seven wild geese in a sky of white and violet as if a storm were coming.

"Shall I turn back?" thought Kirstine, half-afraid.

But the wind was too strong, blowing through her and over her now, and when she looked ahead she saw that the wild geese were going right over the rim of the world like stones dropping.

"The world's end!" cried Kirstine in wonder. "The wild geese have reached the world's end."

And after that Kirstine could remember nothing, except that for a moment everything seemed to stop. Even the waves hung half-furled and the wind went out like a candle flame. Everything stopped, and there was silence.

10

Home

Kirstine felt as if she had been dreaming. She opened her eyes and a white-flowered nettle waved across them. She could smell its sharpness. She sat up, rubbing her eyes with her fists.

"Well," said a deep dark voice, "it's little Kirstine home again."

Looking up she saw the mountainous face of the Old Man of the Stile, with its crags and hollows and sour green eyes.

"And did you reach the place where the wind is always blowing?" he asked, smiling as if he knew a secret.

"Yes," nodded Kirstine, "I reached it."

"And did you see the geese fly to the world's end?" he asked.

"Yes," said Kirstine, "though I only half remember."

"What do you remember?" asked the Old Man of the Stile, huddling from the dew into his tattered leathers.

Kirstine wrinkled her forehead.

"Was the wind blowing there?" asked the Old Man slyly. "Or was it very quiet? Quieter perhaps than the old mill?"

"You have been there too," cried Kirstine suddenly. She knew now why the Old Man's eyes were brimful of secrets.

"Yes," he nodded. "I too."

Kirstine climbed from the wicker boat and began to tie the long green plaits to the trunk of a willow.

"No," said the Old Man of the Stile. "Let it go. You won't need it again."

"No," agreed Kirstine. "Next time I can go alone."

She let the plaited reeds slide through her fingers and they dropped to the water with a soft plash. The wicker boat began to drift slowly into midstream.

"I must go to the mill," said Kirstine, not wanting to watch it out of sight. "Grandfather will be waiting. Good-bye, Old Man of the Stile."

"Good-bye, Kirstine. Remember, I shall always be here."

Kirstine nodded. So he would. Century in and century out, in his tattered leathers, watching the world and the weather.

She ran eagerly through the tangle of wet nettles with their bruised scents and smells of earth until suddenly she was out in the sunlit meadow and the old mill stood there just as she had left it, half-asleep among the jigsawed cows.

And suddenly she did not care that the sails were still,

because she had been where the winds were always blowing and she knew that her grandfather was right. Some days the wind would blow, on others there would be never a whisper. But somewhere the wind was always blowing and now she had it in her bones for ever.

Marigold lay curled like melted butter in the sun and blinked a narrow eye. The mill door groaned on its hinges. At the bleached table sat Grandfather, fast asleep, his powdery head resting on his folded arms. The clock ticked, the pan simmered.

Tiptoe and smiling Kirstine quietly fetched the yellow bowls from the cupboard and filled them with the steaming broth. The dust sailed idly down the long sunbeams and the flies droned in the doorway.

Gently Kirstine shook her grandfather by the shoulder.

"Wake up!" she said softly. "Grandfather, I'm here!"

And he looked up and smiled as he woke, so pleased was he to see her again. And when they had greeted each other they tucked their legs under the table together and drank their broth as if nothing had ever happened.

Grandfather let out a long sigh and wiped his mouth on his sleeve.

"Ah," he said. "That was good. And did you go where the wind blows?"

"Yes," said Kirstine.

"I have never been there myself," said Grandfather. "But it must have been very interesting. What did you say was for supper?"

Kirstine smiled.

"Kippers, I think," she said.

And a sudden rush of wings went by out in the windless meadow.

"Yes, kippers, I think," said Kirstine. The wings had gone and the clock on the wall was ticking again.

Prince Rabbit

A. A. Milne

Once upon a time there was a King who had no children. Sometimes he would say to the Queen, "If only we had a son!" and the Queen would answer, "If only we had!" Another day he would say, "If only we had a daughter!" and the Queen would sigh and answer, "Yes, even if we had a daughter, that would be something." But they had no children at all.

As the years went on, and there were still no children in the Royal palace, the people began to ask each other who would be the next King to reign over them. And some said that perhaps it would be the Chancellor, which was a pity, as nobody liked him very much; and others said that there would be no King at all, but that everybody would be equal. Those who were lowest of all thought that this would be a satisfactory ending of the matter, but those who were higher up felt that, though in some respects it would be a good thing, yet in other respects it would be an ill-advised state of affairs; and they hoped, therefore, that a young Prince would be born in the palace. But no Prince was born.

One day, when the Chancellor was in audience with the King, it seemed well to him to speak what was in the people's minds.

"Your Majesty," he said, and then stopped, wondering how best to put it.

"Well?" said the King.

"Have I Your Majesty's permission to speak my mind?"

"So far, yes," said the King.

Encouraged by this, the Chancellor resolved to put the matter plainly. "In the event of Your Majesty's death—" He coughed and began again. "If Your Majesty ever *should* die," he said, "which in any case will not be for many years – if ever – as, I need hardly say, Your Majesty's loyal subjects earnestly hope – I mean they hope it will be never. But assuming for the moment – making the sad assumption—"

"You said you wanted to speak your mind," interrupted the King. "is that it?"

"Yes, Majesty."

"Then I don't think much of it."

"Thank you, Your Majesty."

"What you are trying to say is, 'Who will be the next King?'"

"Quite so, Your Majesty."

"Ah!" The King was silent for a little. Then he said, "I can tell you who won't be."

The Chancellor did not seek for information on this point, feeling that in the circumstances the answer was obvious.

"What do you suggest yourself?"

"That Your Majesty choose a successor from among the young and the highly born of this country, putting him to whatever test seems good to Your Majesty."

The King pulled at his beard and frowned. "There must be not one test, but many tests. Let all who will offer themselves, provided only they are under the age of twenty and well born. See to it."

He waved his hand in dismissal, and with an accuracy established by long practice, the Chancellor retired backwards out of the palace.

On the following morning, therefore, it was announced that all those who were ambitious to be appointed the King's successor, and who were of high birth and not yet come to the age of twenty, should present themselves a week later for the tests to which His Majesty desired to put them, the first of which would be a running race. Whereat the people rejoiced, for they wished to be ruled by one to whom they could look up, and running was much esteemed in that country.

On the appointed day the excitement was great. All along the course, which was once round the castle, large crowds were massed, and at the finishing point the King and Queen themselves were seated in a specially erected pavilion. And to this the competitors were brought to be introduced to Their Majesties. There were nine young nobles, well-built and handsome and (it was thought) intelligent, who were competitors. And there was also one Rabbit.

The Chancellor had first noticed the Rabbit when he was lining up the competitors, pinning numbers on their backs so that the people should identify them, and giving them such instructions as seemed necessary to him. "Now, now, be off with you," he said. "Competitors only, this way." And he made a motion of impatient dismissal with his foot.

"I *am* a competitor," said the Rabbit. "And I don't think it is usual, " he added with dignity, "for the starter to kick one of the competitors just at the beginning of an important foot race. It looks like favouritism."

"*You* can't be a competitor," laughed all the nobles.

"Why not? Read the rules."

The Chancellor, feeling rather hot suddenly, read the rules. The Rabbit was certainly under twenty; he had a pedigree which showed that he was of the highest birth; and—

"And," said the Rabbit, "I am ambitious to be appointed the King's successor. Those were all the conditions. Now let's get on with the race."

But first came the introduction to the King. One by one the competitors came up ... and at the end—

"This," said the Chancellor, as airily as he could, "is Rabbit."

Rabbit bowed in the most graceful manner possible, first to the King and then to the Queen. But the King only stared at him. The he turned to the Chancellor.

"Well?"

The Chancellor shrugged his shoulders. "His entry does not appear to lack validity," he said.

"He means, Your Majesty, that it is all right," explained Rabbit.

The King laughed suddenly. "Go on," he said. "We can always have a race for a new Chancellor afterwards."

So the race was started. And the young Lord Calomel was much cheered on coming in second, not only by Their Majesties, but also by Rabbit, who had finished the course some time before and was now lounging in the Royal pavilion.

"A very good style, Your Majesty," said Rabbit, turning to the King. "Altogether he seems to be a most promising youth."

"Most," said the King grimly. "So much so that I do not propose to trouble the rest of the competitors. The next test shall take place between you and him."

"Not racing again, please, Your Majesty. That would hardly be fair to His Lordship."

"No, not racing. Fighting."

"Ah! What sort of fighting?"

"With swords," said the King.

"I am a little rusty with swords, but I daresay in a day or two—"

"It will be now," said the King.

"You mean, Your Majesty, as soon as Lord Calomel has recovered his breath?"

The King answered nothing, but turned to his Chancellor. "Tell the young Lord Calomel that in half an hour I desire him to fight with this Rabbit—"

"The young Lord Rabbit," murmured the other competitor to the Chancellor.

"To fight with him for my kingdom."

"*And* borrow me a sword, will you?" said Rabbit. "Quite a small one. I don't want to hurt him."

So, half an hour later, on a level patch of grass in front of the pavilion, the fight began. It was a short but exciting struggle. Calomel, whirling his long sword in his strong right arm, dashed upon Rabbit, and Rabbit, carrying his short sword in his teeth, dodged between Calomel's legs and brought him toppling. And when it was seen that the young lord rose from the ground with a broken arm, and that with the utmost gallantry he had now taken his sword in his left hand, the people cheered. And Rabbit, dropping his sword for a moment, cheered too, and then he picked it up and got it entangled in his adversary's legs again, so that again young Lord Calomel crashed to the ground, this time with a sprained ankle. And so there he lay.

Rabbit trotted into the Royal pavilion and dropped his sword in the Chancellor's lap. "Thank you so much," he said. "Have I won?" And the King frowned and pulled at his beard. "There are other tests," he muttered.

But what were they to be? It was plain that Lord Calomel was in no condition for another physical test. What, then, of an intellectual test?

"After all," said the King to the Queen that night, "intelligence is a quality not without value in a ruler."

"Is it?" asked the Queen doubtfully.

"I have found it so," said the King, a trifle haughtily.

"Oh," said the Queen.

"There is a riddle of which my father was fond, the answer to which has never been revealed save to the Royal House. We might make this the final test between them."

"What is the riddle?"

"I fancy it goes like this." He thought for a moment and then recited it, beating time with his hand."

"My first I *do for your daylight*,
Although 'tis neither black nor white.
My second looks the other way,
Yet always goes to bed by day.
My whole can fly and climb a tree,
And sometimes swims upon the sea."

"What is the answer?" asked the Queen.

"As far as I remember," said His Majesty, "it is either *Dormouse* or *Raspberry*."

"*Dormouse* doesn't make sense," objected the Queen.

"Neither does *Raspberry*," pointed out the King.

"Then how can they guess it?"

"They can't. But my idea is that young Calomel should be secretly told beforehand what the answer is, so that he may win the competition."

"Is that fair?" asked the Queen doubtfully.

"Yes," said the King. "Certainly. Or I wouldn't have suggested it."

So it was duly announced by the Chancellor that the final test between the young Lord Calomel and Rabbit would be the solving of an ancient riddle-me-ree which in the past had baffled all save those of Royal blood. Copies of the riddle had been sent to the competitors, and in a week from that day they would be called upon to give their answers before Their Majesties and the full court. And with Lord Calomel's copy went a message, which said this:

"*From a Friend*. The answer is *Dormouse*. BURN THIS."

The day came around; and Calomel and Rabbit were brought before Their Majesties; and they bowed to Their Majesties and were ordered to be seated, for Calomel's ankle was still painful to him. And when the Chancellor had called for silence, the King addressed those present, explaining the conditions of the test to them.

"And the answer to the riddle," he said, "is in this sealed paper, which I now hand to my Chancellor, in order that he shall open it as soon as the competitors have told us what they know of the matter."

The people, being uncertain what else to do, cheered slightly.

"I will ask Lord Calomel first," His Majesty went on. He looked at His Lordship, and His Lordship nodded slightly. And Rabbit, noticing that nod, smiled suddenly to himself.

The young Lord Calomel tried to look very wise, and he said, "There are many possible answers to this riddle-me-ree, but the best answer seems to me to be *Dormouse*."

"Let someone take a note of that answer," said the King: whereupon the chief secretary wrote down: "LORD CALOMEL – *Dormouse*."

"Now," said the King to Rabbit, "what suggestion have you to make in this matter?"

Rabbit, who had spent an anxious week inventing answers each more impossible than the last, looked down modestly.

"Well?" said the King.

"Your Majesty," said the Rabbit with some apparent hesitation, "I have a great respect for the intelligence of the young Lord Calomel, but I think in this matter he is mistaken. The answer is not, as he suggests, *Wood-louse*, but *Dormouse*."

"I *said Dormouse*," cried Calomel indignantly.

"I thought you said *Wood-louse*," said Rabbit in surprise.

"He certainly said *Dormouse*," said the King coldly.

"*Wood-louse*, I think," said Rabbit.

"'LORD CALOMEL – *Dormouse*,'" read out the chief secretary.

"There you are," said Calomel. "I did say *Dormouse*."

"My apologies," said Rabbit, with a bow. "Then we are both right, for *Dormouse* it certainly is."

The Chancellor broke open the sealed paper and, to the amazement of nearly all present, read out, "*Dormouse* . . . Apparently, Your Majesty," he said in some surprise, "they are both equally correct."

The King scowled. In some way which he didn't quite understand, he had been tricked.

"May I suggest, Your Majesty," the Chancellor went on, "that they be asked now some question of a different order, such as can be answered, after not more than a few minutes' thought, here in Your Majesty's presence? Some problem in the higher mathematics, for instance, such as might be profitable for a future King to know."

"What question?" asked His Majesty, a little nervously.

"Well, as an example – what is seven times six?" And behind his hand he whispered to the King. "Forty-two."

Not a muscle of the King's face moved, but he looked thoughtfully at the Lord Calomel. Supposing His Lordship did not know!

"Well?" he said reluctantly. "What is the answer?"

The young Lord Calomel thought for some time and then said, "Fifty-four."

"And you?" said the King to Rabbit.

Rabbit wondered what to say. As long as he gave the same answers as Calomel, he could not lose in the encounter, yet in this case, "forty-two" was the right answer. But the King, who could do no wrong, even in

arithmetic, might decide, for the purposes of the competition, that "fifty-four" was an answer more becoming to the future ruler of the country. Was it, then, safe to say "forty-two"?

"Your Majesty," he said, "there are several possible answers to this extraordinary novel conundrum. At first sight the obvious solution would appear to be 'forty-two'. The objection to this solution is that it lacks originality. I have long felt that a progressive country such as ours might well strike out a new line in the matter. Let us agree that in future seven sixes are fifty-four. In that case the answer, as Lord Calomel has pointed out, is 'fifty-four'. But if Your Majesty would prefer to cling to the old style of counting, then Your Majesty and Your Majesty's Chancellor would make the answer 'forty-two'."

After saying which, Rabbit bowed gracefully, both to Their Majesties and to his opponent and sat down again.

The King scratched his head in a puzzled sort of way. "The correct answer," he said, "is, or will be in future, 'fifty-four'."

"Make a note of that," whispered the Chancellor to the chief secretary.

"Lord Calomel guessed this at his first attempt; Rabbit at his second attempt. I therefore declare Lord Calomel the winner."

"Shame!" said Rabbit.

"Who said that?" cried the King furiously.

Rabbit looked over his shoulder with the object of identifying the culprit, but was apparently unsuccessful.

"However," went on the King, "in order that there should be no doubt in the minds of my people as to the absolute fairness with which this competition is being conducted, there will be one further test. It happens that a King is often called upon to make speeches and exhortations to his people, and for this purpose the ability to

stand evenly upon two legs for a considerable length of
time is of much value to him. The next test, therefore,
will be—"

But at this point Lord Calomel suddenly cleared his
throat so loudly that the King had perforce to stop and
listen to him.

"Quite so," said the King. "The next test, therefore,
will be held in a month's time, when His Lordship's ankle
is healed, and it will be a test to see who can balance
himself longest upon two legs only."

Rabbit lolloped back to his home in the wood, pondering deeply.

Now, there was an enchanter who lived in the wood, a
man of many magical gifts. He could (it was averred by
the countryside) extract coloured ribbons from his
mouth, cook plum puddings in a hat, and produce as
many as ten handkerchiefs, knotted together, from a
twist of paper. And that night, after a simple dinner of
salad, Rabbit called upon him.

"Can you," he said, "turn a rabbit into a man?"

The enchanter considered this carefully. "I can," he
said at last, "turn a plum pudding into a rabbit."

"That," said Rabbit, "to be frank, would not be a
helpful operation."

"I can turn almost anything into a rabbit," said the
enchanter with growing enthusiasm. "In fact, I like doing
it."

Then Rabbit had an idea. "Can you turn a man into a
rabbit?"

"I did once. At least, I turned a baby into a baby
rabbit."

"When was that?"

"Eighteen years ago. At the court of King Nicodemus.
I was giving an exhibition of my powers to him and his
good Queen. I asked one of the company to lend me a
baby, never thinking for a moment that – The young

Prince was handed up. I put a red silk handkerchief over him and waved my hands. Then I took the handkerchief away ... The Queen was very distressed. I tried everything I could, but it was useless. The King was most generous about it. He said that I could keep the rabbit. I carried it about with me for some weeks, but one day it escaped. Dear, dear!" He wiped his eyes gently with a red silk handkerchief.

"Most interesting," said Rabbit. "Well, this is what I want you to do." And they discussed the matter from the beginning.

A month later the great standing competition was to take place. When all was ready, the King rose to make his opening remarks.

"We are now," he began, "to make one of the most interesting tests between our two candidates for the throne. At the word 'Go!' they will—" and then he stopped suddenly. "Why, what's this?" he said, putting on his spectacles. "Where is the young Lord Calomel? And what is that second rabbit doing? There was no need to bring your brother," he added severely to Rabbit.

"I am Lord Calomel," said the second rabbit meekly.

"Oh!" said the King.

"Go!" said the Chancellor, who was a little deaf.

Rabbit, who had been practising for a month, jumped on his back paws and remained there. Lord Calomel, who had had no practice at all remained on all fours. In the crowd at the back the enchanter chuckled to himself.

"How long do I stay like this?" asked Rabbit.

"This is all very awkward and distressing," said the King.

"May I get down?" said Rabbit.

"There is no doubt that Rabbit has won," said the Chancellor.

"Which rabbit?" cried the King crossly. "They're both rabbits."

"The one with the white spots behind the ears," said Rabbit helpfully. "May I get down?"

There was a sudden cry from the back of the hall. "Your Majesty?"

"Well, well, what is it?"

The enchanter pushed his way forward. "May I look, Your Majesty?" he said in a trembling voice. "White spots behind the ears? Dear, dear! Allow me!" He seized Rabbit's ears and bent them this way and that.

"Ow!" said Rabbit.

"It is! Your Majesty, it is!"

"Is what?"

"The son of the late King Nicodemus, whose country is now joined to your own. Prince Silvio."

"Quite so," said Rabbit airily, hiding his surprise. "Didn't any of you recognize me?"

"Nicodemus only had one son," said the Chancellor, "and he died as a baby."

"Not died," said the enchanter, and forthwith explained the whole sad story.

"I see," said the King, when the story was ended. "But of course that is neither here nor there. A competition like this must be conducted with absolute impartiality." He turned to the Chancellor. "Which of them won that last test?"

"Prince Silvio," said the Chancellor.

"Then, my dear Prince Silvio—"

"One moment," interrupted the enchanter excitedly. "I've just thought of the words. I *knew* there were some words you had to say."

He threw back his red silk handkerchief over Rabbit and cried, "Hey presto!"

And the handkerchief rose and rose and rose ... And there was Prince Silvio!

You can imagine how loudly the people cheered. But the King appeared not to notice that anything surprising had happened.

"Then, my dear Prince Silvio," he went on, "as the winner of this most interesting series of contests, you are appointed successor to our throne."

"Your Majesty," said Silvio, "this is too much." And he turned to the enchanter and said, "May I borrow your handkerchief for a moment? My emotion has overcome me."

So on the following day Prince Rabbit was duly proclaimed heir to the throne before all the people. But not until the ceremony was over did he return the enchanter's red handkerchief.

"And now," he said to the enchanter, "you may restore Lord Calomel to his proper shape."

And the enchanter placed his handkerchief on Lord Calomel's head and said, "Hey presto!" and Lord Calomel stretched himself and said, "Thanks very much." But he said it rather coldly, as if he were not really very grateful.

So they all lived happily for a long time. And Prince Rabbit married the most beautiful Princess of those parts, and when a son was born to them there was much feasting and jollification. And the King gave a great party, whereat minstrels, tumblers, jugglers and suchlike were present in large quantities to give pleasure to the company. But, in spite of a suggestion made by the Princess, the enchanter was not present.

"But I hear he is so clever," said the Princess to her husband.

"He has many amusing inventions," replied the Prince, "but some of them are not in the best of taste."

"Very well, dear," said the Princess.

A Harp of Fishbones

Joan Aiken

Little Nerryn lived in the half-ruined mill at the upper
end of the village, where the stream ran out of the forest.
The old miller's name was Timorash, but she called him
uncle. Her own father and mother were dead, long before
she could remember. Timorash was no real kin, nor was
he particularly kind to her; he was a lazy old man. He
never troubled to grow corn as the other people in the
village did, little patches in the clearing below the village
before the forest began again. When people brought him
corn to grind he took one-fifth of it as his fee and this,
with wild plums which Nerryn gathered and dried, and
carp from the deep millpool, kept him and the child fed
through the short bright summers and the long silent
winters.

Nerryn learned to do the cooking when she was seven
or eight; she toasted fish on sticks over the fire and baked
cakes of bread on a flat stone; Timorash beat her if the
food was burnt, but mostly it was, just the same, because
so often half her mind would be elsewhere, listening to
the bell-like call of a bird or pondering about what made
the difference between the stream's voice in winter and in
summer. When she was a little older Timorash taught her
how to work the mill, opening the sluice-gate so that the
green, clear mountain water could hurl down against the

great wooden paddle-wheel. Nerryn liked this much
better, since she already spent hours watching the stream
endlessly pouring and plaiting down its narrow passage.
Old Timorash had hoped that now he would be able to
give up work altogether and lie in the sun all day, or
crouch by the fire, slowly adding one stick after another
and dreaming about barley wine. But Nerryn forgot to
take flour in payment from the villagers, who were in no
hurry to remind her, so the old man angrily decided that
this plan would not answer, and sent her out to work.

First she worked for one household, then for another.

The people of the village had come from the plains;
they were surly, big-boned, and lank, with tow-coloured
hair and pale eyes; even the children seldom spoke. Little
Nerryn sometimes wondered, looking at her reflection in
the millpool, how it was that she should be so different
from them, small and brown-skinned, with dark hair like
a bird's feathers and hazelnut eyes. But it was no use
asking questions of old Timorash, who never answered
except by grunting or throwing a clod of earth at her.
Another difference was that she loved to chatter, and this
was perhaps the main reason why the people she worked
for soon sent her packing.

There were other reasons too, for, though Nerryn was
willing to work, things often distracted her.

"She let the bread burn while she ran outside to listen
to a curlew," said one.

"When she was helping me cut the hay she asked so
many questions that my ears ached for three days," complained another.

"Instead of scaring off the birds from my corn-patch
she sat with her chin on her fists, watching them gobble
down half a winter's supply and whistling to them!"
grumbled a third.

Nobody would keep her more than a few days, and
she had plenty of beatings, especially from Timorash,

who had hoped that her earnings would pay for a keg of barley wine. Once in his life he had had a whole keg, and he still felt angry when he remembered that it was finished.

At last Nerryn went to work for an old woman who lived in a tumbledown hut at the bottom of the street. Her name was Saroon and she was by far the oldest in the village, so withered and wrinkled that most people thought she was a witch; besides, she knew when it was going to rain and was the only person in the place who did not fear to venture a little way into the forest. But she was growing weak now, and stiff, and wanted somebody to help dig her corn-patch and cut wood. Nevertheless she hardly seemed to welcome help when it came. As Nerryn moved about at the tasks she was set, the old woman's little red-rimmed eyes followed her suspiciously; she hobbled round the hut watching through cracks, grumbling and chuntering to herself, never losing sight of the girl for a moment, like some cross-grained old animal that sees a stranger near its burrow.

On the fourth day she said,

"You're singing, girl."

"I – I'm sorry," Nerryn stammered. "I didn't mean to – I wasn't thinking. Don't beat me, please."

"Humph," said the old woman, but she did not beat Nerryn that time. And next day, watching through the window-hole while Nerryn chopped wood, she said,

"You're not singing."

Nerryn jumped. She had not known the old woman was so near.

"I thought you didn't like me to," she faltered.

"I didn't say so, did I?"

Muttering, the old woman stumped off to the back of the hut and began to sort through a box of mildewy nuts. "As if I should care", Nerryn heard her grumble, "whether the girl sings or not!" But next day she put her

head out of the door, while Nerryn hoed the corn-patch, and said,

"Sing, child!"

Nerryn looked at her, doubtful and timid, to see if she really meant it, but she nodded her head energetically, till the tangled grey locks jounced on her shoulders, and repeated,

"Sing!"

So presently the clear, tiny thread of Nerryn's song began again as she sliced off the weeds; and old Saroon came out and sat on an upturned log beside the door, pounding roots for soup and mumbling to herself in time to the sound. And at the end of the week she did not dismiss the girl, as everyone else had done, though what she paid was so little that Timorash grumbled every time Nerryn brought it home. At this rate twenty years would go by before he had saved enough for a keg of barley wine.

One day Saroon said,

"Your father used to sing."

This was the first time anyone had spoken of him.

"Oh," Nerryn cried, forgetting her fear of the old woman. "Tell me about him."

"Why should I?" old Saroon said sourly. "He never did anything for *me*." And she hobbled off to fetch a pot of water. But later she relented and said,

"His hair was the colour of ash buds, like yours. And he carried a harp."

"A harp, what is a harp?"

"Oh, don't pester, child. I'm busy."

But another day she said, "A harp is a thing to make music. His was a gold one, but it was broken."

"Gold, what is gold?"

"This," said the old woman, and she pulled out a small, thin disc which she wore on a cord of plaited grass round her neck.

"Why!" Nerryn exclaimed. "Everybody in the village has one of those except Timorash and me. I've often asked what they were but no one would answer."

"They are gold. When your father went off and left you and the harp with Timorash, the old man ground up the harp between the millstones. And he melted down the gold powder and made it into these little circles and sold them to everybody in the village, and bought a keg of barley wine. He told us they would bring good luck. But I never had any good luck and that was a long time ago. And Timorash has long since drunk all his barley wine."

"Where did my father go?" asked Nerryn.

"Into the forest," the old woman snapped. "I could have told him he was in for trouble. I could have warned him. But he never asked *my* advice."

She sniffed, and set a pot of herbs boiling on the fire. And Nerryn could get no more out of her that day.

But little by little, as time passed, more came out.

"Your father came from over the mountains. High up yonder, he said, there was a great city, with houses and palaces and temples, and as many rich people as there are fish in the millpool. Best of all, there was always music playing in the streets and houses and in the temples. But then the goddess of the mountain became angry, and fire burst out of a crack in the hillside. And then a great cold came, so that people froze where they stood. Your father said he only just managed to escape with you by running very fast. Your mother had died in the fire."

"Where was he going?"

"The king of the city had ordered him to go for help."

"What sort of help?"

"Don't ask *me*," the old woman grumbled. "You'd think he'd have settled down here like a person of sense, and mended his harp. But no, on he must go, leaving you behind so that he could travel faster. He said he'd fetch

you again on his way back. But of course he never did
come back – one day I found his bones in the forest. The
birds must have killed him."

"How do you *know* they were my father's bones?"

"Because of the tablet he carried. See, here it is, with his
name on it, Heramon the harper."

"Tell me more about the harp!"

"It was shaped like this," the old woman said. They
were washing clothes by the stream, and she drew with
her finger in the mud. "Like this, and it had golden strings
across, so. All but one of the strings had melted in the fire
from the mountain. Even on just one string he could
make very beautiful music, that would force you to stop
whatever you were doing and listen. It is a pity he had to
leave the harp behind. Timorash wanted it as payment for
looking after you. If your father had taken the harp with
him, perhaps he would have been able to reach the other
side of the forest."

Nerryn thought about this story a great deal. For the
next few weeks she did even less work then usual and was
mostly to be found squatting with her chin on her fists by
the side of the stream. Saroon beat her, but not very hard.
Then one day Nerryn said,

"I shall make a harp."

"Hah!" sniffed the old woman. "You! What do you
know of such things?"

After a few minutes she asked,

"What will you make it from?"

Nerryn said, "I shall make it of fishbones. Some of the
biggest carp in the millpool have bones as thick as my
wrist, and they are very strong."

"Timorash will never allow it."

"I shall wait till he is asleep, then."

So Nerryn waited till night, and then she took a chunk
of rotten wood, which glows in the dark, and dived into
the deep millpool, swimming down and down to the

depths where the biggest carp lurk, among the mud and weeds and old sunken logs.

When they saw the glimmer of the wood through the water, all the fish came nosing and nibbling and swimming round Nerryn, curious to find if this thing which shone so strangely was good to eat. She waited as long as she could bear it, holding her breath, till a great barrel-shaped monster slid nudging right up against her; then, quick as a flash, she wrapped her arms round his slippery sides and fled up with a bursting heart to the surface.

Much to her surprise, old Saroon was there, waiting in the dark on the bank. But the old woman only said,

"You had better bring the carp to my hut. After all, you want no more than the bones, and it would be a pity to waste all that good meat. I can live on it for a week." So she cut the meat off the bones, which were coal-black but had a sheen on them like mother-of-pearl. Nerryn dried them by the fire, and then she joined together the three biggest, notching them to fit, and cementing them with a glue which she made by boiling some of the smaller bones together. She used long, thin, strong bones for strings, joining them to the frame in the same manner.

All the time old Saroon watched closely. Sometimes she would say,

"That was not the way of it. Heramon's harp was wider," or "You are putting the strings too far apart. There should be more of them, and they should be tighter."

When at last it was done, she said,

"Now you must hang it in the sun to dry."

So for three days the harp hung drying in the sun and wind. At night Saroon took it into her hut and covered it with a cloth. On the fourth day she said,

"Now, play!"

Nerryn rubbed her finger across the strings, and they gave out a liquid murmur, like that of a stream running

over pebbles, under a bridge. She plucked a string, and the noise was like that a drop of water makes, falling in a hollow place.

"That will be music," old Saroon said, nodding her head, satisfied. "It is not quite the same as the sound from your father's harp, but it is music. Now you shall play me tunes every day, and I shall sit in the sun and listen."

"No," said Nerryn, "for if Timorash hears me playing he will take the harp away and break it or sell it. I shall go to my father's city and see if I can find any of his kin there."

At this old Saroon was very angry. "Here have I taken all these pains to help you, and what reward do I get for it? How much pleasure do you think I have, living among dolts in this dismal place? I was not born here, any more than you were. You could at least play to me at night, when Timorash is asleep."

"Well, I will play to you for seven nights," Nerryn said.

Each night old Saroon tried to persuade her not to go, and she tried harder as Nerryn became more skilful in playing, and drew from the fishbone harp a curious watery music, like the songs that birds sing when it is raining. But Nerryn would not be persuaded to stay, and when she saw this, on the seventh night, Saroon said,

"I suppose I shall have to tell you how to go through the forest. Otherwise you will certainly die, as your father did. When you go among the trees you will find that the grass underfoot is thick and strong and hairy, and the farther you go, the higher it grows, as high as your waist. And it is sticky and clings to you, so that you can only go forward slowly, one step at a time. Then, in the middle of the forest, perched in the branches, are vultures who will drop on you and peck you to death if you stand still for more than a minute."

"How do you know all this?" Nerryn said.

"I have tried many times to go through the forest, but it is too far for me; I grow tired and have to turn back. The vultures take no notice of me, I am too old and withered, but a tender young piece like you would be just what they fancy."

"Then what must I do?" Nerryn asked.

"You must play music on your harp till they fall asleep; then, while they sleep, cut the grass with your knife and go forward as fast as you can."

Nerryn said, "If I cut you enough fuel for a month, and catch you another carp, and gather you a bushel of nuts, will you give me your little gold circle, or my father's tablet?"

But this Saroon would not do. She did, though, break off the corner of the tablet which had Heramon the harper's name on it, and give that to Nerryn.

"But don't blame me," she said sourly, "if you find the city all burnt and frozen, with not a living soul to walk its streets."

"Oh, it will all have been rebuilt by this time," Nerryn said. "I shall find my father's people, or my mother's, and I shall come back for you, riding a white mule and leading another."

"Fairy tales!" old Saroon said angrily. "Be off with you, then. If you don't wish to stay I'm sure *I* don't want you idling about the place. All the work you've done this last week I could have done better myself in half an hour. Drat the woodsmoke! It gets in a body's eyes till they can't see a thing." And she hobbled into the hut, working her mouth sourly and rubbing her eyes with the back of her hand.

Nerryn ran into the forest, going cornerways up the mountain, so as not to pass too close to the mill where old Timorash lay sleeping in the sun.

Soon she had to slow down because the way was so steep. And the grass grew thicker and thicker, hairy,

sticky, all twined and matted together, as high as her
waist. Presently, as she hacked and cut at it with her bone
knife, she heard a harsh croaking and flapping above her.
She looked up, and saw two grey vultures perched on a
branch, leaning forward to peer down at her. Their wings
were twice the length of a man's arm and they had long,
wrinkled, black, leathery necks and little fierce yellow
eyes. As she stood, two more, then five, ten, twenty
others came rousting through the branches, and all
perched round about, craning down their long black
necks, swaying back and forth, keeping balanced by the
way they opened and shut their wings.

Nerryn felt very much afraid of them, but she unslung
the harp from her back and began to play a soft, trickling
tune, like rain falling on a deep pool. Very soon the
vultures sank their necks down between their shoulders,
and closed their eyes. They sat perfectly still.

When she was certain they were asleep, Nerryn made
haste to cut and slash at the grass. She was several
hundred yards on her way before the vultures woke and
came cawing and jostling through the branches to cluster
again just overhead. Quickly she pulled the harp round
and strummed on its fishbone strings until once again,
lulled by the music, the vultures sank their heads between
their grey wings and slept. Then she went back to cutting
the grass, as fast as she could.

It was a long, tiring way. Soon she grew so weary that
she could hardly push one foot ahead of the other, and it
was hard to keep awake; once she only just roused in time
when a vulture, swooping down, missed her with his
beak and instead struck the harp on her back with a loud
strange twang that set echoes scampering through the
trees.

At last the forest began to thin and dwindle; here
the tree-trunks and branches were all draped about
with grey-green moss, like long dangling hanks of

sheepswool. Moss grew on the rocky ground, too, in a thick carpet. When she reached this part, Nerryn could go on safely; the vultures rose in an angry flock and flew back with harsh croaks of disappointment, for they feared the trailing moss would wind round their wings and trap them.

As soon as she reached the edge of the trees Nerryn lay down in a deep tussock of moss and fell fast asleep.

She was so tired that she slept almost till nightfall, but then the cold woke her. It was bitter on the bare mountain-side; the ground was all crisp with white frost, and when Nerryn started walking uphill she crunched through it, leaving deep black footprints. Unless she kept moving she knew that she would probably die of cold, so she climbed on, higher and higher; the stars came out showing more frost-covered slopes ahead and all around, while the forest far below curled round the flank of the mountain like black fur.

Through the night she went on climbing and by sunrise she had reached the foot of a steep slope of ice-covered boulders. When she tried to climb over these she only slipped back again.

What shall I do now? Nerryn wondered. She stood blowing on her frozen fingers and thought "I must go on or I shall die here of cold. I will play a tune on the harp to warm my fingers and my wits."

She unslung the harp. It was hard to play, for her fingers were almost numb and at first refused to obey but, while she had climbed the hill, a very sweet, lively tune had come into her head, and she struggled and struggled until her stubborn fingers found the right notes to play it. Once she played the tune – twice – and the stones on the slope above began to roll and shift. She played a third time and, with a thunderous roar, the whole pile broke loose and went sliding down the mountain-side. Nerryn was only just able to dart aside out of the way before the

frozen mass careered past, sending up a smoking dust of ice.

Trembling a little, she went on up the hill, and now she came to a gate in a great wall, set about with towers. The gate stood open, and so she walked through.

"Surely this must be my father's city," she thought.

But when she stood inside the gate, her heart sank, and she remembered old Saroon's words. For the city that must once have been bright with gold and coloured stone and gay with music was all silent; not a soul walked the streets and the houses, under their thick covering of frost, were burnt and blackened by fire.

And, what was still more frightening, when Nerryn looked through the doorways into the houses, she could see people standing or sitting or lying, frozen still like statues, as the cold had caught them while they worked, or slept, or sat at dinner.

"Where shall I go now?" she thought. "It would have been better to stay with Saroon in the forest. When night comes I shall only freeze to death in this place."

But still she went on, almost tiptoeing in the frosty silence of the city, looking into doorways and through gates, until she came to a building that was larger than any other, built with a high roof and many pillars of white marble. The fire had not touched it.

"This must be the temple," she thought, remembering the tale Saroon had told, and she walked between the pillars, which glittered like white candles in the light from the rising sun. Inside there was a vast hall, and many people standing frozen, just as they had been when they came to pray for deliverance from their trouble. They had offerings with them, honey and cakes and white doves and lambs and precious ointment. At the back of the hall the people wore rough clothes of homespun cloth, but farther forward Nerryn saw wonderful robes, embroidered with gold and copper thread, made of rich materials,

trimmed with fur and sparkling stones. And up in the very front, kneeling on the steps of the altar, was a man who was finer than all the rest and Nerryn thought he must have been the king himself. His hair and long beard were white, his cloak was purple, and on his head were three crowns, one gold, one copper, and one of ivory. Nerryn stole up to him and touched the fingers that held a gold staff, but they were ice-cold and still as marble, like all the rest.

A sadness came over her as she looked at the people and she thought, "What use to them are their fine robes now? Why did the goddess punish them? What did they do wrong?"

But there was no answer to her question.

"I had better leave this place before I am frozen as well," she thought. "The goddess may be angry with me too, for coming here. But first I will play for her on my harp, as I have not brought any offering."

So she took her harp and began to play. She played all the tunes she could remember, and last of all she played the one that had come into her head as she climbed the mountain.

At the noise of her playing, frost began to fall in white showers from the roof of the temple, and from the rafters and pillars and the clothes of the motionless people. Then the king sneezed. Then there was a stirring noise, like the sound of a winter stream when the ice begins to melt. Then someone laughed – a loud, clear laugh. And, just as, outside the town, the pile of frozen rocks had started to move and topple when Nerryn played, so now the whole gathering of people began to stretch themselves, and turn round, and look at one another, and smile. And as she went on playing they began to dance.

The dancing spread, out of the temple and down the streets. People in the houses stood up and danced. Still dancing, they fetched the brooms and swept away the

heaps of frost that kept falling from the rooftops with the sound of the music. They fetched old wooden pipes and tabors out of cellars that had escaped the fire, so that when Nerryn stopped playing at last, quite tired out, the music still went on. All day and all night, for thirty days, the music lasted, until the houses were rebuilt, the streets clean, and not a speck of frost remained in the city.

But the king beckoned Nerryn aside when she stopped playing and they sat down on the steps of the temple.

"My child," he said, "where did you get that harp?"

"Sir, I made it out of fishbones after a picture of my father's harp that an old woman made for me."

"And what was your father's name, child, and where is he now?"

"Sir, he is dead in the forest, but here is a piece of a tablet with his name on it."

And Nerryn held out the little fragment with Heramon the harper's name written. When he saw it, great tears formed in the king's eyes and began to roll down his cheeks.

"Sir," Nerryn said, "what is the matter? Why do you weep?"

"I weep for my son Heramon, who is lost, and I weep for joy because my grandchild has returned to me."

Then the king embraced Nerryn and took her to his palace and had robes of fur and velvet put on her, and there was great happiness and much feasting. And the king told Nerryn how, many years ago, the goddess was angered because the people had grown so greedy for gold from her mountain that they spent their lives in digging and mining, day and night, and forgot to honour her with music, in her temple and in the streets, as they had been used to do. They made tools of gold, and plates and dishes and musical instruments; everything that could be was

made of gold. So at last the goddess appeared among them, terrible with rage, and put a curse on them, of burning and freezing.

"Since you prefer gold, got by burrowing in the earth, to the music that should honour me," she said, "you may keep your golden toys and little good may they do you! Let your golden harps and trumpets be silent, your flutes and pipes be dumb! I shall not come among you again until I am summoned by notes from a harp that is not made of gold, nor of silver, nor any precious metal, a harp that has never touched the earth but came from deep water, a harp that no man has ever played."

Then fire burst out of the mountain, destroying houses and killing many people. The king ordered his son Heramon, who was the bravest man in the city, to cross the dangerous forest and seek far and wide until he should find the harp of which the goddess spoke. Before Heramon could depart a great cold had struck, freezing people where they stood; only just in time he caught up his little daughter from her cradle and carried her away with him.

"But now you are come back," the old king said, "you shall be queen after me, and we shall take care that the goddess is honoured with music every day, in the temple and in the streets. And we will order everything that is made of gold to be thrown into the mountain torrent, so that nobody ever again shall be tempted to worship gold before the goddess."

So this was done, the king himself being the first to throw away his golden crown and staff. The river carried all the golden things down through the forest until they came to rest in Timorash's mill-pool, and one day, when he was fishing for carp, he pulled out the crown. Overjoyed, he ground it to powder and sold it to his neighbours for barley wine. Then he returned to the pool hoping for more gold, but by now he was so drunk that

he fell in and was drowned among a clutter of golden spades and trumpets and goblets and pickaxes.

But long before this Nerryn, with her harp on her back and astride of a white mule with knives bound to its hoofs, had ridden down the mountain to fetch Saroon as she had promised. She passed the forest safely, playing music for the vultures while the mule cut its way through the long grass. Nobody in the village recognized her, so splendidly was she dressed in fur and scarlet.

But when she came to where Saroon's hut had stood, the ground was bare, nor was there any trace that a dwelling had ever been there. And when she asked for Saroon, nobody knew the name, and the whole village declared that such a person had never been there.

Amazed and sorrowful, Nerryn returned to her grandfather. But one day, not long after, when she was alone, praying in the temple of the goddess, she heard a voice that said,

"Sing, child!"

And Nerryn was greatly astonished, for she felt she had heard the voice before, though she could not think where.

While she looked about her, wondering, the voice said again,

"Sing!"

And then Nerryn understood, and she laughed, and, taking her harp, sang a song about chopping wood, and about digging, and fishing, and the birds of the forest, and how the stream's voice changes in summer and in winter. For now she knew who had helped her to make her harp of fishbones.

The Prince and the Goose Girl

Elinor Mordaunt

Once there was a great Prince who was so great a fighter that no one dared to deny him anything that he asked, and people would give up their houses and lands, their children, and even their own freedom rather than offend him.

Everything the people had was his at the asking, they feared him so, and would all tremble and shake when he came thundering past on his war horse, whose hoofs struck great pieces of their fields from the earth as he passed, and whose breath was fire. And they feared his sword, which was so sharp that it wounded the wind as it cut through it, and his battle-axe that could cut the world in half – or so they said – and his frown that was like a cloud, and his voice that was like thunder – or so they said.

Only Erith, the goose girl, feared him not at all.

"He is only a man," she would say. "What you tell of his sword and his battle-axe and his great frown is all a child's tale. He is just a man. He eats and sleeps like other men; if you wounded him, he would bleed. Some day he will love a woman and be her slave for a while just as any other man is. I wouldn't give that for the great bully!" she added, and snapped her little fingers.

"Hee, hee, Erith, that's all very well," the folk would say. "Wait till you meet him thundering over the

common. You will fly as quick as any of your geese, we wager."

"I wouldn't move. It's a man's place to make room for a lady, not a lady's place to make room for a man. I wouldn't move, I tell you." And Erith stamped her little foot. It did not seem to impress the village people much, perhaps because it was bare and made no noise on the soft, dusty road, and one needs to make plenty of noise in this world if one is to be noticed.

"A lady! A lady!" they shrieked. "A lord to make room for a lady! Listen to her. My Lady Goosey Gander! A fine lady indeed, with bare feet and no hat."

"There's lots that have shoes that are not ladies," said Erith. "Shoes won't make one, nor bare feet mar one. I'm a better lady than any of you, though, for I'd not run away for anyone, even that ugly old Prince. Bah! he's not noble or good or brave; he's just ugly – an ugly great bully!"

"Wait a bit, Lady Goosey Gander, wait a bit. If ever you see him, you will forget all your fine tales. Why, he's as tall as the church."

"And as strong as the sea."

"Why, his hands are like oak trees."

"And he cares no more than death whom he attacks."

"Neither do I care," said Erith, setting back her shoulders and tossing her chin. "All men are babies, anyhow!"

The village gasped. That she should dare! She, a chit of a goose girl, to talk of the terror of the whole countryside like that. "All men are babies!" Well, well!

"It's a good thing that you are only what you are, my girl," growled the blacksmith. "For if you were of any account and the Prince heard what you said, I would not give a farthing for your life."

"Hee, hee, Lady Goosey Gander," hooted the children from that day, as they passed her on the way to school,

tending her geese up on the common; but she only laughed at them, for she was really and truly brave, you know, and really and truly brave people do not trouble much about trifles.

One day one of the Prince's men heard the children and asked Erith what they meant.

"They call me Lady Goosey Gander because I said I was as good a lady as the Prince is a gentleman, and better, for I know enough to be civil and kind," answered Erith, quite unconcerned, busy peeling a willow wand with her little bone-handled knife. She wove these willow wands into baskets while she watched her geese, and sold them in the neighbouring market town, for she was poor and had her old mother to keep. She did not stop her work as she spoke; it was more important to her than all the gentlemen or all the Princes in the world. She wanted a bag of meal, and she wanted shoes before the winter began. That was her business; other people might attend to their own.

The gentleman was amused. He told his fellows at supper that night and there was much laughter over the goose girl's words. A page waiting at table told his fellows. And then the Prince's own man told him as he helped him off with his armour that night.

The Prince laughed a great, big, bellowing laugh, but the red swayed up into his face angrily all the same.

"Where does this chit live?" he demanded.

The manservant shrugged his shoulders. "No one knows where she lives; she is of so little importance she might well live nowhere. But she feeds her geese each day on the common above the cliffs to the east, between here and the sea. A bare-footed, common little thing."

"There's one thing uncommon enough about her. She dares to say what she thinks about me, and that's more than any of you do. I hear that she is very ugly, though."

"Most terribly ugly, Your Highness," answered the man.

"And old," said the Prince.

"Very old, Your Highness. Quite, quite old."

"And deaf, too."

"As deaf as a post, Your Highness. It's evident she has never heard what all your subjects say about you," agreed the man, for he always did agree – he was too frightened to do anything else.

"It is too evident, she *has* heard," said the Prince grimly. "And she is not deaf."

"Oh, no, Your Highness."

"And she is young."

"Indeed the merest child, Your Highness."

"And beautiful."

"As beautiful as the day, Your Highness."

"Only a country girl, of course, quite uneducated."

"Quite uneducated, Your Highness, and —"

What else he was going to say remained unsaid, for he was stooping over the Prince's foot unbuckling his spurs while he spoke, and the Prince lifted his foot – quite easily as it seemed – and with it lifted the man, quite easily, but with such force that he bumped against the ceiling, "plump!" and then came to the floor, "bump!"

There were several other men in the room. However, they did not run to pick him up – they were too frightened of their master. But the Prince just put out the toe of his other foot and touched him, and he rolled over and over like a ball and down the stairs, limpitty, limpitty, limp.

Then another came forward to undo the other spur, and he was treated the same.

"Take them both out and bury them!" shouted the Prince. "And if they're not dead, bury them all the same!" Then he got up and stamped round his chamber. He touched no one, but they all fled like hares.

After that he sat down in his great chair, bellowing for wine, and forbade any to go to bed or to sleep, while he sat there himself all night, railing at his men for cowards and fools, and drinking good red wine.

Next morning, directly it was light, the Prince ordered his horse, Sable, to be brought round, mounted it and rode like the wind to the common by the sea.

"That chit of a goose girl is as good as dead," remarked his manservant as best he could with a broken jaw; indeed, you never saw anything so broken; all his legs and arms seemed nothing but splints and bandages. However, it was a common enough sight in the court of that Prince, and no one took much notice.

The Prince thundered along on his great black horse and presently came to the common. In the middle of it he saw a flock of white geese and a patch of faded blue, which was the smock of the goose girl, who was sitting on a bundle of willow rods, busy with her basket-making.

The Prince did not draw rein. He thundered straight on. He scattered the geese in every direction. He would have galloped right over the girl if his horse had not swerved just as its hoofs were upon her. Then he drew rein.

The girl's hands did not stop from her work, but her great blue eyes were straight upon the Prince's fierce black ones.

"The beast is less of a beast than the master," she said, for she knew it was the horse that had refused to tread upon her.

The Prince pulled his reins, rode back a little, then spurred forward at Erith; but again the horse swerved and, being held with too tight a hand to turn, reared back.

The girl was right under his great pawing black hoofs. But she laughed.

The horse dropped to earth so close that his chest was

against hers, his head held high to escape striking her. The foam dropped from his bit; his eye seemed all fire.

The girl's face looked up like a flower from among the thick blackness of his flowing mane. And she laughed again.

This was more than the Prince could stand. He stooped from his saddle. He put his great hand into the leather belt of Erith's smock and swung her up in front of him. There he held her with one hand in its iron glove, shook Sable's rein and put his spurs to his side.

"I have a mind to ride over the cliff with you," said the Prince.

"Ride over," laughed Erith. And she took the willow rod that was still in her hand and smote the horse's neck with it. "Over the cliff, brave horse, and a good riddance of a bad man it will be," said she.

But the horse swerved at the end of the cliff. And the Prince let him swerve. Then they turned and they raced like wind, far, far.

"Are you afraid?" said the Prince.

"Afraid!" laughed the girl. She leaned forward along the neck of the horse, caught one little hand around his ear and cried, "Stop!"

Sable stopped so suddenly that his black mane and a long black tail flew out like a cloud in front of him.

The Prince swore a great oath and smote him, but he did not move.

Then Erith, not willing to see him hurt, whispered: "Go!" And he went – like the wind.

Far, far and fast he went. The Prince was brooding too savagely to heed where they were being carried, so that when at length they came to a swamp, the horse, with one of his mighty strides, was borne far into it and sank to his girths before his rider knew what was happening.

You may picture it. The man and the maid and the horse nearly up to their necks in black mud.

Erith was small and light as a bird. She sprang from the arms which were loosed to pull the reins; she caught at a tuft of grass here, at a shrub there, and in a moment was on dry ground, though black to the knees with mire.

But the Prince was a tall, great man. He was all in his armour, very heavy, and he could not move except downward; but he flung himself from his horse.

"That's not so bad of him," thought Erith. "He cares to save it, for he himself would have a double chance on its back."

The fierce black eyes of the man and the laughing blue eyes of the goose girl met across the strip of swamp. His were as hard as steel, for he did not mean to beg his life from any such chit.

Erith moved away a little. "She is going to leave me," he thought, and grieved, for he did not wish to die.

The girl had disappeared among a group of trees, but in a moment she came back, dragging after her a large, thick bough. Then she picked her way cautiously, as near as possible to the edge of the swamp. A little sturdy tree was growing there. Erith undid her leather belt, pressed her back firmly against the tree and strapped the belt round both it and herself. Then she stretched forward with the bough in both hands.

"Pull," she cried. And the Prince pulled.

The little tree creaked and strained. The goose girl's face grew crimson. It seemed as if her arms must be pulled from her body; but she held on, and at last the Prince crawled out.

Erith had only been muddied a little above her smock, but the Prince was mud up to his armpits, and his face, too, was smeared where he had pushed his helmet back from his forehead with muddy hands. He said no word of thanks to the girl, for he felt that he looked a poor thing, and it made him angry.

"I would I had left you there," said the goose girl. "A thankless boor! You were not worth saving."

The Prince said no word, but began to pull out his horse. Even then the maid had to help him, for it was very heavy and deeply sunk.

Once the horse was free, the maid moved over to a pool which lay at the edge of the swamp and began to bathe her feet and legs and wash the mud from the hem of her smock.

The Prince got on his horse, with a great deal of clatter and grumbling, but she did not turn. They were many, many miles from home, the country was strange and wild, but there she sat, quite untroubled, paddling her feet in the water.

The Prince put his spurs to his horse and galloped away. But the beast would not go freely, spur it as he would. And soon he gave in, let it turn and go back to the goose girl.

She had dried her feet on the grass by now and was standing plaiting her long hair, eyeing herself in the pool and singing softly.

The Prince drew rein close to her and stuck out one foot. "You may come up," he said.

"An' may it please you," corrected the goose girl very quickly, with her blue eyes full upon him.

"May it please you," repeated the Prince with a wry smile at himself; and the maid put her foot on his and jumped lightly to the saddle before him.

Sable needed no spur then, but sprang into a light gallop.

"All this is mine," said the Prince boastfully, waving his arm as they went.

"I would it belonged to a better man," answered the goose girl. "And sit quietly or I will have no comfort riding with you."

"And you belong to me also," said the Prince savagely.

"Not I. I belong to myself, and that is more than you do."

"What do you mean by that?"

"No man belongs to himself who is the slave to evil temper and pride," answered Erith gravely and gently.

After a long ride they came to the common again. On the edge of it was a tiny cottage.

"Stop here," said the goose girl, "and I will get down."

But the Prince clapped his spurs to his horse's side and they were off like the wind. Moreover, he held the goose girl's hands so tightly that she could not touch Sable's ear or lean forward and speak to him. And so they galloped on till they clattered over the drawbridge into the court-yards of the castle.

A curious couple they looked. The Prince all caked with mud, the goose girl with her wet smock clinging round her bare ankles and her long yellow hair loose, hanging below her knees.

The Prince did not get off his horse, but sat like a statue, while all the lords and ladies, the captains and the men-at-arms, the pages and the servingmen – even down to the scullery boy – thronged on the terrace and steps and at every window to look.

There was a long silence. Then one lady, who thought she was pretty enough to do as she liked, tittered loudly.

"The Lady Goosey Gander," she said. "The Lady Goosey Gander."

The Prince's brow grew like a thundercloud. He flung his reins to one of the waiting grooms and alighted, then gave his hand to Erith, who leaped down as lightly as a bird. Still holding her hand, he turned to his people.

"You are always wishing me to choose a wife," he thundered. "Well, I have chosen one, and here she is. You can call the parson to bring his book and get the wedding feast ready, for I will be married in an hour's time."

With that he pulled off his helmet and flung round to kiss the goose girl, but —

"Shame on you," she cried, "to think to marry a maid before you've asked her! You can marry the cat, for all I care." And with that she caught him a great blow across the face and flung free.

Such a slap, such an echoing, sounding slap. The people of the court did not wait to see what would happen, for they knew what the Prince was like in one of his rages all too well, and fled into the palace like rabbits to their burrows – not even a face at the window was left. Only the goose girl did not turn, but stood and laughed at the Prince's reddened face.

He caught at her wrist, yet not roughly. "You *will* marry me!"

"Perhaps some day when you learn to speak civilly," she replied. And feeling her wrist free, she marched off over the drawbridge and over the meadow across the common and so home. She had her own business to attend to.

Some of the Prince's people came creeping back. "Shall we go after her, Your Highness?" they asked, thinking to get into his favour again; but he drove them from him with the flat of his great sword and with oaths and shouting, then flung off to his own chamber and sat there drinking red wine till the night was near over; and none of his court as much as dared to go to bed till he slept.

Next morning he was off again at dawn on his black horse across the common. There sat Erith among her geese, weaving baskets. The very horse neighed with joy at the sight of her sitting there content in the sunshine, but the Prince only scowled.

"Will you marry me?" said he.

"No," said she, "and that's flat – not till you learn manners, at least."

Then he got off his horse and took out his sword and killed all her geese.

"You will have to marry me now or starve, for you have lost all your means of getting a living."

But the girl only laughed and took the dead geese and began plucking them, moving over to the side that the wind blew towards the Prince, so that the feathers flew and stuck all over his armour in every chain and crevice and crack; and threw such handfuls of down in his face that when he went to seize her he was powerless.

Next day Erith, having trussed the plucked geese, took them to the market and sold them for a gold piece.

As she came home singing, she met an army of men bearing osier rods. "What have the osiers done that they should all be cut in one day?" she asked.

"The Prince sent us to cut them, Lady Goosey Gander," they answered, jeering. "There is not one left at the brook's edge now, and your basket-making is spoiled."

But the goose girl only laughed and turned back to the town and bought wool with her gold piece.

Next day as she sat before the fire in her cottage spinning the wool into yarn to sell at the market, the Prince came striding in at the little door, bent half double, for it was so low and he so tall with his helmet on his head.

"It is only old women who remain with covered heads in the house," said the goose girl. "Good morning, old dame."

The Prince took off his helmet. Somehow her ways pleased him, for he was sick of soft speaking.

"Will you marry me?" said he.

"When you kneel to ask me," said she. "Not before."

Then in a rage he took all her yarn, flung it into the fire and was out of the house and away, thundering on his great black horse. But the goose girl only laughed.

Then she took a pair of scissors and cut off her long

hair, yellow as honey in the comb, and fine as silk. This she spun and wove into a scarf, the rarest scarf ever seen.

On the third day, having finished her work, she was up at dawn and walked off to the court of a King, many miles distant. There she sought the Queen and sold her the scarf for twenty pieces of gold.

"But why did you cut off your beautiful hair?" asked the Queen.

"It was just forever in the way," replied the goose girl. She told no tales. To begin with, she did not like them, and to end with she did like the Prince – perhaps because he was as fearless and obstinate as she herself.

Passing through the town, she bought a bag of meal and porridge. "The bag will do to cover my bare poll when it rains," she said to the merchant, and laughed. The gold jangled in the pocket of her petticoat and she felt as gay as a cricket.

On her way back she met the Prince, who pulled up his horse and scowled at her, that she might not see the love in his eyes. Her head was all over little golden curls that shone in the sunlight.

"What have you done with your hair?" he asked.

"What have you done with the osiers and the feathers?" she asked in return, and laughed.

"Are you starving yet?"

"Far from it. I am richer than I ever was," and she shook her pocket till all the gold danced, for she feared nothing. But it was a foolish thing to do, for in a moment he had whipped out his sword and cut the pocket clean from the petticoat.

"Now will you marry me?" he asked, and held the pocket high and rattled the gold.

"Not I," she said, "if you are so poor that you'd have to live on your wife's earnings." And went her way singing.

The Prince was ashamed of himself. He had never felt like it before, and it was very uncomfortable; it made him

feel all tired and hot. It was all the goose girl's fault, of course, and he was very angry. But still he wished he had not stolen her money, and the thought of her little shorn head with its dancing curls made him feel for the first time in his life that he had a heart, and that it hurt.

So wrapped in his shame was the Prince and sitting on his horse so loosely, and so heedless of everything that some robbers coming along the road took courage at the sight of him, for he did not look at all terrible as he usually did, and the gold rattled pleasantly. They had passed him many times before and kept their distance; but now they were emboldened to fall upon him, and so sudden was the attack that he was cast from his horse, the gold was gone, and he bound and gagged before he had thought to resist. Such a poor thing can shame make of any one of us.

Before they had finished, Sable had galloped away. "Shall we ride after him?" asked one of the robbers.

"No, no," answered the others. "He is too well known and we should sure be caught." So they mounted their horses and went off, leaving the Prince bound and more ashamed of himself than ever. But Sable had galloped straight to the goose girl's cottage and struck at the door with his hoof.

When Erith opened the door, she was amazed to see the horse without his master. He muzzled his soft nose over her neck and hand, then trotted a little distance, then neighed as if to call her and returned. This he did several times.

"There must be something wrong," thought the girl; and she put her foot in the stirrup and leaped to the saddle. "Go like the wind," she whispered, leaning along his neck with one little hand around his ear. And like the wind he went.

Now, the robbers had not much rope to spare, so they had bound the Prince kneeling with his arms pulled back and tied to his ankles behind him. And mighty uncom-

fortable it was. Besides, they had stuck one of their own
foul handkerchiefs in his mouth and tied another across
and around it. "Anyone who finds me will make a fine
mock of me," thought the Prince. And he seemed to burn
with rage and shame.

But when the goose girl drew up beside him, *she* did
not laugh, rather gave a little moan of pity, for the
robbers had struck him wantonly over the head and the
blood which he could not reach to staunch ran down over
his face and eyes.

In a moment she was on the ground, had whipped out
the little knife which she still carried in her belt, and cut
the bandage and drew the gag from his mouth. She was
turning to the ropes around the wrists and ankles then,
when – "Stop!" said the Prince. Then, "Will you marry
me, Erith?"

"It's a queer time to be asking that," replied the goose
girl.

"You charged me to ask on my knees," answered the
Prince dryly, "and I am here. Will you marry me now?"

"An' it please you," corrected she, with calm blue eyes.

"An' it please you, dear heart," said he, almost meekly.
"And we will not be living on your money, for it is all
gone."

"Well, I don't mind if I do," answered the goose girl,
and cut the ropes.

So they were trothed and kissed one another. And the
Prince put her on the front of his own horse and rode with
her to the court, where he told the Queen all that had
happened and charged her, by her friendship, to get all
manner of beautiful raiment and jewels ready and command a great feast that he might marry the goose girl one
week from that day, she consenting.

It was the sunniest day ever known in all the world, and
the gayest wedding and the fairest bride. And the feasting
and dancing lasted for seven days, and there was none in

the whole country who went hungry or without a share of the pleasures.

On the seventh day the Prince took his bride back to his own kingdom. They would have no coach, but rode Sable over the hills and pastures and across the common where the geese had once fed, and over the drawbridge and home.

The new Princess had little golden slippers on her feet now, and a robe of rose silk all embroidered with pearls, and a cloak of ermine. But her head was bare, with no crown save that of short golden curls.

A Wind from Nowhere

Nicholas Stuart Gray

Tamsin was picking mushrooms, in a field beside a
stream. She had already collected about thirty real
beauties: as white as snow, silken-skinned, with under-
sides the colour of wild rose petals. And now she was
standing quite still, staring down at the grass between her
feet, hesitating. She was perfectly right to hesitate. The
thing growing there was no true mushroom. It had wavy
edges, tinged with green; its surface was all dappled with
silvery rings, and right in the centre was a tiny orange
spike. It was very large, nearly a foot across. And yet, for
all this, Tamsin stooped and picked it.

She turned it over, and gave a startled cry. Instead of
pink gills, it had a spongy underneath, bright yellow, and
throbbing as though it breathed.

Tamsin dropped it.

"You clumsy and horrible child!" said the fungus, in a
fretfully squeaky voice.

At the far end of the field, Tamsin stopped. In the speed
of her flight, she had dropped her basket, spilling all those
pretty mushrooms in the wet grass. She put both hands
over her mouth, and tried to think clearly. Her mother
was going to cook the mushrooms for breakfast. This
was the only field where they were growing this year in
easy reach of home.

"I can't lose the basket, anyway," said Tamsin, firmly. "And that – that thing can't bite me. Can it? – I've just frightened myself for nothing. A big toadstool!"

She made herself go back.

While collecting the spilled mushrooms, she tried not to look towards the – toadstool? But her eyes seemed drawn to it of their own accord. It was securely rooted in the ground again. As she looked, it gave a slight wriggle, as though to settle itself comfortably.

"Just keep your hands off me, miss," it said, nastily.

Backing away quickly, the girl said she had no intention of touching it. It said it did not believe her. Everyone, it stated, wished to touch it.

"Why?" said Tamsin, bluntly.

"Because of my beauty. Because I'm magic."

"You're what?"

"Beautiful. Magic. And stop playing the innocent!" snapped the tiny voice. "Why did you snatch me from the ground, eh? Why did you stretch your big hand to drag me from my sleep?"

Tamsin was annoyed. She had pretty hands, sun-tanned and slender. She was a very pretty girl, come to that. Fifteen years old, with ash-pale hair tied at the neck with a red ribbon. Her blue eyes were usually merry and kind, but now they sparkled with rage.

"I picked you because you looked so awful!" said she. "I just wanted a closer look."

"Ha! A very likely story!" shrieked the fungus. "You wanted some magic to brush off on your grabbing fingers."

"No, I did not!"

The thing said if she could stop chattering, and lying, perhaps she would go away and leave it in peace.

"Now that I'll be glad to do," said Tamsin.

She took up her basket, now filled again with proper

mushrooms, and turned on her heel, and went off across the field.

Behind her, she could hear spiteful squeaking. It was squeaking in verse.

"Handle magic, even briefly, you will never be the same: From the darkness, from the shadow, somebody will call your name!"

Then there came a series of shrill peals of laughter. Then silence. Tamsin fled.

She crossed the stream by the little plank bridge, and, glancing down into the water, saw the full moon reflected there. She halted abruptly, and looked again. Full moon? Yes, there it was – its reflection – and, looking upwards, she saw it in the night sky overhead. The girl gave a wail of terror. It had been early morning when she left the farmhouse to get mushrooms. Where had the time gone?

Tamsin sat down on a stile, and wailed again. She remembered a moment, just as she had noticed the strange toadstool, when the sunshine had flickered a little, and a cold wind had gusted suddenly. Was that when time had shifted?

Tamsin wondered why no one had come looking for her. Her mother – her sister – no one had searched. Yet she had been away all day, and all the evening. They knew where she'd been going. Had nobody missed her? Had – and her heart gave a terrible jump – had something taken her place at home? Tamsin had heard some very odd tales from old people who liked to make everyone's blood run cold. Tamsin shivered in the bitter wind that was whiffling round her. But, being a sensible person, she decided to get home as quickly as possible, and face whatever was there. She got up and started to run, straight across a field of barley-stubble, and into a little wood.

She noticed, with growing fear, that the stubble's dark gold was aglow in the moonlight, and that the wood

seemed not quite as little as usual. Tamsin put on speed. Then she tripped over a tree-root, and crashed to the ground. When she sat up, rather dizzily, she heard her name being called.

"Tamsin – Tamsin—!"

"Oh, I'm here," cried the girl. "Father – ? Arminal—?"

But the voice that went on calling was not the voice of her father, or her sister.

"What shall I do?" whispered Tamsin.

"Hide!" she told herself.

But where to go?

The whole wood was bathed in green and luminous light, with moonshine dappling the leaves and branches, showing trees – far too many trees, and far too twisted – and creepers covered with huge, white prickles; showing eyes watching from holes in the ground and holes in the tree-trunks; showing a strange object lurching towards Tamsin between two purple bushes. From this object came a voice: a high, whickering voice:

"Tamsin – Tamsin—!"

There was nowhere to hide, and nowhere to run to. The girl stood trembling, facing whatever terrible creature approached.

Half hopping, half dragging itself along the ground, it came towards her; and it shuffled down a mossy bank, and stood swaying in the strange light. It was a besom broom.

"I don't believe it!" said Tamsin, faintly.

"Well, you'd better try," said the broom. "Them as believes nothing, is seldom disappointed. But they do miss a lot of action!"

"I don't want any more action," said the poor girl. "I just want to go home."

"Not a chance!" whickered the broom. "You touched magic, you did. And now you're in it, up to your pretty little ears. My name's Geronomy. I know yours."

"How?" said Tamsin.

"No call to be silly, dear! If you mess about with magic, you should know what to expect. Them that goes it blind, is not only giddy-minded, but in real bad danger!"

"It's not my doing!" said the girl, with a sob. "I only came out to get some mushrooms for breakfast – and – and everything's gone peculiar!"

"Now, now," soothed the broom, "don't cry, Tamsin. Pull yourself together – and do it quickly. Very quickly! She's coming. I can hear the walking!"

So could Tamsin. It was quite far off, but coming nearer every moment. The sound was like someone thumping slowly on a great drum – like rumbles of distant thunder – like the tramping footfalls of a giant ...

"What is it?" cried the girl.

"It's her, of course. Little Madam Mitch!" yelped the besom broom, in panic. "It's me lady! Me terrible mistress! The black witch with two left feet!"

"The two *what*?"

"Feet. Come away, Tamsin. Hurry!"

"Where to? There's no possible hiding-place ..."

The thunderous footsteps were growing louder, coming closer; all the crisp leaves of the autumn trees were rustling; the wind seemed to be blowing from several different directions, all at the same time. The broom came sidling closer to Tamsin, and she snatched her hand away from the touch of its wooden handle.

"Don't be daft, girlie!" snapped Geronomy.

"Go away, please!"

"Look, dear, you've got to ride me."

"No, no! I can't!"

"If you keep acting silly, you'll be overtook by Madam," the besom told her, in a stern voice. "You won't like that. She'll make you her slave – same as she done to me. You wouldn't believe the things you'd

have to do! Horrible things – frightening things. So, quickly now! Don't waste time. Sit on me back, and ride!"

In a haze of bewilderment and terror, the girl seated herself unsurely on the sheaf of long twigs that were bound round the broom-handle. She found a trailing bit of string attached to the head of the shaft, and clutched it with one hand; in the other, she still held tightly to the basket of mushrooms.

"Say the words, then!" whickered the broom, quivering all over.

"What words?"

"Oh, slush! You ignorant thing! Don't you know the simplest spell?"

"No, I do not."

"It goes like this," and the broom lowered its voice to a sinister note, and said:

"Jimp, jump, Geronomy! Up and away! Away!"

Tamsin shakily repeated the words:

"Jimp, jump, Geronomy! Up and away! Away!"

The broom hopped up and down, squealing like an over-excited young colt.

"Up we go! Up we go!"

And up it went. Up into the air, crashing through the leaves and topmost twigs, as fast and easily as any bird. Tamsin gave one high shriek, and shut her eyes.

The wind kept blowing and blowing, first from one side and then from another, in swift and sudden gusts. It threw the broomstick about most alarmingly. And Tamsin lost all sense of direction. She could not tell which way they were going, or from whence they had come. She only knew they were too high up and going much too fast. The sound like footsteps – like thunder – had been left far behind, till it was no more than a nasty muttering in the distance.

"Nearly done it!" gasped Geronomy. "Another burst

of speed – a dive – a swerve to the left – a spin and a twist – and we've escaped!"

It then landed on the ground with a thump. Tamsin tumbled off.

"There!" said the besom, bouncing up and down on its long twigs. "You're home and dry."

Opening her eyes, Tamsin found herself sitting on the grass in her own garden.

"Oh, are we safe?" she gasped. "That – that witch can't find us here?"

The broom said that only time would tell. Then it went on to ask about some cool, dark place, where no one except Tamsin would be likely to find it.

"I don't want your Mum or your sister seeing me," said Geronomy. "For if there's anything I hate more than wood-worms, it's sweeping and cleaning. Housework isn't for the likes of me."

"You mean, you want to stay here? At the farm?"

"Where else? Get thinking clearly, girlie. You come on me in the middle of a wood at spell-time. You took me and you rode me. Finders is keepers, they always say; and so say I."

The last thing on earth Tamsin wanted was a magic broomstick. She tried to explain this, as politely as possible, but it interrupted her with a whinny of anger.

"But I saved you!" it cried. "You can't guess what awfulness I got you out of! Old Madam Mitch would have laid a black cantrap on you, and made you her puppet. Fetching and carrying for demons and worse! Maybe with a pig's face, and ass's ears, and two left feet! Tamsin," said the broomstick, "you're an ungrateful shrew! If you turn me away, I have to go back to Madam. She'll be wild, knowing I tried to escape, and she'll set fire to me tail, and bash me with the fire-irons. Oh, please," it begged, pitifully, "keep me with you, Miss Tamsin, dear. I'll be no sort of trouble to you. Just a drop of water, when

you've the time; maybe a rub over me handle with horse liniment when the weather turns cold and damp. I'll be that grateful. And you'll hardly know I'm hid in that shed over there. At the far end, behind the old cart, with a sack over me to keep out the draughts."

Tamsin was a kind girl. She took the broom to the barn, set it upright in a darkish corner, and draped a patched sack over it. She put a bucket of water at its side, and left it there alone, with only the spiders and mice that lived in the barn – and they were all moving as far away from the broom as they could manage, considering themselves far too domesticated to get mixed up in magic.

As she returned to the garden, Tamsin wondered what her mother would say about her absence all day, and her arrival after midnight – and then she stood still, and rubbed her eyes in disbelief.

Quite low in the eastern sky, the sun was shining. The morning was still very young.

Gasping, Tamsin went into the big farm-kitchen. But she had little appetite for the delicious breakfast that followed.

"You found some beautiful mushrooms," said Arminal, buttering toast.

Tamsin nodded. She hoped her sister would never know what else she had found.

As the days passed, Tamsin also found it was not as simple a matter as it had sounded – giving shelter to Geronomy. It proved rather a handful, and demanded a lot of attention. The poor girl became quite worn out. On top of her home duties, and her work about the little farmstead, she had to water Geronomy twice a day – for the broom drank a good deal, and wanted the bucket freshly scoured each time it was re-filled – and she had to fetch bowlfuls of newly-ground oats, and wisps of hay, and some lumps of sugar, and place them in the barn by

the besom. She never saw it actually eat or drink, but the bowl and bucket were always empty when she went to them.

She stopped thinking of the broomstick as "it". In her mind, he became "he". He was such a little bully that he reminded her of her elder brother, when they had both been children. And this made Tamsin laugh to herself, and become rather fond of Geronomy.

But, one evening, she stopped laughing.

She had gone to the barn, with the usual supplies, only to find Geronomy in a restless and demanding mood. He said he was lonely. He asked how *she* would like being left by herself in a damp, dark cart-shed? Tamsin pointed out that the place was his own choice; and he said he had spoken in the heat of the moment. Then he said he was afraid of the darkness.

"Madam Mitch never treated me so," he muttered, sulkily. "Let me stand by the fire, she did, and sleep in a corner of her best bedroom. Give me cakes, she did, and little sips of ale, and curly green lettuce-leaves..."

"You've never asked for such things," said Tamsin, taken aback.

"I knows me place," the broomstick told her in a prim voice. "It's for you to suggest some treats, isn't it? Never thought you'd turn out *mean*!"

The girl was hurt.

"I'm not! I'll go now and get you a bit of cake—"

"Now wait a minute, can't you?" whickered Geronomy. "Those are only the tiddley things I fancy. My greatest need is exercise. How would you like standing here all the time – alone in the dark – no fresh air – no one to talk to—"

He stopped. Perhaps he thought he had gone too far. His next words were spoken in a sad and gentle voice.

"How I long for the cool fresh air," mourned Geronomy. "I dream of moonlight, and night-birds

singing under the stars. The scent of honeysuckle and primroses—"

"Whatever time of year...?" began Tamsin.

But her heart was touched. It was dull for anybody, she thought, to be stuck under a sack in a barn all the time.

"I'll come out here," she promised, "when everyone is in bed. And I'll take you for a walk."

Then she feared her whole family would come running to see what the uproar was about. Geronomy whinnied and shrieked, bouncing about and nuzzling at Tamsin's hands, and gabbling how kind she was – how noble – how generous and sweet – and how beautiful—

"Ssh!" said Tamsin. "Thank you very much. But, for goodness' sake, be quiet! Someone will hear you. I thought you had to stay hidden, for fear of housework and Madam Mitch—"

Geronomy subsided with a shrill wail. He told her not to say that name.

"She can hear things! See things from afar. *Find* things!"

"You're trying to scare me," said Tamsin, faintly.

The broom said he had scared himself, too.

When Tamsin went to get him, later on, he lolloped out into the night air with great eagerness. The girl's family went early to bed, and she came unobserved from the house, with a shawl hugged closely round her shoulders, feeling nervous and chilled. She shivered now, alone in the blue moonlight with a witch's broomstick. She hurried him into a far paddock, pulling him along by the bit of string attached to his head, while he jumped about and kicked with his twigs. He was wild with excitement, and kept shrieking that he wanted to fly! To fly!

"Who's stopping you?" snapped Tamsin, at last.

The broom halted in front of her. He had been hopping in circles round the meadow. But now he stood quivering, slightly aslant, as though he had put his head on one

side. Almost, Tamsin could imagine bright eyes staring into her face. But the besom was only a straight staff, with an armful of long twigs bound to its base, and the trailing cord at the top.

"I can't fly on me own," said Geronomy. "I has to be ridden. Anyone knows that! I must be ridden – and the words spoken – and then...! Oh, the rush of the magic wind; the whirl upward through the tree-tops, and the whisper of clouds round me. Come on, love," said the broomstick, urgently, "you know you'll enjoy it."

Tamsin stared at him, aghast. Then she said she was going home.

"That's only putting off the moment," said he. "When you brush against black magic – dabble your fingers in sorcery – and ride a broomstick, you can't just shrug it off and stroll away. The powers of darkness will call you, and call you, until you ache to use them once again. Just once! That's what you'll tell yourself. And you'll be lying to yourself. For the more you use witchcraft, the more you need to use it. Until at last, my dear, you'll be a full-fledged sorceress. With evil in your mind, ice in your heart, and a wind from nowhere blowing you to nowhere."

"If," said Tamsin, "you wish to stay in our barn, you're welcome. But I will never ride you, never! Once was quite enough, and that was only in dire emergency."

"Well, here comes another," said Geronomy. "Listen!"

The wind was rising. At first, this was the only sound that Tamsin could hear. A cold, soughing wind, gusty and changeable. A wind that blew from the east – from the north – from the south – from the west – a wind from nowhere. Tamsin gave a small cry. Then she heard distant thunder. Or distant footsteps.

"She heard her name. She knows we're here!" yelped

the broomstick. "Mount and ride, girl! It's our only chance of escape."

"I won't!" said Tamsin, but, even to herself, her voice was only a quavering whisper.

The booming footsteps were coming nearer. Geronomy was plunging and trembling, making terrified small whimpers. And, suddenly, without time for thinking further, the girl was sitting sideways on his twigs, clutching the bit of string in her two fists.

"The words!" whickered Geronomy. "Bet you've forgot the words!"

"How could I ever forget them?"

Tamsin spoke the spell:

"Jimp, jump, Geronomy! Up and away! Away!"

Her hair blew backward with the speed of their rising flight.

As they whirled through the upper leaves of an apple tree, Geronomy said they had only done it by the skin of Tamsin's teeth. And she asked where they were going now to find safety.

"As far as possible," she was told. "It's not so easy to get away from witchcraft."

The broom flew faster and faster; and the wind blew round them, first from one quarter, then from another. Tamsin looked down, and saw starlight reflected from the darkened windows of her home, and of the nearby village. She looked up at the rising yellow moon. She felt dizzy with the buffeting of that strange wind. And then she had an idea.

"Geronomy," she whispered, eagerly, "look – over there – beside the river. Let's go to the rowan coppice."

She almost fell off, as he shied and reared with a great flurry of whickering. "Don't!" cried Tamsin. "Whatever's the matter with you? We'd be safe in the coppice. Rowan berries are a shield against witchcraft."

"What about me?" screamed Geronomy. "The very

name of that tree gives me the all-over creeps! I'd be done a mischief if I got near 'em. For I'm a witchy sort of thing."

"I only thought —"

"Think of *me!*"

But Tamsin was now unable to think of anything, except the noise of thunderous footsteps that was over-taking them, for all the speed of their flight. Then she had to cling tightly to the broomstick as he was hurled side-ways – upwards – downwards – over and over – by great gusts of wind that swept round them cruelly.

Through its whistling, spoke a thin, small voice:

"Dip, dive, Geronomy! Falter and fall! And fall!"

"She's got us!" said the broomstick, despairingly.

And down he went; blown, helpless as a falling leaf, towards the ground. But not to the village; not to the farmhouse. Tumbling in the grip of the wind, to a bare hill where a circle of stones was set.

As they plunged towards it, thunder seemed to be all about them. Or footsteps from every direction, moving to the hilltop. And Geronomy crashed to earth at the foot of a huge, oblong stone, standing upright and ten feet tall. It was one of a ring of such ancient monoliths, some still crowned by dolmen stones laid across their heads. It was a very terrible place in that moonlight, with that wind blowing, and that sound of footsteps. Tamsin gave a faint moan of panic.

"Keep quiet!" whispered Geronomy. "We're hid behind the cromlech and outside the circle. Hush! Maybe – maybe . . ."

He became very silent, huddling with the girl closer into the shadow of the stone.

Up the hill came the sorcerers. Some were tall and thin, and some as fat as pigs. A few strode swiftly; but most of them waddled along with the aid of long, black staffs. And overhead were broomsticks, dark against the stars,

gliding down to allow their riders to dismount in the circle of stones. There were voices, now. Snatches of spells. Horrid fragments of conversation:

> "— and I said to her 'All right, be a spider!'—"
> *"Onery, twoery, tickery, fen!*
> *Hollow bone, crack a bone, ninery, ten!"*
> "— never did fancy earwig-tea, meself."
> *"Dame, what ails your ducks to die?*
> *Eating o' pollywogs – eating an eye!"*
> "— the most divine new familiar, darling —"
> *"Iddle, diddle, duddle, dell;*
> *A yard of pudding's not an ell."*

A few paces ahead of the rest, stumped a tiny figure. Her long, grey hair blew wildly about her thin face. Her clothes were all grey too, streaming with green ribbons and trails of ivy. Her mouth was wide open, and her eyes glinted redly, as she came shouting up the slope. The words she shouted made Tamsin shiver more than she shivered already.

"You've forced me to come on foot! I'll set your twigs afire! I'll chip you to peelings! And I'll have a new slave tonight. A new little witch for training! No longer Tamsin – but Trilly-Tassel!"

Now the dreadful company had filled the stone circle. All about them, twittering at their heels, or perched on their shoulders, or flapping beside their ears, were the familiars. Thin, six-legged dogs – or things that looked like dogs. Black hares with green eyes – or things that looked like hares. Things that resembled snakes, toads, or bats. And things like nothing on earth. Many tiny, ugly, winged monsters. And, of course, cats. But these were aloof, took the first opportunity to leap on to fallen stones, and sit there smiling, seeming amused by the antics of their so-called owners. They were probably real cats. But all were demons.

Madam Mitch was calling now, in a soft and slimy voice:

"Geronomy, my lovely one, where are you? I know you're somewhere near. Come to mother, and I'll give you a sugar-lump – and a thrashing you'll remember! No, no – I mean I'll kiss your head, my sweet pet! Where are you, dear?"

Tamsin felt the broom shaking terribly. He whispered that he would have to go.

"You shan't!" said Tamsin, under her breath. "She'll hurt you. Stay with me."

"You can't save me."

"I can try. Keep still, Geronomy."

The collection of sorcerers had started dancing. Slowly, in a circle, weaving a grand-chain, hand to hand. They were singing a very horrible song.

> *"Maiden, come without delay!*
> *Who shall we send to fetch her away?*
> *Diggelly, cockelly, tickery tea –*
> *Poor little Tamsin, out goes she!"*

The girl felt a strange tugging and pulling in her mind. She stirred and began to get up.

"Try not to hear. Try not to obey," begged the broom-stick.

"I can't help myself," gasped Tamsin. "I must go, I am called ..."

She pushed the broom gently aside, in spite of his frantic moans, and she walked out of the shadow into the circle of witches. It parted, to let her through. In the middle of the ring, she stood still. Her eyes were shut, and there were tears on her face, though she made no sound of crying. A great shout of triumph rose from all the sorcerers. And they stamped their feet on the ground, with a noise like thunder.

"Got her!" shrieked Madam Mitch.

Tamsin heard a curious swishing sound in the air. Then she forgot it, as a young witch came towards her, smiling, with a crown of bryony leaves, jewelled with its own bright berries. She placed it on Tamsin's head. And Tamsin felt her heart go cold, as though the blood that coursed through it was no longer human. She let the witch take her hand and lead her round the inside of the circle of sorcerers, gleefully displaying her, while singing:

> *"Welcome to the coven, love!*
> *And in evil you shall prove*
> *Wickeder than anyone!*
> *Now go on with what's begun."*

Tamsin stood dazed and dumb, wondering with what little sense she had left just exactly how this frightful business *had* begun.

"You should never have grabbed me with your great greedy fingers!" said a voice.

Perched on the shoulder of the young witch was the toadstool that Tamsin had last seen in the mushroom field. It was larger now, and greener; the orange spike was twice as long, and had grown a nasty little face at the top. The whole thing was throbbing.

"Caught! You're caught!" it tittered. "Tamsin is lost! In three minutes' time, you'll be Trilly-Tassel."

"Oh, no ..." whispered the girl, hopelessly.

And a voice, from high overhead, echoed her words. "No! No!"

Tamsin lifted blurred eyes to the sky. Up there among the stars, high and out of reach, flew Geronomy. Circling above the stone ring, tumbling in the wind, curvetting and neighing, he kicked his twigs about in wild excitement.

"There! And there—! And there – there!" he was shrieking. "How's that, for a start? And these – and these – and these —!"

The witches began to scream shrilly, to leap, and to run. Their circle broke as they fled in all directions, clutching their heads in their arms as if to shield them from sparks of fire. And, indeed, sparks of fire were falling from the air. Showers of glowing red sparks, shaken from Geronomy's tail, were blown over the gathering by the wild wind. And the gathering fled, screaming.

"I'm on fire!"

"Me skirt's all charred ..."

"Onery, twoery – ow!"

"— horrid way to end a party —"

"'night, all. Come along, toadlet!"

Off down the hillside they went, at tremendous speed. The thunderous footsteps faded, with the voices, into the darkness. Broomsticks, ridden furiously, whizzed away. The familiars went, too – running, leaping, hopping, flapping – squeaking furiously. The cats slid without haste from their perches and vanished, still smiling.

Now the circle of stones stood quiet in the moonlight. The wind from nowhere went back to nowhere. Tamsin stood blinking at the little crown of bryony, as it withered to ashes at her feet. She felt her blood running warm again. But her face changed as a battered broomstick crashed to the ground nearby.

"Geronomy ..." she faltered.

And then she said:

"What did you do to them?"

Geronomy gave a great shiver.

"Went to the – the rowan coppice," he said hoarsely. "Begged for some – berries. They let 'em fall on me. Flew back here – dropped 'em all over them – and sent those witches off in a fine old flurry – eh? Rowans is truly stronger than ..."

The girl was on her knees beside him, touching very gently and lovingly the blackened handle, the burnt stub

of string, the still-smouldering remnants of the birch-twigs.

"Oh, Geronomy – but you! You carried the berries – and you feared them so."

"For you, girlie. Had to. One last flight – for you. All over, now. No more tree-tops – no moonlight and weird winds – never no more," said Geronomy, and his voice was growing faint. "It was my choice, love. Don't cry. You've a long walk home. I – I can't do any more – better just leave me here – I'm only a broom now – and a useless one at that —"

"You're not! You're wonderful!"

But Geronomy lay quite still, and said no more.

It was a long walk home.

Tamsin's family wondered a little, when she placed a charred old broomstick in a corner of her room.

"He must never be used for sweeping or any house-work," said the girl. "He's a – a sort of pet. And he has to be kept warm and safe, and cherished."

Her family said oh very well.

Every day, Tamsin put a bowl of water beside Geronomy; and, every day, she brought him a wisp of hay, a lump of sugar, a fragment of cake. But they all remained untouched.

Broomsticks neither eat nor drink.

The Woodcutter's Daughter

Alison Uttley

In an old thatched cottage deep in the forest lived the woodcutter, Thomas Furze, and Margaret his wife. They were a homely couple, simple and hardworking. All they wanted was a child, and at last their wish was granted. Late in life, a little girl was born to them.

She was as pretty and dainty a little creature as they were plain and weather-beaten. They gazed upon her with rapture, as if a small angel had come to earth. Her cheeks were pink as the cherries in the wild wood, her skin was white as cherry blossom, and her lips as sweet as honeystalks. So the child was christened by the romantic name of Cherry-blossom, with Cherry for short.

The father was the romantic one of that family, for the mother was practical and matter-of-fact. Between them they managed not to spoil the little girl, and they brought her up very sensibly, considering all things.

Little Cherry helped her mother in the cottage even when she was very tiny. She went to the village school through the clearing in the wood, and her father took her part of the way, past the goblin trees and haunted dells. At night she sat by the fire, listening to the tales he told her while he carved strange beasts from the curiously shaped bits of wood he brought back from the forest. He always had an eye for odd things, and he noticed that some

boughs were shaped like animals, and that faces sometimes seemed to peer from a crooked tree trunk.

The stories he told were very exciting and real to the
little girl. He spoke of dragons that once lived on earth, of
fairies like brilliant winged people flying in the air, and
mermaids dwelling in the coral sea. Cherry never wanted
a book to read while she could hear such legends and folk
tales. As her father talked in his low voice, and her
mother's knitting-needles clicked, half-impatiently, the
girl saw princes and peris, fairies and elves, inhabiting a
world beyond the radiant moon, yet close to her own
forest home.

As she grew taller and older, and perhaps a little wiser,
she hid the fairy tales in a corner of her heart, and she left
the village school. She had to earn her living, but the good
people did not want her to leave home. So she put a little
card, printed in neat characters with her own pen and ink,
in the front parlour window.

"Good plain sewing and ladies' stuffs made up," it said,
for all the world to read. The only ones who saw it were
the tawny squirrels who ran along the low garden fence,
and the robin hopping by the door.

However, there was soon plenty of sewing to be done,
for Cherry's mother spoke to her own friends in the town
and they told their mistresses and patrons. Once in three
months Cherry went to this town, walking many a mile,
and sometimes getting a lift in the carrier's cart for part of
the way. She stayed the night at her grandmother's, a
very ancient woman nearing ninety. She collected sewing
to be done from the ladies, who admired the neat tiny
stitches of the forest girl. At any rate, they said, her
mother had taught her to sew, down there in the back-
woods.

They gave her chemises and petticoats to make from
fine linen, to be tucked and gathered, feather-stitched and
button-holed, ruffled and pleated, and the threads drawn

in lovely patterns. There were handkerchiefs to be hem-
stitched and lace caps to be made. Cherry packed her
parcels in a bundle, bound them with a cord, and carried
them on her back to the cottage.

Then she worked hard with her needle, stitching the
dainty work for the fine ladies, sewing her hopes and
desires and dreams into the linen, embroidering her fan-
cies on the edges with many a smile at her inmost
thoughts.

One night when her parents had gone to bed, the girl
sat late finishing a piece of work. Her needle flashed in
and out of the white linen, and she leaned close to see her
stitches. The lamp flickered out, and as there was no
paraffin in the barrel in the house corner, she lighted a
candle and finished by its slender beam. Then she sat by
the fire, staring into the depths, half-dreaming, watching
the golden castles in the flames, the towers that glowed
and smouldered and fell with a silent clatter of gilded
walls. She gazed at the flames, jagged like the antlers of
the stags in the forest. They were soft as fur, they blew
together in pointed tongues. They changed before her
eyes, and lo! there was a golden bear in the great cave of
the fire.

The girl stared bewitched at the lovely wonder of it,
fearing the beautiful beast would disappear like all the
marvels of enchantment in the world of fire. But he
stayed there, walking slowly through the gateway of the
caves and under the arches of gold. Outside, the wind
howled like a wolf, it snarled and snapped, and the forest
whined back. The door shook, and the shuttered windows rattled and bumped as an icy blast swept through
the crannies and caught up the flames.

Cherry was afraid the fire would break up, and the
pattern of mystery dissolve, but the bear came down the
glowing embers, stepping silently along a track in the
flame. It grew larger, its fur quivered, it raised its head

and walked out of the fire, and stood on the wide hearth-stone, its shaggy feet on the sanded stone.

It shook itself and sparks flew about the room. Its golden eyes gazed at her, questioning her. The girl sprang to her feet in terror and started for the door, but the bear spoke softly to her. Its voice was deep as the wind when it rumbles in the hollows of caves. Its eyes were filled with supplication. Its head was lowered before her in sub-mission.

"Woodcutter's daughter. Give me a drink of cold water, I pray you of your mercy," it said.

Cherry ran to the bucket of spring water standing on the sink, and she carried it to the hearth. The bear drank and drank, and its colour ebbed and flowed, from gold to black, as the coldness of the water touched it.

"Woodcutter's daughter. Give me food, I pray you of your charity," said the bear.

She went to the cupboard and brought out a honey-comb and a newly-baked loaf, which she put on a platter for the bear. It ate with enjoyment, finishing every morsel, while she watched, fascinated.

"Woodcutter's daughter, what is your name?" asked the bear.

"Cherry, if you please," she answered. "Cherry-blossom I was christened, but they call me Cherry for short."

The bear looked around, at the little kitchen, at the young girl, at the white sewing heaped on the oak table near the guttering candle.

"Cherry-red, cherry-white, cherry-blossom on the tree. Will you make a coat for me?" asked the bear, chanting and swaying as it spoke.

"A coat?" she cried, surprised and puzzled.

"Make me a green coat from the nettles in the cherry grove in yon woods," said the bear.

"I know where you mean, but – but – I don't think I can sew nettles," she hesitated.

"Stitch it finely and closely and bring it here for me," said the bear.

"Well, I'll try," said Cherry, "but I've never stitched nettles before. Only linen and lace. Not nettles."

The bear was already moving back into the fire, stepping across the hearthstone, growing smaller, walking into the heart of the flames. Deep in the fire Cherry saw the bear with a thin chain round its neck led by a sprite to the cave. It faded away, the fire burned up with a fierce rush, and she waited. She took the poker and stirred the cave. With a crash it fell, and the cherrywood log lay over the place, hiding everything.

"Am I dreaming, or did I really see a bear?" she asked herself. The empty water-bucket stood on the hearth, and the platter beside it. There was a loaf missing from the cupboard, and the honeycomb gone. She packed up her sewing, took her candle, and went slowly up to bed.

"Father, I dreamed that a great golden bear came out of the fire," she said the next morning.

"Ah! That's a lucky omen. Such dreams come when you burn cherrywood. I've been cutting down some of those great wild cherry trees in the clearing among the nettles. They are very ancient trees and some of them are hollow. That's where I found that wild bees' honeycomb."

"Where is that honeycomb, Cherry? I can't find it. I thought we had four loaves of bread, too, and there are only three," cried Mrs Furze, peering in the bread-mug.

"Mother, I gave them to the bear, in my dream," stammered Cherry.

"You gave them to a bear? Whatever do you mean?" exclaimed her mother.

"Don't ye bother her, Mother," said the placid woodcutter. "This is a strange happening. I've heard of it

before, long ago, when I was a little 'un. It has happened afore, and it brings good luck, they say."

No more was said, for Mrs Furze was a sensible woman. Cherry went out to the grove where her father was thinning old cherry trees. She gathered a great basketful of nettles, which was nothing unusual, for those simple people had nettle broth and boiled nettles as vegetables many days in the spring when their garden had no green stuff.

The woodcutter left his work and joined his pretty daughter.

"See here, Cherry lass," said he, taking her arm and leading her to a place where the nettles were thickest. "Look here. This carved stone has meant something once upon a time."

He showed her a broken pillar of marble, carved with grapes and leaves and strange outlandish beasts.

"There's an old story told that many many years ago a castle stood here, in this clearing. It is country talk that wherever the nettles grow, there was once a dwelling for man. Nowhere in this forest are there nettles save here, among these broken stones and cherry trees."

"Yes, Father. I know," said Cherry. "I used to play under these wild cherry trees when I was coming home from school. I found many a piece of marble carving. I love this spot, Father."

"The cherry trees must have been in the castle grounds," continued her father, poking about in the rubble. "Nobody living knows what happened, or remembers anything about it. Your grandmother knew the tale, but her parents could not remember the castle."

He returned to his work and Cherry took the nettles home. She began to stitch them together with some hesitation at first and then with an eagerness to succeed in the task. Nettles are thick and fibrous, covered with tiny hairs that sting, but a good grasp overcomes the sharp

prickles of poison. The girl sewed every night when her parents were in bed. She dare not let them see what she was making. A coat of nettles for a bear! They would think she was crazed. Although her father would perhaps understand, her mother would scold, so she kept the work secret.

Each night she went to the oak press and took out the nettle coat. She stitched more leaves to it, using tiny stitches, and sewing with extreme care and delicacy.

Many a time she went back to the clearing for more nettles, and as she gathered them she exposed the old foundations of the castle. She could trace the rooms, the great hall, the hearth which was under a yew tree, and the courtyard, where four cherry trees grew. Beyond was the orchard, where the older trees spread their aged branches, and gardens, all wild with primrose and dog roses.

Although she made many inquiries when she went to the town with her bundle of finished garments, nobody could tell her anything of the dwelling that had once stood there.

Sometimes when she sewed the green coat, the golden bear came out of the fire and lay on the hearthstone by her side. Round his neck was a chain. He never spoke, except once when he asked for food and water. He did not answer her questions. He lay with his head on his paws, watching her, and she felt strangely happy when he was with her. Then back he lumbered into the fire, and the thin black sprite caught him and led him into the golden caves.

The coat sleeves were finished, the lapels stitched, and the two large hunting pockets were fixed to the sides. It was a grand coat, fit for a real hunter to wear, with plenty of room for game in those pockets. Cherry spread it out on the floor and looked to see if anything were missing. There were no buttons, of course, and she wondered whether to put some bone buttons from her mother's

work-box down the front. She made three large button-holes ready.

Then she took her needle and some threads of her own silky gold hair and embroidered flowers of the dead-nettle down the front. It was an extra, something special, for the bear's pleasure.

That night she saw three golden buttons glowing in the heart of the fire. She raked them out, and left them to cool on the hearth. Then she stitched them on to the embroidered front of the coat and waited, for she was certain the bear would appear.

Out of the fire he walked, getting larger and larger, till he stood, a great golden bear, by her side.

"It is well done," said he. "Put the coat away till the time comes. Keep it safe until I am ready."

"When will that be?" she asked, disappointed that nothing happened.

"A few more months," he replied. "Now you must make yourself a dress, beautiful as snow. Make a dress fit for a queen."

"How can I?" she laughed. "I have no stuff for a dress, and I couldn't wear one of nettles."

"Make it of cherry blossom, like your name," said the bear, and he went into the fire without another word.

The next day Cherry went to the woods for the flowers of the wild cherry. The trees were full of bloom, but the petals soon fall, and there was little time left before they would all be gone. She carried a basketful of flowers home and set to work at her dress. As she could only work at night, she sewed all through the long hours. It was easier than the nettle coat, for the bunches of flowers clung together with a few stitches, and soon she had a complete dress, sweet-scented and exquisite. The flowers did not fade, they stayed fresh as when they were gathered. Cherry spread out the dress for the bear to see.

Out from the fire he came and praised her work. "A

little longer," said he. "I must wait till winter comes, and the fire roars up the chimney. Keep the cherry-blossom dress and the nettle coat near you till I come again. Be ready for me. You can save me, and only you."

Many days passed and although Cherry looked into the fire each night there was no golden bear in the caves. The flames danced in the fireplace, the smoke, blue as a gentian, billowed among the trees. Cherry sat sewing her ladies' garments. Sometimes she went out to the woods, to visit the deserted castle, with its wild cherry trees, red-gold in the autumn.

"When winter comes I shall see my bear," she thought. "I shall be glad to see him. I miss his company. When he came from the fire and lay by my side, how happy I was! Is it possible to love an animal with all one's heart?"

One winter morning she got ready early to visit the town. Her work was completed, and it was time to take it back before Christmas.

"I wish I could come with you, my dear," said her mother. "It is too far for me to walk, but you can carry a basket of eggs to your grandmother, and give her our love. Take care of yourself, child."

Cherry kissed her mother, and walked away in deep content, with her basket and bundle, for there had been a sprinkling of snow in the night, and the woods were very beautiful. She passed through the grave of old cherry trees, and they seemed to be in blossom. Each tree had round bunches of snow hanging on the knotted boughs, in clusters like real flowers. The shape of the castle walls was clearly outlined by the snow, and she stayed a few minutes to rest there, before she went on her journey. Under the yew tree the ground was clean and dry, with a carpet of yew needles. She thought she saw a shadow pass, and there were footprints in the snow of some large animal. There were chippings of wood left by her father, and she drew them together in a spirit of make believe,

and piled them on the hearth. She placed four carved bits of stone round the kindling wood.

"Father can boil his can of tea here, when he comes," she said to herself. "He will know I got it ready for him."

Then away she walked, with quick light step, laughing to herself as she thought of his surprise. She had brought the nettle coat and the cherry dress in a parcel to show to her grandmother, and this also made her light-hearted. Surely the gold bear would not mind if such an old woman saw what she had made. If she had seen him, she would have asked permission, but it was several months since he had appeared in the fire. Perhaps when she got back home, he would be there. Her heart was warm with the thought of him.

She wore a blue handkerchief tied round her hair, and a thick brown cloak over her old blue frock. Her clothes were shabby, but in the woods they seemed to be exactly right. The snow shadows were blue, and the misty distances were azure, and the tree trunks were brown. The girl went along like a living shadow, moving swiftly in and out of the beeches and oaks and hollies. The carrier's cart never appeared, and she had to walk the whole way to the town. That made her late, and she went straight to her grandmother's house, and rested there for the night.

She showed the old lady the delicate sewing she carried in her pack, but she kept back the nettle coat and the cherry-blossom dress in sudden shyness. She told the news of the forest, how her father had built a new shed by the house, and a squirrel had come to live in it, and the deer had broken into the garden one night, and the pig had been killed to make bacon for the winter months. She gave her grandmother a little carved egg-cup her father had sent, and the eggs from her mother, and some brawn she had made and chitterlings. Still she hesitated to mention the nettle coat and the cherry-blossom dress.

"Did you see anything in the forest when you came through?" asked the grandmother in quavering tones.

"Oh yes. I saw many things, Grandmother. Green woodpeckers, and the deer, and red squirrels, and a white owl, half asleep in a tree, and—"

"Nay, not those things, child. Did you see any queer things? Any strange unco' things?" persisted the grandmother.

"Why yes, Grandmother. I saw the trees all silvered with snow, the dark faces in the trunk of that tree I know very well. Like a gnome it is, all wrinkled and large-mouthed. I saw a shadow move once, in the wild cherry grove. I stayed there a minute among the trees in the clearing where there are carved stones, and, do you know, the trees seemed to be covered with cherry blossom, even in the middle of winter!"

"There's something else," said the old woman slowly. "A bear has been seen. A golden bear, they say. The hunters are after him. Yellow-gold fur, and gold eyes he has. They are after him."

"I'm not afraid of a bear," said Cherry. "I saw one in the fire. A golden bear, right in the flames, and he came out to me."

"Ah! I saw a bear in the fire long ago. It was there in the middle of the fire, and there it stayed. It's a lucky sign, they say. A bear in the fire is a piece of good luck waiting for you, but it's different from one outside in the wood. It might catch you."

The old woman wandered on, and Cherry was half asleep. She decided not to show her nettle coat but only the blosson dress, to her grandmother.

"I made this, Grandmother," said she, turning the skirt and bodice of snowy petals on the rug and shaking out the folds. "Do you like it?"

The grandmother touched the lovely blossom with a shaking finger.

"Is it your wedding dress, my child?" she asked.

"I don't know, Grandmother. I made it out of the cherry blossom growing on the wild trees in our wood," said Cherry.

"Who are you going to marry, Cherry?"

"Nobody has asked me, Grandmother."

"This must be your wedding dress, my Cherry," said the grandmother. "I was asked to make a flower-petal dress when I was a girl, but I never made it."

"Who asked you, Grandmother?" asked Cherry, softly.

"One in a dream, I think. I heard a voice as I sat by the fire, and I never forgot. Life would have been different if I had hearkened and made it, I reckon."

She shook her head, and went off to sleep.

The next day Cherry called at the houses of the rich ladies, the goldsmith's wife, the clergyman's wife, the banker's lady, and the brewer's lady. She received her payment, and the new sewing to be done. They thanked her in their high hard voices, they shook their silken skirts, and sat in their fine rooms as she stood before them in her shabby clothes and took their orders.

"Mind you sew neatly. Take care you don't spoil this silk. This is soft as a flower. You have doubtless never had such fine materials, girl," they said.

"Once I sewed flower petals," said Cherry, curtsying.

"Nonsense. Nobody can sew flower petals," they scolded. There was quite a heap of linen and silk with gold threads woven in it, and soft wools, fine as cobwebs. Cherry's fame had spread and many ladies wanted the woodcutter's daughter to make their clothes, to stitch her pretty patterns on their shifts and nightgowns and petticoats.

It was late before Cherry had collected all the work to be done, but she knew her mother would be anxious if she stayed another night. She wrapped her money in her

handkerchief, and stored it in her bosom. She carried the bundle on her back, tied up in layers of cloth to keep the stuffs clean. In her hand she had a lantern and the small packet with the nettle coat and the cherry-blossom dress.

"You won't get home till after dark, Cherry love," sighed the grandmother, and she gave her a loaf of bread and cheese for the journey, and a pannikin of tea.

"I shall be safe, Grandmother," said Cherry, kissing her on her withered soft cheeks.

"Mind that golden bear. Don't let him catch you. God be with you."

"And God be with you, Grandmother," said Cherry.

She waved the lantern and started off down the road. When she got to the forest she lighted the lantern and walked through the beech trees on the narrow track she knew so well. But the lantern threw strange deceiving shadows as she got deeper into the woods, the trees seemed to be moving this way and that, advancing and retreating to confuse her, and the pathway was hidden in snow. She went on for some miles, then the snow began to fall again, dancing flakes rushed to meet her, blinding her eyes, catching in her hair, lying on the pack till it was heavy as lead.

She struggled on, tired and sleepy, finding her way by the stars, until the snow hid the sky. She realized she was lost, and the only thing to do was to find a shelter and wait till morning. She went on, bewildered by the snow, seeking a tree where she could rest. She was unafraid, for she had often been in the forest at night, and she knew there was nothing to harm her. Then she saw the dark branches of a yew, and her feet stumbled against the stones on the ground. She knew where she was, and this could be no other place than the ruins of the old castle, two or three miles from her home.

Her lantern light fell on the heap of wood she had collected the day before, when she started off for the town. In a minute she had lighted it, and was warming her frozen hands at the blaze. She sat down in the warmth and shelter of the ancient yew tree, and spread out her wet cloak and scarf to dry. The yew needles were soft as a bed under her feet, and she leaned against the red scaly trunk of the tree, and unfastened the bundle with the nettle cloak and the cherry-blossom dress. They were crumpled and flattened, but she shook them so that the petals were fresh, and the nettles were stiff and shapely. Then she hung the two garments in the yew tree, and busied herself, warming her tea in the little pannikin, throwing more wood on the blaze.

The crackle of the fire was so cheerful, she laughed aloud with pleasure.

"Here I am, drinking tea in the ruined castle, and soon I shall be at home. I know my way blindfold from here. What a tale to tell!"

She was startled by the distant sound of shots, and in a minute a great golden bear came towards her, his side bleeding, his eyes half glazed with pain.

"My bear. My golden bear," she cried, running to him. She tore up her scarf and bound it round him. She opened the linen pack and took the choicest pieces to wrap on his wound.

"Drink this," she said, and she poured out the rest of her tea, and offered him food. He shook his head, and lay down by her side.

Then she heard the noise of approaching hooves, and shouts of men. They had seen the light, and were coming, nearer, nearer.

"Into the fire! Quick, or they will catch you," she cried.

"I escaped from the fire, Cherry-blossom, and now you send me back," he said.

"It's your only chance," said Cherry, urgently.

The bear stood by the crackling flames for a moment, and his blood made a pool on the ground. Then he entered the fire, and even as the flames touched him, he became smaller and disappeared in the leaping tongues.

The huntsmen galloped up, surrounding the tree.

"Which way did that bear go? He must have passed quite close. See – his blood is here. He might have killed you, for he was wounded and dangerous," they shouted.

"He went out of sight. He disappeared," said Cherry, standing with her back to the fire.

"And what are you doing here, a young girl alone in the forest at night?" asked one of the men, as the others galloped off.

"I am Cherry, the woodcutter's daughter. This is where my father has been cutting wood. I got lost coming from the town, and I am going home," explained Cherry.

"Then get on my horse and ride with me, Cherry, for you are a pretty girl, and I shall enjoy taking you home," said the young man.

"No, sir." Cherry thought of her bear, caught in his woodland fire.

"What? You don't want to go home? Then I shall stay here and take care of you. It isn't safe with a bear in the woods," he said impudently, and he flung himself from his horse, tied it to a branch of the tree, and sat down by the fire. He threw fresh boughs on it, and Cherry stood looking anxiously at him. Far away they could hear the horses galloping.

"Now tell me what you are doing here in the forest," he continued. "That wounded bear came very close to you. Here is its blood."

Even as he spoke, pointing to the ground, Cherry could see the golden bear moving in the flames. She went towards the man, lest he should notice, but the horse was

aware of the presence of the wild beast. It reared and plunged in terror, neighing shrilly.

"What's the matter with you?" called the man, but he went to calm it. "The bear must be somewhere near, he's so frightened."

"Oh, golden bear! Come out and rescue me," whispered Cherry, leaning to the fire.

Out from the flames stepped the bear, growing tall and splendid as he left the fire, but already the horse had broken away and the man ran after it.

"Throw the nettle coat into the fire," commanded the bear. "Throw it into the flames, now."

She tossed the green coat upon the burning wood, expecting to see it shrivel up. The leaves were burnt away, but the strong fibres of the nettles remained. It became a coat of gold, a web of gleaming threads like a coat of mail. The bear picked it from the embers and put it on his shoulders. Immediately he changed to a man, tall and fair, strong and valiant.

"Now throw your cherry-petal dress on the fire," commanded the bear-man, pointing to the white dress hanging in the yew tree.

Cherry obeyed, and the dress became white as silver, with every petal clear and bright.

"Wear it, Cherry. It is for your wedding. Now look around."

Then Cherry saw that she was standing in the hall of the castle, and the yew tree was the wide chimney stack, growing up, with dark boughs curving to the roof. The fire glowed on the hearth, shining up to the great timbers of the roof, to the lovely branches of the tree. The floor was covered with the carpet of yew needles, and seats of carved stone and rugs of fur were in their places. Through the high windows of the. spreading yew tree Cherry could see the stars, and at the far end there was a great door of carved wood.

"All this was destroyed hundreds of years ago," said the bear-man. "My enemy broke the castle walls and enchanted me, so that nobody knew what had happened. In a night all disappeared, and the memory of the place went. Into the flames I was cast and I was held there until a girl should release me. I became a bear of fire, doomed to lie in the gold cave, from which I could come forth at times to seek a rescuer. I tried to escape, but nobody helped me, until I found you. You made me the burning coat of nettles which had sprung up from the bones of my home. You brought me home to life again by lighting this fire on the hearthstone, from which it had been banished for centuries. You sat in the hall and played in the castle when you were a little child, among the broken stones. I loved you then, as I watched you with the cherry blossom falling upon your hair. I saw you unafraid, playing your childish games in my house."

"Yes," said Cherry, staring round in wonder and delight. "I used to play here. I always thought there was somebody watching me, sharing my games. I never felt alone."

"Woodcutter's daughter, will you marry me?" asked the bear-man.

"Yes, golden bear," said Cherry. "I will marry you."

"We will go back to your father and mother and bring them here to the castle. For long years I have been like one dead, held within the fire by the spirit of evil. Now I am alive and I love you, Cherry-blossom."

"And I love you, golden bear," answered Cherry, holding up her face to his.

He put his arms around her, and down upon their heads fell a shower of snow which was cherry petals. The cherry trees in the grove were in flower again that winter's day. The turtle dove cooed in the boughs of the yew tree, and a charm of goldfinches flew across the open chamber. Together the bear-man and Cherry-blossom

walked out into the moonlit wood, to the thatched cottage of the old people. They looked back, and in the place of the cherry wood stood a great house, white as snow, shining like fire, with a yew tree rising from its walls.

The Lord Fish

Walter de la Mare

Once upon a time there lived in the village of Tussock in
Wiltshire a young man called John Cobbler. Cobbler
being his name, there must have been shoemaking in his
family. But there had been none in John's lifetime; nor
within living memory either. And John cobbled nothing
but his own old shoes and his mother's. Still, he was a
handy young man. He could have kept them both with
ease, and with plenty of butter to their bread, if only he
had been a little different from what he was. He was lazy.

Lazy or not, his mother loved him dearly. She had
loved him ever since he was a baby, when his chief joy
was to suck his thumb and stare out of his saucer-blue
eyes at nothing in particular except what he had no words
to tell her about. Nor had John lost this habit, even when
he was being a handy young man. He could make baskets
– of sorts; he was a wonder with bees; he could mend pots
and pans, if he were given the solder and could find his
iron; he could grow cabbages, hoe potatoes, patch up a
hen-house or lime-wash a sty. But he was only a jack of
such trades, and master of none. He could seldom finish
off anything; not at any rate as his namesake the Giant
Killer could finish off his giants. He began well; he went
on worse; and he ended, yawning. And unless his mother
had managed to get a little washing and ironing and

mending and sweeping and cooking and stitching from
the gentry in the village, there would often have been less
in the pot for them both than would keep their bodies and
souls – and the two of them – together.

Yet even though John was by nature idle and a day-
dreamer, he might have made his mother far easier about
his future if only he could have given up but one small
pleasure and pastime; he might have made not only good
wages, but also his fortune – even though he would have
had to leave Tussock to do it quick. It was his love of
water that might some day be his ruin. Or rather, not so
much his love of water as his passion for fishing in it. Let
him but catch sight of a puddle, or of rain gushing from a
waterspout, or hear in the middle of the night a leaky tap
singing its queer ding-dong-bell as drop followed drop
into a basin in the sink, let the wind but creep an inch or
two out of the east and into the south; and every other
thought would instantly vanish out of his head. All
he wanted then was a rod and a line and a hook and
a worm and a cork; a pond or a stream or a river – or
the deep blue sea. And it wasn't even fish he pined for,
merely fishing.

There would have been little harm in this craving of his
if only he had been able to keep it within bounds. But he
couldn't. He fished morning, noon and even night.
Through continually staring at a float, his eyes had come
to be almost as round as one, and his elbows stood out
like fins when he walked. The wonder was his blood had
not turned to water. And though there are many kinds of
tasty English fish, his mother at least grew very tired of
having any kind at every meal. As the old rhyme goes:

> *A Friday of fish*
> *Is all man could wish.*
> *Of vittles the chief*
> *Is mustard and beef.*

It's only a glutton
Could live on cold mutton;
And bacon when green
Is too fat or too lean.
But all three are sweeter
To see in a dish
By any wise eater
Than nothing but FISH!

Quite a little fish, too, even a roach, may take as many hours to catch and almost as many minutes to cook as a full-sized one; and they both have the same number of bones. Still, in spite of his fish and his fishing, his mother went on loving her son John. She hoped in time he might weary of them himself. Or was there some secret in his passion for water of which she knew nothing? Might he some day fish up something really worth having – something to keep? A keg perhaps of rubies and diamonds, or a coffer full of amber and gold? Then all their troubles would be over.

Meanwhile John showed no sign at all of becoming less lazy or of growing tired of fishing, though he was no longer content to fish in the same places. He would walk miles and miles in hope to find pond, pool or lake that he had never seen before, or a stream strange to him. Wherever he heard there was water within reach between dawn and dark, off he would go to look for it. Sometimes in his journeyings he would do a job of work, and bring home to his mother not only a few pence but a little present for herself – a ribbon, or a needle-case, a bag of jumbles or bull's-eyes, or a duck's egg for her tea; any little thing that might take her fancy. Sometimes the fish he caught in far-off waters tasted fresher, sweeter, richer, juicier than those from nearer home; sometimes they tasted worse – dry, poor, rank and muddy. It depended partly on the sort of fish, partly on how long he had taken

to carry them home, and partly on how his mother felt at the moment.

Now there was a stream John Cobbler came to hear about which for a long time he could never find. For whenever he went to look for it – and he knew that it lay a good fourteen miles and more from Tussock – he was always baulked by a high flintstone wall. It was the highest wall he had ever seen. And, like the Great Wall of China, it went on for miles. What was more curious, although he had followed the wall on and on for hours at a stretch, he had never yet been able to find a gate or door to it, or any way in.

When he asked any stranger whom he happened to meet at such times if he knew what lay on the other side of this mysterious wall, and whether there were any good fish in the stream which he had been told ran there, and if so, of what kind, shape, size and flavour they might be – every single one of them told him a different tale. Some said there was a castle inside the wall, a good league or so away from it, and that a sorcerer lived in it who had mirrors on a tower in which he could detect any stranger that neared his walls. Others said an old, old Man of the Sea had built himself a great land mansion there in the middle of a Maze – of water and yew trees; an old Man of the Sea who had turned cannibal, and always drowned anybody who trespassed over his wall before devouring him. Others said water-witches dwelt there, in a wide lake made by the stream beside the ruinous walls of a palace which had been the abode of princes in old times. All agreed that it was a dangerous place, and that they would not venture over the wall, dark or daylight, for a pocketful of guineas. On summer nights, they said, you could hear voices coming from away over it, very strange voices, too; and would see lights in the sky. And some avowed they had heard hunting-horns at the rise of the moon. As for the fish, all agreed they must be monsters.

There was no end to the tales told John of what lay beyond the wall. And he, being a simple young man, believed each one of them in turn. But none made any difference to the longing that had come over him to get to the other side of this wall and to fish in the stream there. Walls that kept out so much, he thought, must keep something well worth having in. All other fishing now seemed tame and dull. His only hope was to find out the secret of what lay beyond this high, grey, massive, mossy, weed-tufted, endless wall. And he stopped setting out in its direction only for the sake of his mother.

But though for this reason he might stay at home two or three days together, the next would see him off again, hungering for the unknown waters.

John not only thought of the wall all day, he dreamed of it and of what might be beyond it by night. If the wind sighed at his window he saw moonlit lakes and water in his sleep; if a wild duck cried overhead under the stars, there would be thousands of wild duck and wild swans too and many another water-bird haunting his mind, his head on his pillow. Sometimes great whales would come swimming into his dreams. And he would hear mermaids blowing in their hollow shells and singing as they combed their hair.

With all this longing he began to pine away a little. His eyes grew less clear and lively. His rib-bones began to show. And though his mother saw a good deal more of her son John since he had given up his fishing, at last she began to miss more and more and more what she had become accustomed to. Fish, that is – boiled, broiled, baked, fried or Dutch-ovened. And her longing came to such a pass at last that she laid down her knife and fork one supper-time beside a half-eaten slice of salt pork and said, "My! John, how I would enjoy a morsel of tench again! Do you remember those tench you used to catch up at Abbot's Pool? Or a small juicy trout, John! Or some

stewed eels! Or even a few roach out of the moat of the
old Grange, even though they are mostly mud! It's funny,
John, but sea-fish never did satisfy me even when we
could get it; and I haven't scarcely any fancy left for meat.
What's more, I notice cheese now gives you nightmares.
But fish? – never!"

This was enough for John. For weeks past he had been
sitting on the see-saw of his mind, so that just the least
little tilt like that bumped him clean into a decision. It
was not fear or dread indeed, all this talk of giants and
wizardry and old bygone princes that had kept him from
scaling the great wall long ago, and daring the dangers
beyond it. It was not this at all. But only a half-hidden
feeling in his mind that if once he found himself on the
other side of it he might never be quite the same creature
again. You may get out of your bed in the morning, the
day's usual sunshine at the window and the birds singing
as they always sing, and yet know for certain that in the
hours to come something is going to happen – something
that hasn't happened before. So it was with John Cobbler.
At the very moment his mother put down her knife and
fork on either side of her half-eaten slice of salt pork and
said, "My! John, how I would enjoy a morsel of tench
again! ... Or a small juicy trout, John!" his mind was
made up.

"Why, of course, Mother dear," he said to her, in a
voice that he tried in vain to keep from trembling. "I'll see
what I can do for you to-morrow." He lit his candle there
and then, and scarcely able to breathe for joy at the
thought of it, clumped up the wooden stairs to his attic to
look out his best rod and get ready his tackle.

While yet next morning the eastern sky was pale blue
with the early light of dawn, wherein tiny clouds like a
shoal of silver fishes were quietly drifting on – before,
that is, the flaming sun had risen, John was posting along
out of Tussock with his rod and tackle and battered old

creel, and a hunk of bread and cheese tied up in a red spotted handkerchief. There was not a soul to be seen. Every blind was down; the chimneys were empty of smoke; the village was still snoring. He whistled as he walked, and every now and again took a look at the sky. That vanishing fleecy drift of silver fishes might mean wind, and from the south, he thought. He plodded along to such good purpose, and without meeting a soul except a shepherd with his sheep and dog and an urchin driving a handful of cows – for these were solitary parts – that he came to the wall while it was still morning and a morning as fresh and green as even England can show.

Now John wasn't making merely for the wall, but for a certain place in it. It was where, one darkening evening some little time before, he had noticed the still-sprouting upper branches of a tree that had been blown down in a great wind over the edge of the wall and into the narrow grassy lane that skirted it. Few humans seemed ever to come this way, but there were hosts of rabbits, whose burrows were in the sandy hedgerow, and, at evening, nightjars, croodling in the dusk. It was too, John had noticed, a favourite resort of bats.

After a quick look up and down the lane to see that the coast was clear, John stood himself under the dangling branches – like the fox in the fable that was after the grapes – and he jumped, and jumped. But no matter how high he jumped, the lowermost twigs remained out of his reach. He rested awhile looking about him, and spied a large stone half-buried in the sandy hedgerow. He trundled it over until it was under the tree, and after a third attempt succeeded in swinging himself up into its branches, and had scrambled along and dropped quietly in on the other side almost before news of his coming had spread among the wild things that lived on the other side of it. Then blackbird to blackbird sounded the alarm. There was a scurry and scamper among the leaves and

bracken. A host of rooks rose cawing into the sky. Then all was still. John peered about him; he had never felt so lonely in his life. Never even in his dreams had he been in a place so strange to him as this. The foxgloves and bracken of its low hills and hollows showed bright green where the sunshine struck through the great forest trees. Else, so dense with leaves were their branches that for the most part there was only an emerald twilight beneath their boughs. And a deep silence dwelt there.

For some little time John walked steadily on, keeping his eyes open as he went. Near and far he heard jays screaming one to the other, and wood-pigeons went clattering up out of the leaves into the sun. Ever and again, too, the hollow tapping of a woodpecker sounded out in the silence, or its wild echoing laughter, and once he edged along a glade just in time to see a herd of deer fleeting in a multitude before him at sight and scent of man. They sped soundlessly out of view across the open glade into covert. And still John kept steadily on, lifting his nose every now and again to snuff the air; for his fisherman's wits had hinted that water was near.

And he came at length to a gentle slope waist-high with spicy bracken, and at its crest found himself looking down on the waters of a deep and gentle stream flowing between its hollow banks in the dingle below him. "Aha!" cried John out loud to himself; and the sound of his voice rang so oddly in the air that he whipped round and stared about him as if someone else had spoken. But there was sign neither of man nor bird nor beast. All was still again. So he cautiously made his way down to the bank of the stream and began to fish.

For an hour or more he fished in vain. The trees grew thicker on the farther bank, and the water was deep and dark and slow. None the less, though he could see none, he knew in his bones that it was fairly alive with fish. Yet not a single one of them had as yet cheated him with even

a nibble. Still, John had often fished half a day through without getting so much as a bite, and so long as the water stole soundlessly on beneath him and he could watch the reflection of the tree boughs and of the drifts of blue sky between them in this dark looking-glass, he was happy and at ease. And then suddenly, as if to mock him, a fish with a dappled green back and silver belly and of a kind he never remembered to have seen before, leapt clean out of the water about three yards from his green and white float, seemed to stare at him a moment with fishy lidless eyes, and at once plunged back into the water again. Whether it was the mere noise of its water-splash, or whether the words had actually sounded from out of its gaping jaws he could not say, but it certainly seemed as if before it vanished he had heard a strange voice cry, "Ho, there! John! ... Try lower down!"

He laughed to himself; then listened. Biding a bit, he clutched his rod a little tighter, and keeping a more cautious look-out than ever on all sides of him, he followed the flow of the water, pausing every now and again to make a cast. And still not a single fish seemed so much as to have sniffed (or even sneered) at his bait, while yet the gaping mouths of those leaping up out of the water beyond his reach seemed to utter the same hollow and watery-sounding summons he had heard before: "Ho, John! Ho! Ho, you, John Cobbler, there! Try lower down!" So much indeed were these fish like fish enchanted that John began to wish he had kept to his old haunts and had not ventured over the wall; or that he had at least told his mother where he meant to go. Supposing he never came back? Where would she be looking for him? Where? Where? And all she had asked for, and perhaps for his own sake only, was a fish supper!

The water was now flowing more rapidly in a glass-green heavy flood, and before he was ready for it John suddenly found himself staring up at the walls of a high

dark house with but two narrow windows in the stone surface that steeped up into the sky above. And the very sight of the house set his heart beating faster. He was afraid. Beyond this wall to the right showed the stony roofs of lesser buildings, and moss-clotted fruit trees gone to leaf. Busying to and fro above the roof were scores of rooks and jackdaws, their jangled cries sounding out even above the roaring of the water, for now close beneath him the stream narrowed to gush in beneath a low-rounded arch in the wall, and so into the silence and darkness beyond it.

Two thoughts had instantly sprung up in John's mind as he stared up at his strange solitary house. One that it must be bewitched, and the other that except for its birds and the fish in its stream it was forsaken and empty. He laid his rod down on the green bank and stole from one tree-trunk to another to get a better view, making up his mind that if he had time he would skirt his way round the walled garden he could see, but would not yet venture to walk out into the open on the other side of the house.

It was marvellously quiet in this dappled sunshine, and John decided to rest awhile before venturing farther. Seating himself under a tree he opened his handkerchief, and found not only the hunk of bread and cheese he had packed in it, but a fat sausage and some cockled apples which his mother must have put in afterwards. He was uncommonly hungry, and keeping a wary eye on the two dark windows from under the leaves over his head, he continued to munch. And as he munched, the jackdaws, their black wings silvered by the sun, continued to jangle, and the fish silently to leap up out of their watery haunts and back again, their eyes glassily fixed on him as they did so, and the gathering water continued to gush steadily in under the dark rounded tunnel beneath the walls of the house.

But now as John listened and watched he fancied that

above all these sounds interweaving themselves into a gentle chorus of the morning, he caught the faint strains as of a voice singing in the distance – and a sweet voice too. But water, as he knew of old, is a curious deceiver of the ear. At times, as one listens to it, it will sound as if drums and dulcimers are ringing in its depths; at times as if fingers are plucking on the strings of a harp, or invisible mouths calling. John stopping eating to listen more intently.

And soon there was no doubt left in his mind that this was no mere water-noise, but the singing of a human voice, and that not far away. It came as if from within the walls of the house itself, but he could not detect any words to the song. It glided on from note to note as though it were an unknown bird piping in the first cold winds of April after its sea-journey from Africa to English shores; and though he did not know it, his face as he listened puckered up almost as if he were a child again and was going to cry.

He had heard tell of the pitiless sirens, and of sea-wandering nereids, and of how they sing among their island rocks, or couched on the oceanic strands of their sunny islands, where huge sea-fish disport themselves in the salt water: porpoise and dolphin, through billows clear as glass, and green and blue as precious stones. His mother too had told him as a child – and like Simple Simon himself he had started fishing in her pail! – what dangers there may be in listening to such voices; how even sailors have stopped up their ears with wax lest they should be enticed by this music to the isles of the sirens and never sail home again. But though John remembered this warning, he continued to listen, and an intense desire came over him to discover who this secret singer was, and where she lay hid. He might peep perhaps, he thought to himself, through some lattice or cranny in the dark walls and not be seen.

But though he stole on, now in shadow, now in sun, pushing his way through the tangled brambles and briars, the bracken and bryony that grew close in even under the walls of the house, he found – at least on this side of it – no doorway or window or even slit in the masonry through which to look in. And he came back at last, hot, tired and thirsty, to the bank of the stream where he had left his rod.

And even as he knelt down to drink by the waterside, the voice which had been silent awhile began to sing again, as sad as it was sweet; and not more than an arm's length from his stooping face a great fish leapt out of the water, its tail bent almost double, its goggling eyes fixed on him, and out of its hook-toothed mouth it cried, "A-whoof! Oo-ougoolkawott!" That at least to John was what it seemed to say. And having delivered its message, it fell back again into the dark water and in a wild eddy was gone. Startled by this sudden noise John drew quickly back, and in so doing dislodged a large moss-greened stone on the bank, which rolled clattering down to its plunge into the stream; and the singing again instantly ceased. He glanced back over his shoulder at the high wall and vacant windows, and out of the silence that had again descended he heard in mid-day the mournful hooting as of an owl, and a cold terror swept over him. He leapt to his feet, seized his rod and creel, hastily tied up what was left of his lunch in his red-spotted handkerchief, and instantly set out for home. Nor did he once look back until the house was hidden from view. Then his fear vanished, and he began to be heartily ashamed of himself.

And since he had by now come into sight of another loop of the stream, he decided, however long it took him, to fish there until he had at least caught something – if only a stickleback – so that he should not disappoint his mother of the supper she longed for. The minnow smeared with pork marrow which he had been using for

bait on his hook was already dry. None the less he flung it into the stream, and almost before the float touched the water a swirl of ripples came sweeping from the farther bank, and a greedy pike, grey and silver, at least two feet long if he was an inch, had instantly gobbled down bait and hook. John could hardly believe his own eyes. It was as if it had been actually lying in wait to be caught. He stooped to look into its strange motionless eye as it lay on the grass at his feet. Sullenly it stared back at him as though, even if it had only a minute or two left to live in, it were trying heroically to give him a message, yet one that he could not understand.

Happy at heart, he stayed no longer. Yet with every mile of his journey home the desire grew in him to return to the house, if only to hear again that dolorous voice singing from out of the darkness within its walls. But he told his mother nothing about his adventures, and the two of them sat down to as handsome a dish of fish for supper as they had ever tasted.

"What's strange to me, John," said his mother at last, for they had talked very little, being so hungry, "is that though this fish here is a pike, and cooked as usual, with a picking of thyme and marjoram, a bit of butter, a squeeze of lemon and some chopped shallots, there's a good deal more to him that just that. There's a sort of savour and sweetness to him, as if he had been daintily fed. Where did you catch him, John?"

But at this question John was seized by such a fit of coughing – as if a bone had stuck in his throat – that it seemed at any moment he might choke. And when his mother had stopped thumping him on his back she had forgotten what she had asked him. With her next mouthful, too, she had something else to think about; and it was fortunate that she had such a neat strong row of teeth, else the crunch she gave to it would certainly have broken two or three of them in half.

"Excuse me, John," she said, and drew out of her mouth not a bone, but something tiny, hard and shiny, which after being washed under the kitchen tap proved to be a key. It was etched over with figures of birds and beasts and fishes, that might be all ornament or might, thought John, his cheeks red as beetroot, be a secret writing.

"Well I never! Brass!" said his mother, staring at the key in the palm of her hand.

"Nor didn't I," said John. "I'll take it off to the blacksmith's at once, Mother, and see what he makes of it."

Before she could say Yes or No to this, John was gone. In half an hour he was back again.

"He says, Mother," said he, "it's a key, Mother; and not brass but solid gold. A gold key! Whoever? And in a fish!"

"Well, John," said his mother, who was a little sleepy after so hearty a supper, "I never – mind you – did see much good in fishing except the fish, but if there are any more gold keys from where that pike came from, let's both get up early, and we'll soon be as rich as Old Creatures."

John needed no telling. He was off next morning long before the sun had begun to gild the dewdrops in the meadows, and he found himself, rod, creel and bait, under the magician's wall a good three hours before noon. There was not a cloud in the sky. The stream flowed quiet as molten glass, reflecting the towering forest trees, the dark stone walls, and the motionless flowers and grass-blades at its brim. John stood there gazing awhile into the water, just as if today were yesterday over again, then sat himself down on the bank and fell into a kind of daydream, his rod idle at his side. Neither fish nor key nor the freshness of the morning nor any wish or thought was in his mind but only a longing to hear again the voice of the secret one. And the shadows

around him had crept even less than an inch on their daily
round, and a cuckoo under the hollow sky had but thrice
cuckoo'd in some green dell of the forest, when there slid
up into the air the very notes that had haunted him,
waking and sleeping, ever since they had first fallen on his
ear. They rang gently on and on, in the hush, clear as a
cherub in some quiet gallery of paradise, and John knew
in his heart that she who sang was no longer timid in his
company, but out of her solitude was beseeching his aid.

He rose to his feet, and once more searched the vast
frowning walls above his head. Nothing there but the
croaking choughs and jackdaws among the chimneys,
and a sulphur-coloured butterfly wavering in flight along
the darkness of their stones. They filled him with dread,
these echoing walls, and still the voice pined on. And at
last he fixed his eyes on the dark arch beneath which
coursed in heavy leaden flow the heaped-up volume of
the stream. No way in, indeed! Surely, where water could
go, mightn't *he*?

Without waiting a moment to consider the dangers
that might lie in wait for him in the dark water beneath
the walls, he had slipped out of his coat and shoes and had
plunged in. He swam on with the stream until he was
within a little way of the yawning arch; then took a deep
breath and dived down and down. When he could hold it
no longer he slipped up out of the water – and in the nick
of time. He had clutched something as he came to the
surface, and found himself in a dusky twilight looking up
from the foot of a narrow flight of stone steps – with a
rusty chain dangling down the middle of it. He hauled
himself up out of the water and sat down a moment to
recover his breath, then made his way up the steps. At the
top he came to a low stone corridor. There he stayed
again.

But here the voice was more clearly to be heard. He
hastened down the corridor and came at last to a high

narrow room full of sunlight from the window in its walls looking out over the forest. And, reclining there by the window, the wan green light shining in on her pale face and plaited copper-coloured hair, was what John took at first to be a mermaid; and for the very good reason that she had a human head and body, but a fish's tail. He stayed quite still, gazing at her, and she at him, but he could think of nothing to say. He merely kept his mouth open in case any words should come, while the water-drops dripped from his clothes and hair on to the stone flags around him. And when the lips in the odd small face of this strange creature began to speak to him, he could hardly make head or tail of the words. Indeed she had been long shut up alone in this old mansion from which the magician who had given her her fish's tail, so that she should not be able to stray from the house, had some years gone his way, never to come back. She had now almost forgotten her natural language. But there is a music in the voice that tells more to those who understand it than can any words in a dictionary. And it didn't take John very long to discover that this poor fish-tailed creature, with nothing but the sound of her own sad voice to comfort her, was mortally unhappy; that all she longed for was to rid herself of her cold fish's tail, and so win out into the light and sunshine again, freed from the spell of the wizard who had shut her up in these stone walls.

John sat down on an old wooden stool that stood beside the table, and listened. And now and then he himself sighed deep or nodded. He learned – though he learned it very slowly – that the only company she had was a deaf old steward who twice every day, morning and evening, brought her food and water, and for the rest of the time shut himself up in a tower on the farther side of the house looking out over the deserted gardens and orchards that once had flourished with peach and quince

and apricot, and all the roses of Damascus. Else, she said,
sighing, she was always alone. And John, as best he could,
told her in turn about himself and about his mother.
"She'd help you all she could to escape away from here – I
know *that*, if so be she *could*. The only question is, How?
Since, you see, first it's a good long step for Mother to
come and there's no proper way over the wall, and next if
she managed it, it wouldn't be easy with nothing but a tail
to walk on. I mean, lady, for you to walk on." At this he
left his mouth open, and looked away, afraid that he
might have hurt her feelings. And in the same moment he
bethought himself of the key, which, if he had not been
on the verge of choking, his mother might have swal-
lowed in mistake for a mouthful of fish. He took it out of
his breeches' pocket and held it up towards the window,
so that the light should shine on it. And at sight of it it
seemed that something between grief and gladness had
suddenly overcome the poor creature with the fish's tail,
for she hid her face in her fingers and wept aloud.

This was not much help to poor John. With his idle
ways and love of fishing, he had been a sad trial at times to
his mother. But she, though little to look at, was as brave
as a lion, and if ever she shed tears at all, it was in secret.
This perhaps was a pity, for if John had but once seen her
cry he might have known what to do now. All that he
actually did do was to look very glum himself and turn
his eyes away. And as they roved slowly round the bare
walls he perceived what looked like the crack of a little
door in the stones and beside it a tiny keyhole. The one
thing in the world he craved was to comfort this poor
damsel with the fish's tail, to persuade her to dry her eyes
and smile at him. But as nothing he could think to say
could be of any help, he tiptoed across and examined the
wall more closely. And cut into the stone above the
keyhole he read the four letters – CAVE! What they meant
John had no notion, except that a cave is something

hollow – and usually empty. Still, since here was a lock and John had a key, he naturally put the key into the lock with his clumsy fingers to see if it would fit. He gave the key a gentle twist. And lo and behold, there came a faint click. He tugged, drew the stone out upon its iron hinges, and looked inside.

What he had expected to see he did not know. All that was actually within this narrow stone cupboard was a little green pot, and beside it a scrap of what looked like parchment, but was actually monkey skin. John had never been much of a scholar at his books. He was a dunce. When he was small he had liked watching the clouds and butterflies and birds flitting to and fro and the green leaves twinkling in the sun, and found frogs and newts and sticklebacks and minnows better company than anything he could read in print on paper. Still he had managed at last to learn all his letters and even to read, though he read so slowly that he sometimes forgot the first letters of a long word before he had spelled out the last. He took the piece of parchment into the light, held it tight between his fingers, and, syllable by syllable, muttered over to himself what it said – leaving the longer words until he had more time.

And now the pale-cheeked creature reclining by the window had stopped weeping and between the long strands of her copper hair was watching him through her tears. And this is what John read:

> *Thou who wouldst dare*
> *To free this Fair*
> *From fish's shape,*
> *And yet escape*
> *O'er sea and land*
> *My vengeful hand: —*
> *Smear this fish-fat on thy heart,*
> *And prove thyself the jack thou art!*

With tail and fin
Then plunge thou in!
And thou shalt surely have thy wish
To see the great, the good Lord Fish!

Swallow his bait in haste, for he
Is master of all wizardry.
And if he gentle be inclined,
He'll show thee where to seek and find
The Magic Unguent that did make
This human maid a fish-tail take.

But have a care
To make short stay
Where wields his sway,
The Great Lord Fish;
'Twill be too late
To moan your fate
When served with sauce
Upon his dish!

John read this doggerel once, he read it twice, and though he couldn't understand it all even when he read it a third time, he understood a good deal of it. The one thing he could not discover, though it seemed the most important, was what would happen to him if he did as the rhyme itself bade him do – smeared the fish-fat over his heart. But this he meant to find out.

And why not at once, thought John, though except when he hooked a fish, he was seldom as prompt as that. He folded up the parchment very small, and slipped it into his breeches' pocket. Then imitating as best he could the motion of descending the steps and diving into the water, he promised the maid he would return to her the first moment he could, and entreated her not to sing again until he came back. "Because..." he began, but could get no further. At which, poor mortal, she began to weep

again, making John, for very sadness to see her, only the more anxious to be gone. So he took the little pot out of the stone cupboard, and giving her for farewell as smiling and consoling a bob of his head as he knew how, hurried off along the long narrow corridor, and so down the steep stone steps to the water.

There, having first very carefully felt with his fingertips exactly where his heart lay beating, he dipped his finger into the green ointment and rubbed it over his ribs. And with that, at once, a dreadful darkness and giddiness swept over him. He felt his body narrowing and shortening and shrinking and dwindling. His bones were drawing themselves together inside his skin; his arms and legs ceased at last to wave and scuffle, his eyes seemed to be settling into his head. The next moment, with one convulsive twist of his whole body, he had fallen plump into the water. There he lay a while in a motionless horror. Then he began to stir again, and after a few black dreadful moments found himself coursing along so swiftly that in a trice he was out from under the arch and into the green gloaming of the stream beyond it. Never before had he slipped through the water with such ease. And no wonder!

For when he twisted himself about to see what had happened to him, a sight indeed met his eye. Where once had been arms were now small blunt fins. A gristly little beard or barbel hung on either side of his mouth. His short dumpy body was of a greeny brown, and for human legs he could boast of nothing now but a fluted wavering tail. If he had been less idle in his young days he might have found himself a fine mottled trout, a barble, a mullet, or a lively eel, or being a John he might well have become a jack. But no, he was fisherman enough to recognize himself at sight – a common tench, and not a very handsome one either! A mere middling fish, John judged. At this horrifying discovery, though the rhyme

should have warned him of it, shudder after shudder ran along his backbone and he dashed blindly through the water as if he were out of his senses. Where could he hide himself? How flee away? What would his mother say to him? And alackaday, what had become of the pot of ointment? "Oh mercy me, oh misery me!" he moaned within himself, though not the faintest whisper sounded from his bony jaws. A pretty bargain this!

He plunged on deeper and deeper, and at length, nuzzling softly the sandy bed of the stream with his blunt fish's snout, he hid his head between two boulders at the bottom. There, under a net of bright green water-weed, he lay for a while utterly still, brooding again on his mother and on what her feelings would be if she could see him no more – or in the shape he was! Would that he had listened to her counsel, and had never so much as set eyes on rod or hook or line or float or water. He had wasted his young days in fishing, and now was fish for evermore.

But as the watery moments sped by, this grief and despondency began to thin away and remembrance of the crafty and cruel magician came back to mind. Whatever he might look like from outside, John began to be himself again within. Courage, even a faint gleam of hope, welled back into his dull fish's brains. With a flick of his tail he had drawn back out of the gloomy cranny between the boulders, and was soon disporting himself but a few inches below the surface of the stream, the sunlight gleaming golden on his scales, the cold blood coursing through his body, and but one desire in his heart.

These high spirits indeed almost proved the end of him. For at this moment a prowling and hungry pike having from its hiding-place spied this plump young tench, came flashing through the water like an arrow from a bow, and John escaped the snap of its sharp-toothed jaws by less than half an inch. And when on land he had always supposed that the tench who is the fishes'

doctor was safe from any glutton! After this dizzying experience he swam on more heedfully, playing a kind of hide-and-seek among the stones and weeds, and nibbling every now and again at anything he found to his taste. And the world of trees and sky in which but a few hours before he had walked about on his two human legs was a very strange thing to see from out of the rippling and distorting wavelets of the water.

When evening began to darken overhead he sought out what seemed to be a safe lair for the night, and must have soon fallen into a long and peaceful fish's sleep – a queer sleep too, for having no lids to his eyes they both remained open, whereas even a hare when he is asleep shuts only one!

Next morning very early John was about again. A south wind must be blowing, he fancied, for there was a peculiar mildness and liveliness in the water, and he snapped at every passing tit-bit carried along by the stream with a zest and hunger that nothing could satisfy. Poor John, he had never dreamed a drowned fly or bee or a grub or caterpillar, or even water-weed, could taste so sweet. But then he had never tried to find out. And presently, dangling only a foot or two above his head, he espied a particularly juicy-looking and wriggling red worm.

Now though, as has been said already, John as a child or even as a small boy, had refrained from tasting caterpillars or beetles or snails or woodlice, he had once – when making mud pies in his mother's garden – nibbled at a little earthworm. But he had not nibbled much. For this reason only perhaps, he stayed eyeing this wriggling coral-coloured morsel above his head. Memory too had told him that it is not a habit of worms to float wriggling in the water like this. And though at sight of it he grew hungrier and hungrier as he finned softly on, he had the good sense to cast a glance up out of the water. And there

– lank and lean upon the bank above – he perceived the strangest shape in human kind he had ever set eyes on. This bony old being had scarcely any shoulders. His grey glassy eyes bulged out of his head above his flat nose. A tuft of beard hung from his cod-like chin, and the hand that clutched his fishing rod was little else but skin and bone.

"Now," thought John to himself, as he watched him steadily from out of the water, "if that old rascal there ain't the Lord Fish in the rhyme, I'll eat my buttons." Which was an easy thing to promise, since at this moment John hadn't any buttons to eat. It was by no means easy to make up his hungry fishy mind to snap at the worm and chance what might come after. He longed beyond words to be home again; he longed beyond words to get back into his own body again – but only (and John seemed to be even stubborner as a fish than he had been as a human), *only* if the beautiful lady could be relieved of her tail. And how could there be hope of any of these things if he gave up this chance of meeting the Lord Fish and of finding the pot of "unguent" he had read of in the rhyme? The other had done its work with him quick enough!

If nothing had come to interrupt these cogitations, John might have cogitated too long. But a quick-eyed perch had at this moment finned into John's pool and had caught sight of the savoury morsel wriggling and waggling in the glass-clear water. At the very first glimpse of him John paused no longer. With gaping jaws and one mad swirl of his fish-tail he sprang at the worm. A dart of pain flashed through his body. He was whirled out of the water and into the air. He seemed on the point of suffocation. And the next instant found him gasping and floundering in the lush green grass that grew beside the water's brink. But the old angler who had caught him was even more skilful in the craft of fishing than John Cobbler was himself. Almost before John could sob twice, the hook

had been extracted from his mouth, he had been swathed up from head to tail in cool green moss, a noose had been slipped around that tail, and poor John, dangling head downwards from the fisherman's long skinny fingers, was being lugged away he knew not where. Few, fogged and solemn were the thoughts that passed through his gaping, gasping head on this dismal journey.

Now the Lord Fish who had caught him lived in a low stone house which was surrounded on three sides by a lake of water, and was not far distant from his master's — the Sorcerer. Fountains jetted in its hollow echoing chambers, and water lapped its walls on every side. Not even the barking of a fox or the scream of a peacock or any sound of birds could be heard in it; it was so full of the suffling and sighing, the music and murmuration of water, all day, all night long. But poor John being upside down had little opportunity to view or heed its marvels. And still muffled up in his thick green overcoat of moss he presently found himself suspended by his tail from a hook in the Lord Fish's larder, a long cool dusky room or vault with but one window to it, and that only a hole in the upper part of the wall. This larder too was of stone, and apart from other fish as luckless as John who hung there gaping from their hooks, many more, plumper and heavier than he, lay still and cold on the slate slab shelves around him. Indeed, if he could have done so, he might have hung his head a little lower at being so poor a fish by comparison.

Now there was a little maid who was in the service of this Lord Fish. She was the guardian of his larder. And early next morning she came in and set about her day's work. John watched her without ceasing. So fish-like was the narrow face that looked out from between the grey-green plaits of her hair that he could not even guess how old she was. She might, he thought, be twelve; she *might*, if age had not changed her much, be sixty. But he guessed

she must be about seventeen. She was not of much beauty to human eyes – so abrupt was the slope of her narrow shoulders, so skinny were her hands and feet.

First she swept out the larder with a besom and flushed it out with buckets of water. Then, with an earthenware watering pot, and each in turn, she sprinkled the moss and weed and grasses in which John and his fellows were enwrapped. For the Lord Fish, John soon discovered, devoured his fish raw, and liked them fresh. When one of them, especially of those on the shelves, looked more solemn and motionless than was good for him, she dipped him into a shallow trough of running water that lay outside the door of the larder. John indeed heard running water all day long – while he himself could scarcely flick a fin. And when all this was done, and it was done twice a day, the larder-maid each morning chose out one or two or even three of her handsomest fish and carried them off with her. John knew – to his horror – to what end.

But there were two things that gave him heart and courage in this gruesome abode. The first was that after her second visit the larder-maid treated him with uncommon kindness. Perhaps there was a look on his face not quite like that of her other charges. For John with his goggling ogling eyes would try to twist up his poor fish face into something of a smile when she came near him, and – though very faintly – to waggle his tail tips, as if in greeting. However that might be, there was no doubt she had taken a liking to him. She not only gave him more of her fish-pap than she gave the rest, to fatten him up, but picked him out special dainties. She sprinkled him more slowly than the others with her water-pot so that he could enjoy the refreshment the more. And, after a quick, sly glance over her shoulder one morning she changed his place in the larder, and hung him up in a darker corner all to himself. Surely, surely, this must mean, John thought,

that she wished to keep him as long as she could from
sharing her master's table. John did his best to croak his
thanks, but was uncertain if the larder-maid had heard.

This was one happy thing. His other joy was this.
Almost as soon as he found himself safe in his corner, he
had discovered that on a level with his head there stood
on a shelf a number of jars and gallipots and jorams of
glass and earthenware. In some were dried roots, in some
what seemed to be hanks of grass, in others black-veined
lily bulbs, or scraps of twig, or dried-up buds and leaves,
like tea. John guessed they must be savourings his
cook-maid kept for the Fish Lord to soak his fish in, and
wondered sadly which, when his own turn came, would
be his. But a little apart from the rest and not above
eighteen inches from his nose, there stood yet another
small glass jar, with greenish stuff inside it. And after
many attempts and often with eyes too dry to read,
John spelled out at last from the label of this jar these
outlandish words: UNGUENTUM AD PISCES HOMINIBUS
TRANSMOGRIFICANDOS. And he went over them again and
again until he knew them by heart.

Now John had left school very early. He had taken up
crow-scaring at seven, pig-keeping at nine, turnip-
hoeing at twelve – though he had kept up none of them
for very long. But even if John had stayed at school until
he was grown-up, he would never have learned any Latin
– none at all, not even dog Latin – since the old dame who
kept the village school at Tussock didn't know any herself. She could cut and come again as easily as you please
with the cane she kept in her cupboard, but this had never
done John much good, and she didn't know any Latin.

John's only certainty then, even when he had learned
these words by heart, was that they were not good honest
English words. Still, he had his wits about him. He
remembered that there had been words like these written
in red on the parchment over the top of the rhyme that

now must be where his breeches were, since he had
tucked it into his pocket – though where that was he
hadn't the least notion. But unguent was a word he now
knew as well as his own name; and it meant ointment.
Not many months before this, too, he had mended a chair
for a great lady that lived in a high house on the village
green – a queer lady too though she was the youngest
daughter of a marquis of those parts. It was a job that had
not taken John very long, and she was mightily pleased
with it. "Sakes, John," she had said, when he had taken
the chair back and put it down in the light of a window,
"sakes, John, what a *transmogrification!*" And John had
blushed all over as he grinned back at the lady, guessing
that she meant that the chair showed a change for the
better.

Then, too, when he was a little boy, his mother had
often told him tales of the *piskies*. "Piskies, PISCES,"
muttered John to himself on his hook. It sounded even
to *his* ear poor spelling, but it would so. Then too,
HOMINIBUS. If you make a full round O of the first syllable
it sounds uncommonly like *home*. So what the Lord Fish,
John thought at last, had meant by this lingo on his glass
pot must be that it contained an UNGUENT to which some
secret PISKY stuff or what is known as wizardry had been
added, and that it was useful for "changing" for the better
anything or anybody on which it was rubbed when away
from HOME. Nobody could call the stony cell in which the
enchanted maid with the fish-tail was kept shut up a
home; and John himself at this moment was a good many
miles from his mother!

Besides, the stuff in the glass pot was uncommonly like
the ointment which he had taken from the other pot and
had smeared on his ribs. After all this thinking John was
just clever enough to come to the conclusion that the one
unguent had been meant for turning humans into fish,
and that this in the pot beside him was for turning fish

into humans again. At this his flat eyes bulged indeed in his head, and in spite of the moss around them his fins stood out stiff as knitting needles. He gasped to himself – like a tench out of water. And while he was still brooding on his discovery, the larder-maid opened the door of the larder with her iron key to set about her morning duties.

"*Ackh*," she called softly, hastening towards him, for now she never failed to visit him first of all her charges, "*ackh*, what's wrong with 'ee? What's amiss with 'ee?" and with her lean finger she gently stroked the top of his head, her narrow bony face crooked up with care at seeing this sudden change in his looks. She did not realize that it was not merely a change but a transmogrification! She sprinkled him twice, and yet a third time, with her ice-cold water, and with the tips of her small fingers pushed tiny gobbet after gobbet of milk-pap out of her basin into his mouth until John could swallow no more. Then with gaspings and gapings he fixed his nearer eye on the jar of unguent or ointment, gazed back rapidly at the little larder-maid, then once again upon the jar.

Now this larder-maid was a great-grandniece of the Lord Fish, and had learned a little magic. "Aha," she whispered, smiling softly and wagging her finger at him. "So that's what you are after, Master Tench? That's what you are after, you crafty Master Sobersides. Oh, what a scare you gave me!"

Her words rang out shrill as a whistle, and John's fellow fish, trussed up around him in their moss and grass and rushes on their dishes, or dangling from their hooks, trembled at sound of it. A faint chuffling, a lisping and quiet gaggling, tiny squeaks and groans filled the larder. John had heard these small noises before, and had supposed them to be fish talk, but though he had tried to imitate them he had never been sure of an answer. All he could do, then, was what he had done before – he fixed again his round glassy eye first on the jar and then on the

little larder-maid, and this with as much gentle flattery and affection as he could manage. Just as when he was a child at his mother's knee he would coax her to give him a slice of bread pudding or a spoonful of jam.

"Now I wonder," muttered the larder-maid as if to herself, "if you, my dear, are the one kind or the other. And if you are the *other*, *shall* I, my gold-green Tinker, take the top off the jar?"

At this John wriggled might and main, chapping with his jaws as wide and loud as he could, looking indeed as if at any moment he might burst into song.

"Ah," cried the maid, watching him with delight, "he understands! That he does! But if I did, precious, what would my lord the Lord Fish say to me? What would happen to *me*, eh? You, Master Tench, I am afraid, are thinking only of your own comfort."

At this John sighed and hung limp as if in sadness and dudgeon and remorse. The larder-maid eyed him a few moments longer, then set about her morning work so quickly and with so intense a look on her lean narrow face, with its lank dangling tresses of green–grey hair, that between hope and fear John hardly knew how to contain himself. And while she worked on, sprinkling, feeding, scouring, dipping, she spoke to her charges in much the same way that a groom talks to his horses, a nurse to a baby, or a man to his dogs. At last, her work over, she hastened out of the larder and shut the door.

Now it was the habit of the Lord Fish on the Tuesdays, Thursdays and Saturdays of every week, to make the round of his larder, eyeing all it held, plump fish or puny, old or new, ailing or active; sometimes gently pushing his finger in under the moss to see how they were prospering for his table. This was a Thursday. And sure enough the larder-maid presently hastened back, and coming close whispered up at John, "Hst, he comes! The Lord Fish! Angry and hungry. Beware! Stay mum as mum can be,

you precious thing. Flat and limp and sulky, look 'ee, for if the Lord Fish makes his choice of 'ee now, it is too late and all is over. And above all things, don't so much as goggle for a moment at that jar!"

She was out again like a swallow at nesting-time, and presently there came the sound of slow scraping footsteps on the flagstones and there entered the Lord Fish into the larder, the maid at his heels. He was no lord to look at, thought John; no marquis, anyhow. He looked as glum and sullen as some old Lenten cod in a fishmonger's, in his stiff drab-coloured overclothes. And John hardly dared to breathe, but hung – mouth open and eyes fixed – as limp and lifeless from his hook in the ceiling as he knew how.

"*Hoy, hoy, hoy,*" grumbled the Lord Fish, when at last he came into John's corner. "Here's a dullard. Here's a rack of bones. Here's a sandy gristly-trap. Here's a good-as-dead-and-gone-and-useless! Ay, now my dear, you can't have seen him. Not this one. You must have let him go by, up there in the shadows. A quick eye, my dear, a quick watchful eye! He's naught but muddy slug-gard tench 'tis true. But, oh yes, we can better him! He wants life, he wants exercise, he wants cosseting and feeding and *fattening*. And then – why then, there's the makings in him of as comely a platter of fish as would satisfy my Lord Bishop of the Seven Sturgeons himself."

And the little larder-maid, her one hand clutching a swab of moss and the other demurely knuckled over her mouth, sedately nodded.

"Ay, master," said she, "he's hung up there in the shadows, he is. In the dark. He's a mumper, that one, he's a moper. He takes his pap but poorly. He shall have a washabout and a dose of sunshine in the trough. Trust me, master, I'll soon put a little life into him. Come next Saturday, now!"

"So, so, so," said the Lord Fish. And having made the

round of John's companions he retired at last from out of
his larder, well content with his morning's visit. And
with but one quick reassuring nod at John over her narrow shoulder, his nimble larder-maid followed after him.
John was safe until Saturday.

Hardly had the Lord Fish's scuffling footsteps died
away when back came the little maid, wringing her hands
in glee, and scarcely able to speak for laughing. "Ay,
Master Tench, did you hear that? 'Up there in the
shadows. Here's a dullard; here's a rack of bones; here's a
gristle-trap. He wants cosseting and feeding and fattening.' – Did he not now? Was I sly? Was I cunning? Did the
old Lord nibble my bait, Master Tench? Did he not now?
Oho, my poor beautiful; 'fatten', indeed!" And she
lightly stroked John's snout again. "What's wrong with
the old Lord Fish is that he eats too much and sleeps
too long. Come 'ee now, let's make no more ado about
it."

She dragged up a wooden stool that stood close by,
and, holding her breath, with both hands she carefully
lifted down the jar of green fat or grease or unguent. Then
she unlatched John from his hook, and laid him gently on
the stone slab beside her, bidding him meanwhile have no
fear at all of what might happen. She stripped off his
verdant coat of moss, and, dipping her finger in the
ointment, smeared it on him, from the nape of his neck
clean down his spine to the very tip of his tail.

For a few moments John felt like a cork that, after
bobbing softly along down a softly-flowing river, is
suddenly drawn into a roaring whirlpool. He felt like a
firework squib when the gushing sparks are nearly all out
of it and it is about to burst. Then gradually the fog in his
eyes and the clamour in his ears faded and waned away,
and lo and behold, he found himself returned safe and
sound into his own skin, shape and appearance again.
There he stood in the Lord Fish's fish larder, grinning

down out of his cheerful face at the maid who in stature reached not much above his elbow.

"Ah," she cried, peering up at him out of her small water-clear eyes, and a little dazed and dazzled herself at this transmogrification. "So you *were* the other kind, Master Tench!" And the larder-maid looked at him so sorrowfully and fondly that poor John could only blush and turn away. "And now," she continued, "all you will be wanting, I suppose, is to be gone. I beseech you then make haste and be off, or my own skin will pay for it."

John had always been a dullard with words. But he thanked the larder-maid for all she had done for him as best he could. And he slipped from off his little finger a silver ring which had belonged to his father, and put it into the palm of the larder-maid's hand; for just as when he had been changed into a fish, all his clothes and everything about him had become fish itself, so now when he was transformed into human shape again, all that had then been his returned into its own place, even to the parchment in his breeches' pocket. Such it seems is the law of enchantment. And he entreated the maid, if ever she should find herself on the other side of the great wall, to ask for the village of Tussock, and when she came to Tussock to ask for Mrs Cobbler.

"That's my mother," said John, "is Mrs Cobbler. And she'll be mighty pleased to see you, I promise you. And so will I."

The larder-maid looked at John. Then she took the ring between finger and thumb, and with a sigh pushed it into a cranny between the slabs of stone for a hiding-place. "Stay there," she whispered to the ring, "and I'll come back to 'ee anon."

Then John, having nothing else handy, and knowing that for the larder-maid's sake he must leave the pot behind him, took out of the fob in his breeches' pocket a great silver watch that had belonged to his grandfather. It

was nothing now but a watch case, since he had one day taken out the works in hopes to make it go better, and had been too lazy to put them back again. Into this case he smeared as much of the grease out of the pot as it would hold.

"And now, Master Tench, this way," said the larder-maid, twisting round on him. "You must be going, and you must be going for good. Follow that wall as far as it leads you, and then cross the garden where the Lord Fish grows his herbs. You will know it by the scent of them in the air. Climb the wall and go on until you come to the river. Swim across that, and turn sunwards while it is morning. The Lord Fish has the nose of a she-wolf. He'd smell 'ee out across a bean field. Get you gone at once then, and meddle with him no more. Ay, and I know it is not on *me* your thoughts will be thinking when you get to safety again."

John, knowing no other, stooped down and kissed this little wiseacre's lean cold fingers, and casting one helpless and doleful look all about the larder at the fish on hook and slab, and seeing none, he fancied, that could possibly be in the same state as his had been, he hastened out.

There was no missing his way. The Lord Fish's walls and water conduits were all of stone so solid that they might have been built by the Romans, though, truly, they were chiefly of magic, which has nothing to do with time. John hurried along in the morning sunshine, and came at length to the stream. With his silver watch between his teeth for safety he swam to the other side. Here grew very tall rough spiny reeds and grasses, some seven to nine feet high. He pushed his way through them, heedless of their clawing and rasping, and only just in time. For as soon as he was safely hidden in the low bushes beyond them, whom did he now see approaching on the other side of the stream, rod in hand, and creel at his elbow, but the Lord Fish himself – his lank face

erected up into the air and his nose sniffing the morning as if it were laden with the spices of Arabia. The larder-maid had told the truth indeed. For at least an hour the Lord Fish stood there motionless on the other side of the stream immediately opposite John's hiding-place. For at least an hour he pried and peeped about him, gently sniffing on. And, though teased by flies and stung with nettles, John dared not stir a finger. At last even the Lord Fish grew weary of watching and waiting, and John, having seen him well out of sight, continued on his way....

What more is there to tell? Sad and sorrowful had been the maid's waiting for him, sad beyond anything else in the fish-tailed damsel's memory. For, ever since she had so promised him, she had not even been able to sing to keep herself company. But when, seventeen days after he had vanished, John plunged in again under the stone arch and climbed the steep stone steps to her chamber, he spent no time in trying to find words and speeches that would not come. Having opened the glass of his watch, he just knelt beside her, and said, "*Now*, if you please lady. If you can keep quite still, I will be quick. If only *I* could bear the pain I'd do it three times over, but I promise 'ee it's soon gone." And with his finger he gently smeared the magic unguent on the maid's tail down to the very tip.

Life is full of curiosities, and curious indeed it was though at one moment John's talk to the enchanted creature had seemed to her little better than Double Dutch, and she could do his bidding only by the signs he had made to her, at the next they were chattering together as merrily as if they had done nothing else all their lives. But they did not talk for long, since of a sudden there came the clatter of oars, and presently a skinny hand was thrust over the window-sill, and her daily portion of bread and fruit and water was laid out on the sill. The sound of the Lord Fish's "Halloo!" when he had lowered his basket

into the boat made the blood run cold again in John's body. He waited only until the rap and grinding of the oars had died away. Then he took the maid by the hand, and they went down the stone steps together. There they plunged into the dark water, and presently found themselves breathless but happy beyond words seated together on the green grass bank in the afternoon sunshine. And there came such a chattering and cawing from the rooks and jackdaws over their heads that it seemed as if they were giving thanks to see them there. And when John had shaken out the coat he had left under the tree seventeen days before, brushed off the mildew, and dried it in the sun, he put it over the maid's shoulders.

It was long after dark when they came to Tussock, and not a soul was to be seen in the village street or on the green. John looked in through the window at his mother. She sat alone by the hearthside, staring into the fire, and it seemed to her that she would never get warm again. When John came in and she was clasped in his arms, first she thought she was going to faint, then she began to cry a little, and then to scold him as she had never scolded him before. John dried her tears and hushed her scoldings. And when he had told her a little of his story, he brought the maid in. And John's mother first bobbed her a curtsey, then kissed her and made her welcome. And she listened to John's story all over again from the beginning to the end before they went to bed – though John's bed that night was an old armchair.

Now before the bells of Tussock church – which was a small one and old – rang out a peal for John's and the fish-maid's wedding, he set off as early as ever one morning to climb the wall again. In their haste to be gone from the Sorcerer's mansion she had left her belongings behind her, and particularly, she told John, a leaden box or casket, stamped with a great A – for Almanara; that being her name.

Very warily John stripped again, and, diving quietly, swam in under the stone arch. And lo, safe and sound, in the far corner of the room of all her grief and captivity, stood the leaden casket. But when he stooped to lift it, his troubles began. It was exceedingly heavy, and to swim with it even on his shoulders would be to swim to the bottom! He sat awhile and pondered, and at last climbed up to the stone window, carved curiously with flowers and birds and fish, and looked out. Water lay beneath him in a moat afloat with lilies, though he couldn't tell how deep. But by good fortune a knotted rope hung from a hook in the window-sill – for the use, no doubt, of the Lord Fish in his boat. John hauled the rope in, tied one end of it to the ring in the leaden casket and one to a small wooden stool. At last after long heaving and hoisting he managed to haul the casket on to the sill. He pushed it over, and – as lively as a small pig – away went the stool after it. John clambered up to the window again and again looked out. The stool, still bobbing, floated on the water beneath him. Only a deeper quiet had followed the splash of the casket. So, after he had dragged it out of the moat and on to the bank, John ventured on beyond the walls of the great house in search of the Lord Fish's larder. He dearly wanted to thank the larder-maid again. When at last he found it, it was all shut up and deserted. He climbed up to the window and looked in, but quickly jumped down again, for every fish that hung inside it hung dead as mutton. The little larder-maid was gone. But whether she had first used the magic unguent on the Lord Fish himself and then in dismay of what followed had run away, or whether she had tried it on them both and now was what John couldn't guess, he never knew and could never discover. He grieved not to see her again, and always thought of her with kindness.

Walking and resting, walking and resting, it took him three days, even though he managed to borrow a

wheelbarrow for the last two miles, to get the casket home. But it was worth the trouble. When he managed at last to prise the lid open, it was as though lumps of a frozen rainbow had suddenly spilled over in the kitchen, the casket was crammed so full of precious stones. And after the wedding Almanara had a great J punched into the lead of the box immediately after her great A – since now what it held belonged to them both.

But though John was now married, and not only less idle but as happy as a kingfisher, *still* when the sweet south wind came blowing, and the leaves were green on the trees, and the birds in song, he could not keep his thoughts from hankering after water. So sometimes he made himself a little paste or dug up a few worms, and went off fishing. But he made two rules for himself. First, whenever he hooked anything – and especially a tench – he would always smear a speck or two of the unguent out of his grandfather's silver watch-case on the top of its head; and next, having made sure that his fish was fish, wholly fish, and nothing but fish, he would put it back into the water again. As for the mansion of the Sorcerer, he had made a vow to Almanara and to his mother that he would never go fishing *there*. And he never did.

The Prince with the Nine Sorrows

Laurence Housman

A long time ago there lived a King and a Queen, who had an only son. As soon as he was born his mother gave him to the forester's wife to be nursed; for she herself had to wear her crown all day and had no time for nursing. The forester's wife had just given birth to a little daughter of her own; but she loved both children equally and nursed them together like twins.

One night the Queen had a dream that made the half of her hair turn grey. She dreamed that she saw the Prince her son at the age of twenty lying dead with a wound over the place of his heart; and near him his foster-sister was standing, with a royal crown on her head, and his heart bleeding between her hands.

The next morning the Queen sent in great haste for the family Fairy, and told her of the dream. The Fairy said, "This can have but one meaning, and it is an evil one. There is some danger that threatens your son's life in his twentieth year, and his foster-sister is to be the cause of it; also, it seems she is to make herself Queen. But leave her to me, and I will avert the evil chance; for the dream coming beforehand shows that the Fates mean that he should be saved."

The Queen said, "Do anything; only do not destroy the forester's wife's child, for, as yet at least, she has done

no wrong. Let her only be carried away to a safe place and made secure and treated well. I will not have my son's happiness grow out of another one's grave."

The Fairy said, "Nothing is so safe as a grave when the Fates are about. Still, I think I can make everything quite safe within reason, and leave you a clean as well as a quiet conscience."

The little Prince and the forester's daughter grew up together till they were a year old; then, one day, when their nurse came to look for them, the Prince was found, but his foster-sister was lost; and though the search for her was long, she was never seen again, nor could any trace of her be found.

The baby Prince pined and pined, and was so sorrowful over her loss that they feared for a time that he was going to die. But his foster-mother, in spite of her grief over her own child's disappearance, nursed him so well and loved him so much that after a while he re-covered his strength.

Then the forester's wife gave birth to another daughter, as if to console herself for the loss of the first. But the same night that the child was born the Queen had just the same dream over again. She dreamed that she saw her son lying dead at the age of twenty; and there was the wound in his breast, and the forester's daughter was standing by with his heart in her hand and a royal crown upon her head.

The poor Queen's hair had gone quite white when she sent again for the family Fairy, and told her how the dream had repeated itself. The Fairy gave her the same advice as before, quieting her fears, and assuring her that however persistent the Fates might be in threatening the Prince's life, all in the end should be well.

Before another year was passed the second of the forester's daughters had disappeared; and the Prince and his foster-mother cried themselves ill over a loss that had

been so cruelly renewed. The Queen, seeing how great were the sorrow and the love that the Prince bore for his foster-sisters, began to doubt in her heart and say, "What have I done? Have I saved my son's life by taking away his heart?"

Now every year the same thing took place, the forester's wife giving birth to a daughter, and the Queen on the same night having the same fearful dream of the fate that threatened her son in his twentieth year; and afterwards the family Fairy would come, and then one day the forester's wife's child would disappear, and be heard of no more.

At last when nine daughters in all had been born to the forester's wife and lost to her when they were but a year old, the Queen fell very ill. Every day she grew weaker and weaker, and the little Prince came and sat by her, holding her hand and looking at her with a sorrowful face. At last one night (it was just a year after the last of the forester's children had disappeared) she woke suddenly, stretching out her arms and crying. "Oh, Fairy," she cried, "the dream, the dream!" And covering her face with her hands, she died.

The little Prince was now more than ten years old, and the very saddest of mortals. He said that there were nine sorrows hidden in his heart, of which he could not get rid; and that at night, when all the birds went home to roost, he heard cries of lamentation and pain; but whether these came from very far away, or out of his own heart he could not tell.

Yet he grew slenderly and well, and had such grace and tenderness in his nature that all who saw him loved him. His foster-mother, when he spoke to her of his nine sorrows, tried to comfort him, calling him her own nine joys; and, indeed, he was all the joy left in life for her.

When the Prince neared his twentieth year, the King his father felt that he himself was becoming old and

weary of life. "I shall not live much longer," he thought: "very soon my son will be left alone in the world. It is right, therefore, now that he should know of the danger ahead that threatens his life." For till then the Prince had not known anything; all had been kept a secret between the Queen and the King and the family Fairy.

The old King knew of the Prince's nine sorrows, and often he tried to believe that they came by chance, and had nothing to do with the secret that sat at the root of his son's life. But now he feared more and more to tell the Prince the story of those nine dreams, lest the knowledge should indeed serve but as the crowning point of his sorrows, and altogether break his heart for him.

Yet there was so much danger in leaving the thing untold that at last he summoned the Prince to his bedside, meaning to tell him all. The King had worn himself so ill with anxiety and grief in thinking over the matter, that now to tell all was the only means of saving his life.

The Prince came and knelt down, and leaned his head on his father's pillow; and the King whispered into his ear the story of the dreams, and of how for his sake all the Prince's foster-sisters had been spirited away.

Before his tale was done he could no longer bear to look into his son's face, but closed his eyes, and, with long silences between, spoke as one who prayed.

When he had ended he lay quite still, and the Prince kissed his closed eyelids and went softly out of the room.

"Now I know," he said to himself; "now at last!" And he came through the wood and knocked at his foster-mother's door. "Other mother," he said to her, "give me a kiss for each of my sisters, for now I am going out into the world to find them, to be rid of the sorrows in my heart."

"They can never be found!" she cried, but she kissed him nine times. "And this," she said, "was Monica, and this was Ponica, and this was Veronica," and she went

over every name. "But now they are only names!" she
wept, as she let him go.

He went along, and he went along, mile after mile.
"Where may you be going to, fair sir?" asked an old
peasant, at whose cabin the Prince sought shelter when
night came to the first day of his wanderings. "Truly,"
answered the Prince, "I do not know how far or whither I
need to go; but I have a finger-post in my heart that keeps
pointing me."

So that night he stayed there, and the next day he went
on.

"Where to so fast?" asked a woodcutter when the
second night found him in the thickest and loneliest parts
of the forest. "Here the night is so dark and the way so
dangerous, one like you should not go alone."

"Nay, I know nothing," said the Prince, "only I feel
like a weather-cock in a wind that keeps turning me to its
will!"

After many days he came to a small long valley rich in
woods and water-courses, but no road ran through it.
More and more it seemed like the world's end, a place
unknown, or forgotten of its old inhabitants. Just at the
end of the valley, where the woods opened into clear
slopes and hollows towards the west, he saw before him,
low and overgrown, the walls of a little tumble-down
grange. "There," he said to himself when he saw it, "I can
find shelter for tonight. Never have I felt so tired before,
or such a pain at my heart!"

Before long he came to a little gate, and a winding path
that led in among lawns and trees to the door of an old
house. The house seemed as if it had been once lived in,
but there was no sign of any life about it now. He pushed
open the door, and suddenly there was a sharp rustling of
feathers, and nine white peahens rose up from the ground
and flew out of the window into the garden.

The Prince searched the whole house over, and found it

a mere ruin; the only signs of life to be seen were the white feathers that lifted and blew about over the floors.

Outside, the garden was gathering itself together in the dusk, and the peahens were stepping daintily about the lawns, picking here and there between the blades of grass. They seemed to suit the gentle sadness of the place, which had an air of grief that has grown at ease with itself.

The Prince went out into the garden, and walked about among the quietly stepping birds; but they took no heed of him. They came picking up their food between his very feet, as though he were not there. Silence held all the air, and in the cleft of the valley the day drooped to its end.

Just before it grew dark, the nine white peahens gathered together at the foot of a great elm, and lifting up their throats they wailed in chorus. Their lamentable cry touched the Prince's heart: "Where," he asked himself, "have I heard such sorrow before?" Then all with one accord the birds sprang rustling up to the lowest boughs of the elm, and settled themselves to roost.

The Prince went back to the house, to find some corner amid its half-ruined rooms to sleep in. But there the air was close, and an unpleasant smell of moisture came from the floor and walls: so, the night being warm, he returned to the garden, and folding himself in his cloak lay down under the tree where the nine peahens were at roost.

For a long time he tried to sleep, but could not, there was so much pain and sorrow in his heart.

Presently when it was close upon midnight, over his head one of the birds stirred and ruffled through all its feathers; and he heard a soft voice say:

"Sisters, are you awake?"

All the other peahens lifted their heads, and turned towards the one that had spoken, saying, "Yes, sister, we are awake."

Then the first one said again, "Our brother is here."

They all said, "He is our enemy; it is for him that we endure this sorrow."

"Tonight," said the first, "we may all be free."

They answered, "Yes, we may all be free! Who will go down and peck out his heart? Then we shall be free."

And the first who had spoken said, "I will go down!"

"Do not fail, sister!" said all the others. "For if you fail you can speak to us no more."

The first peahen answered, "Do not fear that I shall fail!" And she began stepping down the long boughs of the elm.

The Prince lying below heard all that was said. "Ah! poor sisters," he thought, "have I found you at last; and are all these sorrows brought upon you for me?" And he unloosed his doublet, and opened his vest, making his breast bare for the peahen to come and peck out his heart.

He lay quite still with his eyes shut, and when she reached the ground the peahen found him lying there, as it seemed to her fast asleep, with his white breast bare for the stroke of her beak.

Then so fair he looked to her, and so gentle in his youth, that she had pity on him, and stood weeping by his side, and laying her head against his, whispered, "O, brother, once we lay as babes together and were nursed at the same breast! How can I peck out your heart?"

Then she stole softly back into the tree, and crouched down again by her companions. They said to her, "Our minute of midnight is nearly gone. Is there blood on your beak! Have you our brother's heart for us?" But the other answered never a word.

In the morning the peahens came rustling down out of the elm, and went searching for fat carnation buds and anemone seeds among the flower-beds in the garden. To the Prince they showed no sign either of hatred or fear, but went to and fro carelessly, pecking at the ground about his feet. Only one came with drooping head and

wings, and sleeked itself to his caress, and the Prince, stooping down, whispered in her ear, "O sister, why did you not peck out my heart?"

At night, as before, the peahens all cried in chorus as they went up into the elm; and the Prince came and wrapped himself in his cloak, and lay down at the foot of it to watch.

At midnight the eight peahens lifted their heads, and said, "Sister, why did you fail last night?" But their sister gave them not a word.

"Alas!" they said, "now she has failed, unless one of us succeed, we shall never hear her speak with her human voice again. Why is it that you weep so," they said again, "now when deliverance is so near?" For the poor peahen was shaken with weeping, and her tears fell down in loud drops upon the ground.

Then the next sister said, "I will go down! He is asleep. Be certain, I will not fail!" So she climbed softly down the tree, and the Prince opened his shirt and laid his breast bare for her to come and take out his heart.

Presently she stood by his side, and when she saw him, she too had pity on him for the youth and kindness of his face. And at once she shut her eyes, and lifted her head for the stroke; but then weakness seized her, and she laid her head softly upon his heart and said, "Once the breast that gave me milk gave milk also to you. You were my sister's brother, and she spared you. How can I peck out your heart?" And having said this she went softly back into the tree, and crouched down again among her sisters.

They said to her, "Have you blood upon your beak? Is his heart ours?" But she answered them no word.

The next day the two sisters, who because their hearts betrayed them had become mute, followed the Prince wherever he went, and stretched up their heads to his caress. But the others went and came indifferently, careless except for food; for until midnight their human

hearts were asleep; only now the two sisters who had given their voices away had regained their human hearts perpetually.

That night the same thing happened as before. "Sisters," said the youngest, "tonight I will go down, since the two eldest of us have failed. My wrong is fresher in my heart than theirs! Be sure I shall not fail!" So the youngest peahen came down from the tree, and the Prince laid his heart bare for her beak; but the bird could not find the will to peck it out. And so it was the next night, and the next, until eight nights were gone.

So at last only one peahen was left. At midnight she raised her head, saying, "Sisters, are you awake?"

They all turned, and gazed at her weeping, but could say no word.

Then she said, "You have all failed, having all tried but me. Now if I fail we shall remain mute and captive for ever, more undone by the loss of our last remaining gift of speech than we were at first. But I tell you, dear sisters, I will not fail; for the happiness of you all lies with me now!"

Then she went softly down the tree; and one by one they all went following her, and weeping, to see what the end would be.

They stood some way apart, watching with upturned heads, and their poor throats began catching back a wish to cry as the little peahen, the last of the sisters, came and stood by the Prince.

Then she, too, looked in his face, and saw the white breast made bare for her beak; and the love of him went deep down into her heart. And she tried and tried to shut her eyes and deal the stroke, but could not.

She trembled and sighed, and turned to look at her sisters, where they all stood weeping silently together. "They have spared him," she said to herself: "why should not I?"

But the Prince, seeing that she, too, was about to fail like the rest of them, turned and said, as if in his sleep, "Come, come, little peahen, and peck out my heart!"

At that she turned back again to him, and laid her head down upon his heart and cried more sadly than them all.

Then he said, "You have eight sisters, and a mother who cries for her children to return!" Yet still she thought he was dreaming, and speaking only in his sleep. The other peahens came no nearer, but stood weeping silently. She looked from him to them. "O," she cried, "I have a wicked heart, to let one stand in the way of nine!" Then she threw up her neck and cried lamentably with her peafowl's voice, wishing that the Prince would wake up and see her, and so escape. And at that all the other peahens lifted up their heads and wailed with her: but the Prince never turned, nor lifted a finger, nor uttered a sound.

Then she drew in a deep breath, and closed her eyes fast.

"Let my sisters go, but let me be as I am!" she cried; and with that she stooped down, and pecked out his heart.

All her sisters shrieked as their human shapes returned to them. "Oh, sister! O, wicked little sister!" they cried. "What have you done?"

The little white peahen crouched close down to the side of the dead Prince. "I loved him more than you all!" she tried to say: but she only lifted her head, and wailed again and again the peafowl's cry.

The Prince's heart lay beating at her feet, so glad to be rid of its nine sorrows that mere joy made it live on, though all the rest of the body lay cold.

The peahen leaned down upon the Prince's breast, and there wailed without ceasing: then suddenly, piercing with her beak her own breast, she drew out her own living heart and laid it in the place where his had been.

And, as she did so, the wound where she had pierced him closed and became healed; and her heart was, as it

were, buried in the Prince's breast. In her death agony she could feel it there, her own heart leaping within his breast for joy.

The Prince, who had seemed to be dead, flushed from head to foot as the warmth of life came back to him; with one deep breath he woke, and found the little white peahen lying as if dead between his arms.

Then he laughed softly and rose (his goodness making him wise), and taking up his own still beating heart he laid it into the place of hers. At the first beat of it within her breast, the peahen became transformed as all her sisters had been, and her own human form came back to her. And the pain and the wound in her breast grew healed together, so that she stood up alive and well in the Prince's arms.

"Dear heart!" said he: and "Dear, dear heart!" said she; but whether they were speaking of their own hearts or of each other's, who can tell? for which was which they themselves did not know.

Then all round was so much embracing and happiness that it is out of reach for tongue or pen to describe. For truly the Prince and his foster-sisters loved each other well, and could put no bounds upon their present contentment. As for the Prince and the one who had plucked out his heart, of no two was the saying ever more truly told that they had lost their hearts to each other; nor was ever love in the world known before that carried with it such harmony as theirs.

And so it all came about according to the Queen's dream, that the forester's daughter wore the royal crown upon her head, and held the Prince's heart in her hand.

Long before he died the old King was made happy because the dream he had so much feared had become true. And the forester's wife was happy before she died. And as for the Prince and his wife and his foster-sisters, they were all rather happy; and none of them is dead yet.

The Great Quillow

James Thurber

Once upon a time, in a far country, there lived a giant
named Hunder. He was so enormous in height and girth
and weight that little waves were set in motion in distant
lakes when he walked. His great fingers could wrench a
clock from its steeple as easily as a child might remove a
peanut from its shell. Every morning he devoured three
sheep, a pie made of a thousand apples, and a chocolate as
high and as wide as a spinning wheel. It would have taken
six ordinary men to lift the great brass key to his front
door, and four to carry one of the candles with which he
lighted his house.

It was Hunder's way to strip a town of its sheep and
apples and chocolate, its leather and cloth, its lumber and
tallow and brass, and then move on to a new village and
begin his depredations again. There had been no men
strong enough to thwart his evil ways in any of the towns
he had set upon and impoverished. He had broken their
most formidable weapons between his thumb and forefinger, laughing like the hurricane. And there had been no
men cunning enough in any of the towns to bring about
his destruction. He had crushed their most ingenious
traps with the toe of his mammoth boot, guffawing like a
volcano.

One day Hunder strode hundreds and hundreds of

leagues and came to a little town in a green valley. It was a staunch little town and a firm little valley, but they quaked with the sound of his coming. The houses were narrow and two stories high; the streets were narrow and cobbled. There were not many people in the town: a hundred men, a hundred women, a hundred children.

Every Tuesday night at seven o'clock a council of ten met to administer the simple affairs of the community. The councillors were the most important tradesmen and artisans of New Moon Street, a short, narrow, cobbled street that ran east and west. These men were the tailor, the butcher, the candymaker, the blacksmith, the baker, the candlemaker, the lamplighter, the cobbler, the carpenter, and the locksmith. After the small business of the tranquil town had been taken care of, the council members sat around and speculated as to the number of stars in the sky, discussed the wonderful transparency of glass, and praised the blueness of violets and the whiteness of snow. Then they made a little fun of Quillow, the toymaker (whose work they considered a rather pretty waste of time), and went home.

Quillow, the toymaker, did not belong to the council but he attended all its meetings. The councilmen were fond of Quillow because of the remarkable toys he made, and because he was a droll and gentle fellow. Quillow made all kinds of familiar playthings on his long and littered workbench: music boxes, jumping jacks, building blocks; but he was famous for a number of little masterpieces of his own invention: a clown who juggled three marbles, a woodman who could actually chop wood, a trumpeter who could play seven notes of a song on a tiny horn, a paperweight in which roses burst into bloom in falling snow.

Quillow was as amusing to look at as any of his toys. He was the shortest man in town, being only five feet tall. His ears were large, his nose was long, his mouth was

small, and he had a shock of white hair that stood straight up like a dandelion clock. The lapels of his jacket were wide. He wore a red tie in a deep-pointed collar, and his pantaloons were baggy and unpressed. At Christmas time each year Quillow made little hearts of gold for the girls of the town and hearts of oak for the boys. He considered himself something of a civic figure, since he had designed the spouting dolphins in the town fountain, the wooden animals on the town merry-go-round, and the twelve scarlet men who emerged from the dial of the town clock on the stroke of every hour and played a melody on little silver bells with little silver hammers.

It was the custom of Quillow's colleagues to shout merrily, "Why, here comes the Great Quillow!" when the toy-maker appeared. The lamplighter or the tailor or the locksmith would sometimes creep up behind him and pretend to wind a key in his back as if he were a mechanical figure of his own devising. Quillow took all this in good part, and always, when the imaginary key in his back was turned, he would walk about stiff-legged, with jerky movements of his arms, joining in the fun and increasing laughter.

It was different on the day the giant arrived. Laughter was hushed and the people hid in their houses and talked in frightened whispers when Hunder's great bulk appeared like a cyclone in the sky and the earth shook beneath him. Panting a little after his thousand-league walk, Hunder pulled up four trees from a hillside to make room for his great hulk, and sat down. Hunder surveyed the town and grunted. There was no one to be seen in the street. Not even a cat crept over the cobblestones.

"Ho, town!" bawled Hunder. The doors shook and the windows rattled. "Ho, town! Send me your clerk that you may hear Hunder's will!"

The town clerk gathered up quill and ink and

parchment. "There are ninety-nine other men in town," he grumbled, "but it's the town clerk this, and the town clerk that, and the town clerk everything." He walked out of his house, still grumbling, and trudged across the valley to hear the giant's will.

An hour later the town clerk sat at the head of a long table in the council room and began to call the roll. "We're all here," snapped the blacksmith. "You can see that."

The clerk continued with the roll call.

"Baker," he called. "Here," said the baker. "Blacksmith," he droned. "Here," said the blacksmith sourly.

The clerk finished calling the roll and looked over his spectacles. "We have a visitor tonight, as usual," he said, "Quillow, the toymaker. I will make the proper entry in the minutes."

"Never mind the minutes," said the blacksmith. "Read us the demands of Hunder the giant."

The clerk entered Quillow's name in the minutes.

"Now," he said, "I will read the minutes of the last meeting."

The candymaker stood up. "Let's dispense with the minutes of the last meeting," he said.

The clerk looked over his spectacles. "It must be properly moved and duly seconded," he said. It was properly moved and duly seconded. "Now read the demands of Hunder the giant!" shouted the blacksmith.

The clerk rapped on the table with his gavel. "Next," he said, "comes unfinished business. We have before us a resolution to regulate the speed of merry-go-rounds."

"Dispense with it!" bawled the blacksmith.

"It must be properly moved and duly seconded," said the clerk. It was properly moved and duly seconded and the clerk at last unrolled a long scroll of parchment. "We come now," he said, "to the business of the day. I have here the demands of Hunder the giant. The document is

most irregular. It does not contain a single 'greeting' or 'whereas' or 'be it known by these presents'!"

Everyone sat motionless as the clerk began to read the scroll. "I, Hunder, must have three sheep every morning," he read.

"That would use up all the sheep in the valley in a week and a fortnight," said the butcher, "and there would be no mutton for our own people."

"I, Hunder, must have a chocolate a day as high and as wide as a spinning wheel," read the town clerk.

"Why, that would exhaust all the chocolate in my storeroom in three days!" cried the candymaker.

The town clerk read from the parchment again. "I, Hunder, must have a new jerkin made for me in a week and a fortnight."

"Why, I would have to work night and day to make a jerkin in a week and a fortnight for so large a giant," gasped the tailor, "and it would use up all the cloth on my shelves and in my basement."

"I, Hunder," went on the town clerk, "must have a new pair of boots within a week and a fortnight."

The cobbler moaned as he heard this. "Why, I would have to work night and day to make a pair of boots for so large a giant in a week and a fortnight," he said. "And it would use up all the leather in my workshop and in my back room."

The council members shook their heads sadly as each demand was read off by the town clerk. Quillow had folded his arms and crossed his legs and shut his eyes. He was thinking, but he looked like a sleeping toy.

"I, Hunder," droned the town clerk, "must have an apple pie each morning made of a thousand apples."

The baker jumped from his chair. "Why, that would use up all the apples and flour and shortening in town in a week and a fortnight," he cried. "And it would take me night and day to make such a pie, so that I could bake no

more pies or cakes or cookies, or blueberry muffins or cinnamon buns or cherry boats or strawberry tarts or plum puddings for the people of the town."

All of the councilmen moaned sadly because they loved the list of good things the baker had recited. Quillow still sat with his eyes closed.

"I, Hunder," went on the town clerk, "must have a house to live in by the time a week and a fortnight have passed."

The carpenter wept openly. "Why, I would have to work night and day to build a house for so large a giant in a week and a fortnight," sobbed the carpenter. "All my nephews and uncles and cousins would have to help me, and it would use up all the wood and pegs and hinges and glass in my shop and in the countryside."

The locksmith stood up and shook his fist in the direction of the hillside on which the giant lay snoring. "I will have to work night and day to make a brass key large enough to fit the keyhole in the front door of the house of so large a giant," he said. "It will use up all the brass in my shop and in the community."

"And I will have to make a candle for his bedside so large it will use up all the wick and tallow in my shop and the world!" said the candlemaker.

"This is the final item," said the town clerk. "I, Hunder, must be told a tale each day to keep me amused."

Quillow opened his eyes and raised his hand. "I will be the teller of tales," he said. "I will keep the giant amused."

The town clerk put away his scroll.

"Does anyone have any idea of how to destroy the giant Hunder?" asked the candymaker.

"I could creep up on him in the dark and set fire to him with my lighter," said the lamplighter.

Quillow looked at him. "The fire of your lighter

would not harm him any more than a spark struck by a colt-shoe in a meadow," said Quillow.

"Quillow is right," said the blacksmith. "But I could build secretly at night an enormous catapult which would cast a gigantic stone and crush Hunder."

Quillow shook his head. "He would catch the stone as a child catches a ball," said Quillow, "and he would cast it back at the town and squash all our homes."

"I could put needles in his suit," said the tailor.

"I could put nails in his boots," said the cobbler.

"I could put oil in his chocolates," said the candy-maker.

"I could put stones in his mutton," said the butcher.

"I could put tacks in his pies," said the baker.

"I could put gunpowder in his candles," said the candlemaker.

"I could make the handle of his brass key as sharp as a sword," said the locksmith.

"I could build the roof of his house insecurely so that it would fall on him," said the carpenter.

"The plans you suggest," said Quillow, "would merely annoy Hunder as the gadfly annoys the horse and the flea annoys the dog."

"Perhaps the Great Quillow has a plan of his own," said the blacksmith with a scornful laugh.

"Has the Great Quillow a plan?" asked the candy-maker, with a faint sneer.

The little toymaker did not answer. The councillors got up and filed slowly and sadly from the council room. That night none of them wound the imaginary key in Quillow's back.

Quillow did not leave the council chamber for a long time, and when he walked through New Moon Street, all the shops of the councilmen were brightly lighted and noisily busy. There was a great ringing and scraping and thumping and rustling. The blacksmith was helping the

locksmith make the great brass key for Hunder's house.
The carpenter was sawing and planing enormous boards.
The baker was shaping the crust for a gigantic pie, and his
wife and apprentice were peeling a thousand apples. The
butcher was dressing the first of the three sheep. The
tailor was cutting the cloth for Hunder's jerkin. The
cobbler was fitting together mammoth pieces of leather
for Hunder's boots. The candymaker was piling all his
chocolate upon his largest table, while his wife and his
daughter made soft filling in great kettles. The
candlemaker had begun to build the monumental candle
for Hunder's bedside.

As Quillow reached the door of his shop, the town
clock in its steeple began to strike, the moon broke out of
a patch of cloud, and the toymaker stood with his hand on
the door latch to watch the twelve little men in scarlet
hats and jackets and pantaloons emerge, each from his
own numeral, to make the night melodious with the
sound of their silver hammers on the silver bells of the
round white dial.

Inside his shop, Quillow lighted the green-shaded
lamp over his workbench, which was littered with odds
and ends and beginnings and middles of all kinds of toys.
Working swiftly with his shining tools, Quillow began
to make a figure eight inches high out of wire and cloth
and leather and wood. When it was finished it looked like
a creature you might come upon hiding behind a tulip or
playing with toads. It had round eyes, a round nose and a
wide mouth, and no hair. It was blue from head to foot.
Its face was blue, its jacket was blue, its pantaloons were
blue, and its feet were blue.

As Quillow stood examining the toy, the lamplighter
stuck his head in the door without knocking, stared for a
moment, and went away. Quillow smiled with satisfac-
tion and began to make another blue man. By the time
the first cock crowed he had made ten blue men and put

them away in a long wooden chest with a heavy iron clasp.

The lamplighter turned out the last street light, the sun rose, the crickets stopped calling and the clock struck five. Disturbed by the changing pattern of light and sound, the giant on the hillside turned in his sleep. Around a corner into New Moon Street tiptoed the town crier. "Sh!" he said to the lamplighter. "Don't wake the giant."

"Sh!" said the lamplighter. "His food may not be ready."

The town crier stood in the cobbled street and called softly, "Five o'clock and all's well!"

All the doors in New Moon Street except Quillow's flew open.

"The pie is baked," said the baker.

"The chocolate is made," said the candymaker.

"The sheep are dressed," said the butcher.

"I worked all night on the great brass key," said the locksmith, "and the blacksmith helped me with his hammer and anvil."

"I have scarcely begun the enormous candle," said the candlemaker.

"I am weary of sawing and planing," said the carpenter.

"My fingers are already stiff," said the tailor, "and I have just started the giant's jerkin."

"My eyes are tired," said the cobbler, "and I have hardly begun to make his boots."

The sun shone full on the giant's face, and he woke up and yawned loudly. The councillors jumped, and a hundred children hid in a hundred closets.

"Ho!" roared Hunder. It was the sign the blacksmith had waited for. He drove his wagon drawn by four horses into New Moon Street and climbed down.

"Ho!" roared the giant.

"Heave," grunted the councillors as they lifted the sheep on to the wagon.

"Ho!" roared the giant.

"Heave," grunted the councillors, and up went the pie.

"Ho!" roared the giant.

"Heave," grunted the councillors, and they set the great chocolate in place.

Hunder watched the loading of the wagon, licking his lips and growling like a cave full of bulldogs.

The councillors climbed up on the wagon and the blacksmith yelled "Giddap!", and then "Whoa!" He glared about him. "Where is Quillow?" he demanded. "Where is that foolish little fellow?"

"He was in his shop at midnight," said the lamplighter, "making toys."

The nine other councillors snorted.

"He could have helped with the key," said the locksmith.

"The pie," said the baker.

"The sheep," said the butcher.

"The boots," said the cobbler.

At this Quillow bounced out of his shop like a bird from a clock, bowing and smiling.

"Well!" snarled the blacksmith.

"Ho!" roared Hunder.

"Good morning," said Quillow. He climbed up on the wagon and the blacksmith spoke to each horse in turn. (Their names were Lobo, Bolo, Olob, and Obol.)

"I worked all night with my hammer and anvil," said the blacksmith as the horses lurched ahead, "helping the locksmith with the great brass key." He scowled at Quillow. "The lamplighter tells us you spent the night making toys."

"Making toys," said Quillow cheerily, "and thinking up a tale to amuse the giant Hunder."

The blacksmith snorted. "And a hard night you must have spent hammering out your tale."

"And twisting it," said the locksmith.

"And levelling it," said the carpenter.

"And rolling it out," said the baker.

"And stitching it up," said the tailor.

"And fitting it together," said the cobbler.

"And building it around a central thread," said the candlemaker.

"And dressing it up," said the butcher.

"And making it not too bitter and not too sweet," said the candymaker.

When the wagon came to a stop at Hunder's feet, the giant clapped his hands, and Quillow and the councillors were blown to the ground. Hunder roared with laughter and unloaded the wagon in half a trice.

"Tell me your silly names," said Hunder, "and what you do."

The new slaves of Hunder, all except Quillow, bowed in turn and told the giant who they were and what they did. Quillow remained silent.

"You, smallest of men, you with the white hair, who are you?" demanded Hunder.

"I am Quillow, the teller of tales," said the toymaker, but unlike the others he did not bow to the giant.

"Bow!" roared Hunder.

"Wow!" shouted Quillow.

The councillors started back in dismay at the toymaker's impertinence, their widening eyes on Hunder's mighty hands, which closed and then slowly opened. The black scowl cleared from the giant's brow and he laughed suddenly.

"You are a fairly droll fellow," he said. "Perhaps your tales will amuse me. If they do not, I will put you in the palm of my hand and blow you so far it will take men five

days to find you. Now be off to your work, the rest of you!"

As the wagon carried the frightened councillors back to town, Quillow sat on the ground and watched the giant eat a sheep as an ordinary man might eat a lark. "Now," said Hunder, "tell me a tale."

"Once upon a time," began Quillow, crossing his legs and tickling a cricket with a blade of grass, "a giant came to our town from a thousand leagues away, stepping over the hills and rivers. He was so mighty a giant that he could stamp upon the ground with his foot and cause the cows in the fields to turn flip-flops in the air and land on their feet again."

"Garf," growled Hunder, "I can stamp upon the ground with my foot and empty a lake of its water."

"I have no doubt of that, O Hunder," said Quillow, "for the thunder is your plaything and the mountains are your stool. But the giant who came over the hills and rivers many and many a year ago was a lesser giant than Hunder. He was weak. He fell ill of a curious malady. He was forced to run to the ocean and bathe in the yellow waters, for only the yellow waters in the middle of the sea could cure the giant."

"Rowf," snarled Hunder, picking up another sheep. "That giant was a goose, that giant was a grasshopper. Hunder is never sick." The giant smote his chest and then his stomach mighty blows without flinching, to show how strong he was.

"This other giant," said Quillow, "had no ailment of the chest or the stomach or the mouth or the ears or the eyes or the arms or the legs."

"Where else can a giant have an ailment?" demanded Hunder.

Quillow looked dreamily across the green valley toward the town, which was bright in the sun. "In the mind," said Quillow, "for the mind is a strange and

intricate thing. In lesser men than Hunder, it is subject to mysterious maladies."

"Wumf," said the giant, beginning his third sheep. "Hunder's mind is strong like the rock." He smote himself heavily across the forehead without wincing.

"No one to this day knows what brought on this dreadful disease in the mind of the other giant," said Quillow. "Perhaps he killed a turtle after sundown, or ran clockwise thrice around a church in the dark of the moon, or slept too close to a field of asphodel."

Hunder picked up the pie and began to devour it. "Did this goose, this grasshopper, have pains in his head?" he asked. "Look, teller of tales!" Hunder banged his head savagely against a tree and the trunk of the tree snapped in two. The giant grinned, showing his jagged teeth.

"This other giant," said Quillow, "suffered no pain. His symptoms were marvellous and dismaying. First he heard the word. For fifteen minutes one morning, beginning at a quarter of six, he heard the word."

"Harumph!" said Hunder, finishing his pie and reaching for his chocolate. "What was the word the giant heard for fifteen minutes one day?"

"The word was 'woddly'," said Quillow. "All words were one word to him. All words were 'woddly'."

"All words are different to Hunder," said the giant. "And do you call this a tale you have told me? A blithering goose of a giant hears a word and you call that a tale to amuse Hunder?"

Quillow arose as the clock in the steeple struck six and the scarlet figures came out to play the silver bells.

"I hear all words," said Hunder. "This is a good chocolate; otherwise I should put you in the palm of my hand and blow you over the housetops."

"I shall bring you a better tale tomorrow," said Quillow. "Meanwhile, be sure to see the first star over

your left shoulder, do not drink facing downstream, and always sleep with your heart to the east."

"Why should Hunder practise this foolish rigmarole?" asked the giant.

"No one knows to this day," said Quillow, "what caused the weird illness in the mind of the other giant." But Hunder gave only a murmurous growl in reply, for he had lain down again on the hillside and closed his eyes. Quillow smiled as he saw that the giant lay with his heart to the east.

The toymaker spent the day making twenty more little blue men and when the first owl hooted he stood in the doorway of his shop and whistled. The hundred children collected in the cobbled street before the toyshop from every nook and corner and cranny and niche of the town. "Go to your homes," said Quillow, "each Sue and John of you, each Nora and Joe, and tell your fathers and mothers to come to the merry-go-round in the carnival grounds one quarter-hour before the moon comes over the hill. Say that Quillow has a plan to destroy the giant Hunder."

The group of children broke like the opening of a rose and the cobbled streets rang with the sound of their running.

Even the scowling blacksmith, the scornful lamplighter, the mumbling town crier, and the fussy town clerk (who had spent the day searching for an ancient treaty the people of the town had once signed with a giant) came at the appointed hour to hear what Quillow had to say.

"What is this clown's whim that brings us here like sheep?" demanded the blacksmith.

Quillow climbed up on the merry-go-round, sat on a swan, and spoke. At first there was a restless stir like wind in the grass, but as Quillow explained his plan, even the chattering wives fell silent. Quillow finished speaking as

the moon peeped over the hill, and the hundred men and the hundred women and the hundred children straggled away from the carnival grounds.

"It will never work," said the lamplighter.

"It is worth trying," said the candymaker.

"I have a better plan," said the town crier. "Let all the women and the children stand in the streets and gaze sorrowfully at the giant, and perhaps he will go away.

His wife took him by the arm and led him home. "We will try Quillow's plan," she said. "He has a magic, the little man."

The next morning, just as the clock in the steeple struck five, the weary blacksmith, with Quillow sitting beside him, drove the wagon loaded with three sheep and a fresh apple pie and another monster chocolate to where the giant sat on the hillside. Hunder unloaded the wagon in a third of a trice, placed the food beside him on the hill, and began to gnaw at a sheep. "Tell me a tale, smallest of men," he said, "and see to it that I do not nod, or I shall put you in the palm of my hand and blow you through yonder cloud."

"Once upon a time," began Quillow, "there was a king named Anderblusdaferafan, and he had three sons named Ufabrodoborobe, Quamdelrodolanderay, and Tristolcomofarasee."

"Those are hard names," said Hunder. "Tell me those names again that I may remember them." So Quillow started over slowly with "Once upon a time," and again the giant made him repeat the names.

"Why did this king and his sons have such long and difficult names?" demanded Hunder, eating his second sheep.

"Ah," said Quillow, "it was because of the king's mother, whose name was Isoldasadelofandaloo."

"Tell me her name once more," said Hunder, "that I

may remember it." So Quillow told him the name again slowly.

Thus the wily Quillow, who really had thought of no tale to tell, wasted the long minutes as the hands of the clock in the steeple crept around the dial. As they neared a quarter to six o'clock, Quillow went on. "One day as the king and his sons were riding through the magical forest," he said, "they came upon a woddly. Woddly woddly woddly. Woddly woddly woddly."

The giant's eyes grew narrow, then wide.

"Woddly woddly woddly," said Quillow, "woddly woddly woddly woddly."

The giant dropped the chocolate he was eating. "Say it with words!" he bellowed. "You say naught but 'woddly'".

Quillow looked surprised. "Woddly woddly woddly woddly woddly woddly woddly woddly," he said. "Woddly woddly woddly."

"Can this be the malady come upon me?" cried the giant. He caught the toymaker up in his hand. "Or do you seek to frighten Hunder?" he roared.

"Woddly woddly woddly," said Quillow, trembling in spite of himself, as he pointed to a farmer in a field and to a child gathering cowslips and to the town crier making his rounds. "Woddly woddly woddly," repeated Quillow.

The giant dropped Quillow and arose. He strode to where the farmer stood and picked him up. "Say words!" bawled Hunder. "Say many words!"

"Woddly," said the farmer, and Hunder dropped him in the field and turned to the child.

"What is your name?" roared Hunder.

"Woddly woddly," said the child.

Hunder stepped over to the town crier. "What is the time of day?" he bellowed.

"Woddly woddly," said the town crier.

Then Hunder shouted questions at men and women and children who came running into the streets. He asked them how old they were, and what day it was, and where they were going, and how they were feeling. And they said "Woddly" and "Woddly woddly" and "Woddly woddly woddly."

Hunder strode across the green valley to where Quillow sat brushing flies off the half-eaten chocolate. "It is the malady! I have heard the word! It is the malady!" cried Hunder. "What am I to do to cure the malady?"

Just then the clock in the steeple struck six, and as the scarlet men came out to play the bells, Quillow spoke reproachfully. "I was telling you how the king and his three sons rode through the magical forest," he said, "when you picked me up and flung me to the earth and ran away, leaving your chocolate uneaten."

The giant sat on the ground, panting heavily, his lower teeth showing. "I heard the word," he said. "All men said the word."

"What word?" asked Quillow.

"Woddly," said the giant.

"That is but the first symptom," said Quillow reassuringly, "and it has passed. Look at the chimneys of the town. Are they not red?"

Hunder looked. "Yes, the chimneys are red," said Hunder. "Why do you ask if the chimneys are red?"

"So long as the chimneys are red," said Quillow, "you have no need to worry, for when the second symptom is upon you, the chimneys of the town turn black."

"I see only red chimneys," said the giant. "But what could have caused Hunder to hear the word?" he asked as he hurled the half-eaten chocolate far away over the roofs of the town.

"Perhaps," said Quillow, "you stepped on a centaur's grave or waked the sleeping unicorn or whistled on Saint Nillin's Day."

Hunder the giant rested badly on the hillside that night, twisting and turning in his sleep, tormented by ominous dreams. While he slept, the youngest and most agile men of the town, in black smocks and slippered feet, climbed to the roofs of the houses and shops, each carrying a full pail and a brush, and painted all the chimneys black.

Quillow, the toymaker, worked busily all night, and by the dark hour before the dawn, had made twenty more blue men so that he now had fifty blue men in all. He put the new ones with the others he had made, in the large chest with the iron clasp.

As the first birds twittered in the trees, the lamplighter and the town crier came into the toyshop. Quillow was repairing a doll for a little girl who was ill. He smiled and bowed to his friends confidently, but the palms of their hands were moist and the roofs of their mouths were dry.

"Perhaps he will detect your trick," said the lamplighter.

"Perhaps he will smash all our houses," said the town crier.

As the three men talked, they heard the giant stirring on the hillside. He rubbed his eyes with his great knuckles, yawned with the sound of a sinking ship, and stretched his powerful arms. The toymaker and the lamplighter and the town crier watched through a window and held their breath.

Hunder sat up, staring at the ground and running his fingers through his hair. Then slowly he lifted his head and looked at the town. He closed his eyes tightly and opened them again and stared. His mouth dropped open and he lurched to his feet. "The chimneys!" he bellowed. "The chimneys are black! The malady is upon me again!"

Quillow began to scamper through the cobbled streets and across the green valley as the giant's eyes rolled and his knees trembled. "Teller of tales, smallest of men!" bellowed Hunder. "Tell me what I must do. The chim-

neys are black!" Quillow reached the feet of the giant, panting and flushed. "Look, teller of tales," said the giant, "name me fairly the colour of yonder chimneys."

Quillow turned and looked toward the town. "The chimneys are red, O Hunder," he said. "The chimneys are red. See how they outdo the red rays of the sun."

"The rays of the sun are red," said Hunder, "but the chimneys of the town are black."

"You tremble," said Quillow, "and your tongue hangs out, and these are indeed the signs of the second symptom. But still there is no real danger, for you do not see the blue men. Or do you see the blue men, O Hunder?" he asked.

"I see the men of the town standing in the streets and staring at me," said Hunder. "But their faces are white and they wear clothes of many colours. Why do you ask me if I see blue men?"

Quillow put on a look of grave concern. "When you see the blue men," he said, "it is the third and last symptom of the malady. If that should happen, you must rush to the sea and bathe in the yellow waters or your strength will become the strength of a kitten." The giant groaned. "Perhaps if you fast for a day and a night," said Quillow, "the peril will pass."

"I will do as you say, teller of tales," said the giant, "for you are wise beyond the manner of men. Bring me no food today, tell me no tale." And with a moan Hunder sat back upon the hillside and covered his eyes with his hands.

When Quillow returned to the town, the people cheered him softly and the children flung flowers at his feet. But the blacksmith was sceptical. "The giant is still there on the hillside," he said. "I shall save my cheers and my flowers until the day he is gone, if that day shall ever come." And he stalked back to his smithy to help the

locksmith make the great brass key for Hunder's front door.

That noon there was enough mutton and pie and chocolate for all the people of the town, and they ate merrily and well.

Hunder the giant fretted and worried so profoundly during the day that he fell quickly to sleep as the night came. It was a night without moon or stars, as Quillow had hoped. A town owl who lived on the roof of the tavern – at the Sign of the Clock and Soldier – was surprised at the soft and shadowy activities of the toymaker. The bat and the firefly hovered about him in wonder as he worked secretly and swiftly in the green valley at the feet of the snoring giant. The squirrel and the nightingale watched like figures in a tapestry as he dug and planted in the woods at the giant's head. If the giant thrashed suddenly in his sleep or groaned, the cricket and frog fell silent in high anxiety. When Quillow's work was finished and he returned to his shop, the bat and the firefly moved in dreamy circles, the squirrel and the nightingale stirred freely again, and the cricket and the frog began to sing. The owl on the roof of the Clock and Soldier nodded and slept. Quillow lay down on his workbench and closed his eyes.

When the scarlet men played the bells of five o'clock, and the first birds twittered in the trees and the grey light came, Quillow awoke and opened his door. The town crier stood in the cobbled street in front of the shop. "Cry the hour," said Quillow. "Cry all's well."

"Five o'clock!" cried the town crier. "Five o'clock and all's well!"

The people crept out of their houses and on the hillside across the green valley, Hunder the giant stirred and yawned and stretched and rubbed his eyes and sat up. He saw that the chimneys were still black, but he grinned at them and winked. "The malady passes," said Hunder. "I

see men with white faces wearing clothes of many
colours, but I see no blue men." He flexed the muscles of
his powerful arms and he smote himself mighty blows
upon his brow and chest and stomach. "Ho, councillors!"
roared Hunder, "bring me my sheep and my pie and my
chocolate, for I have a vast hunger."

The people fled from the streets, and behind the barred
doors and shuttered windows of their houses they
listened and trembled. The baker, the butcher, and the
candymaker hid under their beds. They had prepared no
meal for the giant and they were afraid for their lives. But
the brave little toymaker, his white hair flowing like the
dandelion clock in the morning wind, ran through the
cobbled streets and across the green valley and stood at
the giant's feet.

"Behold, I am still a whole man!" bellowed the giant,
thumping his brow. "I have heard the word and I have
seen the black chimneys, but I have not beheld the blue
men."

"That is well," said Quillow, "for he who beholds the
blue men must bathe in the yellow waters in the middle of
the sea, or else he will dwindle, first to the height of the
pussy willow, then to the height of the daffodil, then to
the height of the violet, until finally he becomes a small
voice in the grass, lost in the thundering of the crickets."

"But I shall remain stronger than the rock and taller
than the oak," said Hunder, and he clapped his hands
together.

"If you are stronger than the rock and taller than the
oak," said Quillow, "then stamp on the ground and make
yonder cow in the field turn a flip-flop."

Hunder stood up and chortled with glee. "Behold,
smallest of men," he said, "I will make the cow turn twice
in the air." He brought his right foot down upon the earth
sharply and heavily. The cow turned a double flip-flop in
the field, Quillow bounced as high as the giant's belt, and

great boughs fell from trees. But the giant had no eyes for these familiar wonders. He stared at something new under the sun, new and small and terrible. The blue men had come. The blue men were popping high into the air. They popped up in the valley and they popped up in the woods. They popped up from behind stones and they popped up from behind cowslips. They popped up in front of Hunder and they popped up behind him and under him and all around him.

"The blue men!" cried Hunder. "The blue men have come! The world is filled with little blue men!"

"I see no blue men," said Quillow, "but you have begun to shrink like the brook in dry weather, and that is the sign of the third symptom."

"The sea! The sea! Point me to the sea!" bellowed Hunder, who now stood shivering and shaking.

"It is many leagues to the east," said Quillow. "Run quickly towards the rising sun and bathe in the yellow waters in the middle of the sea."

Hunder the giant ran toward the rising sun, and the town trembled as he ran. Pictures fell from walls and plates from plate rails and bricks from chimneys. The birds flew and the rabbits scampered. The cows turned flip-flops in the fields and the brook jumped out of its bed.

A fortnight later a traveller from afar, stopping at the Sign of the Clock and Soldier, told the innkeeper of a marvellous tale of how a giant, panting and moaning like a forest on fire, had stumbled down out of the mountains and plunged into the sea, flailing and threshing, and babbling of yellow waters and black chimneys and little blue men; and of how he had floundered farther and farther out to sea until at last he sank beneath the waves, starting a mighty tide rolling to the shore and sending up water spouts as high as the heavens. Then the giant was

seen no more, and the troubled waters quieted as the sea resumed its inscrutable cycle of tides under the sun and the moon.

The innkeeper told this tale to the blacksmith, and the blacksmith told it to the locksmith, and the locksmith told it to the baker, and the baker told it to the butcher, and the butcher told it to the tailor, and the tailor told it to the cobbler, and the cobbler told it to the candymaker, and the candymaker told it to the candlemaker, and the candlemaker told it to the town crier, and the town crier told it to the lamplighter, and the lamplighter told it to the toymaker.

As the lamplighter spoke, Quillow put the finishing touches on a new toy, whistling softly, his eyes sparkling. The lamplighter saw that the toy was a tiny replica of Quillow himself.

"What do you do with that?" he asked.

"You put it in the palm of your hand, like this," said Quillow, and he put the figure in the palm of his hand. "And then you blow, like this." He blew, and the miniature Quillow floated slowly through the air and drifted gently to the floor. "I think it will amuse the children," said the little toymaker. "I got the idea from a giant."

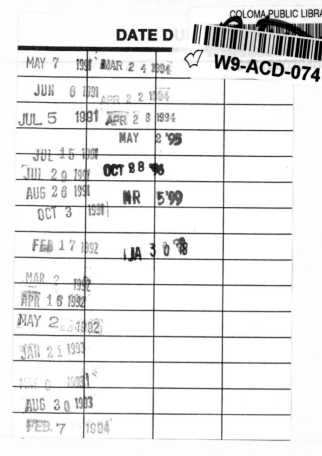